P9-DNC-116

LOOK WHAT YOU MADE ME DO

LOOK WHAT YOU MADE ME DO

ELAINE MURPHY

GRAND CENTRAL
PUBLISHING

NEW YORK   BOSTON

This book is a work of fiction. Names, characters, places, and incidents are the product of the author's imagination or are used fictitiously. Any resemblance to actual events, locales, or persons, living or dead, is coincidental.

Copyright © 2021 by Elaine Murphy

Cover design by Elizabeth Connor. Cover photo © Jane Morley/Trevillion Images. Compositing and retouching by Scott Nobles.
Cover copyright © 2021 by Hachette Book Group, Inc.

Hachette Book Group supports the right to free expression and the value of copyright. The purpose of copyright is to encourage writers and artists to produce the creative works that enrich our culture.

The scanning, uploading, and distribution of this book without permission is a theft of the author's intellectual property. If you would like permission to use material from the book (other than for review purposes), please contact permissions@hbgusa.com. Thank you for your support of the author's rights.

Grand Central Publishing
Hachette Book Group
1290 Avenue of the Americas, New York, NY 10104
grandcentralpublishing.com
twitter.com/grandcentralpub

First Edition: July 2021

Grand Central Publishing is a division of Hachette Book Group, Inc. The Grand Central Publishing name and logo is a trademark of Hachette Book Group, Inc.

The publisher is not responsible for websites (or their content) that are not owned by the publisher.

The Hachette Speakers Bureau provides a wide range of authors for speaking events. To find out more, go to www.hachettespeakersbureau.com or call (866) 376-6591.

Library of Congress Cataloging-in-Publication Data
Names: Murphy, Elaine, 1981–.
Title: Look what you made me do / Elaine Murphy.
Description: First edition. | New York, NY : Grand Central Publishing, 2021. |
Identifiers: LCCN 2021006852 | ISBN 9781538704158 (trade paperback) | ISBN 9781538704165 (ebook)
Subjects: GSAFD: Suspense fiction.
Classification: LCC PR9199.4.M86744 L66 2021 | DDC 813/6—dc23
LC record available at https://lccn.loc.gov/2021006852

ISBNs: 978-1-5387-0415-8 (trade paperback); 978-1-5387-0416-5 (ebook)

Printed in the United States of America

LSC-C

Printing 1, 2021

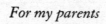

For my parents

LOOK WHAT YOU MADE ME DO

CHAPTER 1

I've been expecting the call, but when my phone rings, the sound is still too sharp, more alarm than alert. The personalized ringtone grinds the world to a halt, turning my knees to gel and my stomach to mush. I should be safe in the produce section of a grocery store, but I've never been safe anywhere. The sound trills from my pocket, the coat vibrating against my hip, and like any awful thing, it feels like a shock, an offense. An unfairness.

Another ring and I look around guiltily, a lemon clutched in my left hand, but the other shoppers ignore me, preoccupied with getting their groceries and getting home, away from the October cold. I consider letting the call go to voicemail, but I know she'll just call back. She's been getting antsy lately, and after a decade of experience, I know the signs. There's no way to escape it. To escape her. There never has been.

I pull the phone from my pocket to see Becca's name transposed over a picture we took three years ago. She's standing in front of a mailbox painted to resemble a cartoon castle, with brightly colored turrets and arched windows. Her arms are folded like a sentry, eyes glaring, daring anyone to approach. As soon as the camera clicked, she'd doubled over laughing, like any goofy, fun older sister. The one I'd always wanted.

I answer the call, losing sight of the picture. "Hey."

"It's me," she says. "I need help. I'm moving furniture."

I knew what she was going to say, of course, but my knees weaken further, like they do when we go to amusement parks and she insists I get on the roller coaster even though she knows I hate roller coasters. You're thirty, Carrie, she says. Suck it up. Little kids are doing it—what's your problem? You can't be afraid of *everything*.

I'm twenty-eight, I correct her every time. *You're* thirty. But every time, I get on the roller coaster. And my head spins and my stomach lurches and I feel sick and hot for the rest of the day, and the trip to the amusement park ends as they all do—with Becca being amused.

I want to say no now, too. I want to tell her it's my one-year anniversary dinner with Graham and I'm making dinner, but I don't. I don't tell her because she already knows, which is probably why she picked this date to "move furniture," and we both know I'll cancel my plans. It's not like I have a choice.

"I'm at the grocery store," I say, for the sake of it, staring at the lemon in my hand.

"So?"

"So it's my anniversary. I'm making—"

"Don't say lemon spaghetti," she snaps. Even when Becca needs you, she can't be nice, not really. It's not in her genetic makeup to be kind. We share 50 percent of our DNA, but we could be complete strangers for how unalike we are. She's blond; I'm brunette. She has blue eyes; mine are brown. She's a murderer; I'm not.

"It's Graham's favorite." I'm not actually the biggest fan of lemon spaghetti either, but Graham is pretty much perfect apart from this one thing, so I can live with it. I grew up with Becca, after all. I've dealt with worse.

"Tell him to choose something else."

"I—"

"And choose another night, too," she says. "I need help. Moving—"

"Furniture," I say. "I know."

"Kilduff Park. West entrance. Hurry up."

She disconnects before I can say anything else, and I stand in the produce section and stare between the phone and the basket in my hand, as though weighing my options. As though I have options.

I text Graham a lame apology. *Work emergency. So sorry.*

It's a believable lie. He knows what my job is like because we met at work. Weston Stationery is a small, business-casual office at the edge of an industrial park,

and while a job designing and marketing novelty office
supplies might not sound exciting, I like it. Right now
I'm even up for a promotion, which *is* exciting. It's down
to me and another girl named Angelica, though she's not
at all angelic. Which, in our office, mostly means she puts
her recyclables in the trash and takes too long to sign
birthday cards and got a tattoo on her ankle of a polka-
dot binder clip to suck up to our boss. When I talk to
Graham about the promotion, he tells me I have it in the
bag because I'm the best person for the job. When I talk
about it to Becca, she yawns.

Graham replies to my text right away. He's disappointed, but of course he understands. He'll order takeout. *Come over later?*

I'll try.

I won't try. Not after this. I can't.

I empty my basket, reluctantly returning my fresh
pasta to the deli counter and the French loaf to the bakery,
exchanging the warmth of the store and my boyfriend for
a dark park four days before Halloween to help my sister
move furniture.

———

The first time Becca killed somebody, she was seventeen. I was fifteen, a sophomore in high school, and only
vaguely aware of a cheerleader named Missy Vanscheer.
Missy and Becca were on the cheerleading team together

but didn't get along so I only heard Missy's name when it was followed by something like "skank" or "bee-otch." I thought nothing of it when I heard whispers that Missy was missing. First, she skipped cheer practice, and the next day she wasn't at school. Then her parents reported her missing, and that's when it became real.

That's also when the rumor started that Missy was pregnant, and the father was an older man and they'd run away together. Her friends swore she'd never mentioned a boyfriend, certainly not an older guy, and nobody knew she was pregnant. But the rumor persisted, and though the police investigated, they never found any mentions of a boyfriend in her social media pages, her phone, or her diary.

They never found Missy either.

It was two years later, the day after my high school graduation and a week before my eighteenth birthday, that I learned the truth. Becca called me, panicked and near tears, totally out of character for my sister. When people described Becca, they used terms like *beautiful*, *aloof*, and *manipulative*. Hearing her say she *needed* me eroded a lifetime of lessons to the contrary and had me reaching for a pencil, asking her for the address.

"Don't write it down!" she'd shrieked, as though she could see my notepad. "Don't write it down," she repeated, more calmly. "Don't use GPS. Don't even bring your phone. Just remember it."

It was only when I got to the abandoned hiking trail that I learned why.

Becca leaned against the hood of her car, smoking a cigarette, looking like the Queen Bee in every high school movie with her tight jeans and T-shirt, her blond hair in a high, shiny ponytail. Not even the towering trees and mountains could compete with her beauty.

I parked my dented little Volvo, the car I'd worked overtime at the diner to pay for, saving up my measly tips and depositing them at the bank on my way home. For months, I'd been collecting them in an envelope in my underwear drawer, until one day I went to get the money and all that remained was a five-dollar bill. Becca swore she hadn't taken it, my $1,287, but I knew she had. I went to the bank and opened an account, and Becca came home from the mall with a new wardrobe. My parents knew but were too wary of her to do anything, which probably had a lot to do with how we came to be at the hiking trail.

"It's about time." She tossed her burning cigarette on the ground, heedless of the nearby trash can and dry leaves that littered the area.

"Um…" I looked around. We were alone. The air was clean and warm, scented with dirt and pine, but there was something else there, too. An undercurrent that made me more uncomfortable than normal.

"What are you wearing?" Becca groaned at my jeans and T-shirt, Cookie Monster printed on the front, gobbling a cookie.

I resisted the urge to tug at the hem of my shirt,

the fabric clinging to my muffin top just a little too tightly. If I drew her attention there, she'd make a snide comment about my weight, the extra ten pounds everyone swore was baby fat until I was too old for the excuse.

"Just…clothes."

She rolled her eyes. "Well, come on."

But when I started for the mouth of the trail, ready to follow even without knowing the destination, Becca didn't budge.

"What?" I asked, staring back at her.

She sighed, her glossy lips turning down in a pout. "We have to get something."

I glanced around again. Apart from the ignored trash can and a wooden sign with a map of the trail dangling by a single rusty nail, there was nothing to "get."

"Where is it?"

Her pout deepened, as though my question disappointed her, and Becca yanked open the back door of her car—my parents bought it for her as a graduation gift—to retrieve a yellow bag with a garden store logo stamped on the side. She dumped out two pairs of garden gloves printed with bright-purple flowers, still held together with the tags. While I was surprised to see the gloves, I was more surprised to see the bag. Becca didn't normally "pay" for things. She just took what she wanted, and always got away with it. I shoplifted a pack of gum when I was twelve, got caught seconds later, and had my picture posted on the wall of shame at the front of the store for a year. My parents were very disappointed.

I accepted a pair of gloves and copied Becca, snapping them apart and pulling them on, though there was almost certainly no garden in the vicinity. With one more heavily exaggerated sigh, like this was the most tedious day of her whole life, Becca reached in through the open driver's-side window and pressed a button to pop the trunk. The lid lifted slowly, and even from my position in front of the car, my heart started to pound, and nausea roiled in my gut.

I'd never seen inside Becca's trunk before. It had never occurred to me to check; there was no reason. But in that moment, I knew I definitely did not want to know what was in there.

"Well, come on," she said, like I was the problem.

I didn't budge. "What is it?"

"Come on."

"What is it?" My voice rose an octave, and Becca finally looked at me, really looked at me, and a little furrow appeared between her perfectly arched brows. She opened her mouth to speak but then closed it, her cheek twitching while she chewed on it. She always chewed on the inside of her cheek, was always spitting blood. Her blue eyes grew shiny with tears.

"Something bad happened," she whispered.

My feet propelled me forward automatically, the need

to help, to fix, so ingrained I didn't even have to think about it.

"What?" I was also whispering, though there was no one around to hear. The trail had been deemed unsafe years ago after three hikers fell to their deaths, and no one came out here anymore since Brampton boasted plenty of other, less deadly, trails to enjoy.

Becca's wet eyes flickered to the trunk, and again my feet moved, one step, then two, until I could just see the edge of the black carpet lining. I couldn't see anything more than that, but the smell I'd noticed earlier, the one that felt out of place in the clean, bright forest, was stronger.

I inched forward and saw a foot. A human foot. In an orange-and-white canvas sneaker, laces neatly tied, a pale ankle peeking out beneath the hem of a pair of black pants.

I recognized the sneaker as Shanna's before I recognized her face, covered in crusted blood and bruises, lips and eyes swollen shut, dark hair matted and stuck to torn flesh. She was the person in a movie who'd been hit by a bus and barely survived, so brutally damaged it was almost impossible to believe. Except the way she was folded into the space, limbs at weird, crumpled angles, her neck clearly askew, made it all too believable that my sister had a dead girl in her trunk.

More specifically, she had her dead co-worker in her trunk. I recognized Shanna because we'd gone to school together. She'd been in Becca's class, two years ahead of me, but that hadn't stopped her from flirting with my tenth-grade crush. I'd been obvious and awkward, and the whole school knew my feelings, though I'd have rather died than admit them. Shanna invited him to the winter dance and he happily accepted, and I wore mourning black for a week and cried myself to sleep for two. When the tires on Shanna's car were slashed the night of the dance, I'd even gotten a visit from the police, but I'd been home with my parents and had an embarrassingly ironclad alibi. I'd endured a month of taunts of "loser" and "psycho" in the hallways until eventually the school moved onto a new teenage scandal, Shanna graduated, and I never thought of her again. Until now.

I gagged, the combination of the sight and the smell and the knowledge more than I was ever going to be ready for. I lurched toward the tree line, fingers gripping the nearest trunk for balance, and dragged in breath after breath, nose running, mind reeling, trying to understand.

I had a lot of questions, but somehow, deep inside, I knew that the most basic, essential answer was this: Becca had killed somebody.

I don't know how much time passed before I mustered the nerve to face my sister. She'd lit another cigarette and was pacing the length of the car, lifting an irritated brow when I finally looked at her.

"Are you ready now?"

"Ready for what?"

"To help me move…" She gestured toward the trunk. Toward Shanna's broken body. "It."

"That's Shanna!"

"Obviously," Becca snapped, then glanced into the trunk and pursed her lips with distaste. "Anyway. Let's go."

"Go where?"

She jerked her chin toward the mouth of the trail, already darker and more ominous than it had been minutes earlier. "Up there."

"Why?"

"Well, she can't stay here, can she?"

"She—but—you—I—" My stomach attempted another escape through my mouth, but I swallowed it down, eyes watering at the effort. "What happened?"

Becca heaved a petulant sigh. "We had a misunderstanding."

Though I wanted to look anywhere but, I found myself looking at the dead girl—at Shanna—again. It was almost impossible to catalog the magnitude of her injuries, the sheer scope of the damage. And looking at Becca, tall, beautiful, and unscathed, told me she didn't do this. At least, not with her hands.

I held her stare as I passed, walking around to the front of the car where she'd been standing so casually when I arrived, the paint gleaming in the afternoon sunlight. I glared at the shiny silver bumper and it winked back at me, like we were in on a secret. The secret being, I belatedly realized, that it was brand new because the other one had been used to kill somebody earlier that day.

"Did you—"

"Yes," Becca said tersely. "I accidentally hit her with my car."

My stomach lurched. "What was the misunderstanding?"

"C'mon," she muttered, gripping Shanna's ankles and yanking them over the lip of the trunk, things cracking and popping as the locked joints tried to straighten.

"What was the misunderstanding?" I repeated.

Becca paused, holding a dead girl's feet, and stared me down. Tried to, anyway. When I didn't relent, she huffed. "She said she saw me taking money from the till, and she misunderstood. Then she misunderstood how fast I was driving and stepped in front of my car."

"You—" I'd once hit a parked car, not hard enough to leave a mark, and was shaken for days.

"Accidentally," she added, as an afterthought. Or a reminder. "Now let's go."

When I still didn't move, she scuffed her foot in the dirt and released Shanna's ankles. They dropped against the edge of the car with an empty thud.

"Carrie," Becca said, fingers curling into her palms, "*please*." I could see her chewing on her cheek again, the inside of her bottom lip stained crimson, like she'd eaten a cherry Popsicle. She drew in a breath through her nose, nostrils flaring, and blinked rapidly, tears clinging to the ends of her lashes. "She was so horrible to me. She lied to our co-workers about me, to our boss. She knows how much I love this job, and she wanted—she wanted to destroy me." A single fat tear rolled down her cheek, glinting in the sunlight like a diamond. "And if anyone finds out about this, they'll think I did it on purpose, and I'll—I'll—" She gulped dramatically. "I could go to jail."

Becca worked at the jewelry store at the mall, fancy enough that not everybody could afford to shop there but not so fancy that they had guards. She got minimum wage and earned commission and regularly bitched about neither being enough, though her looks helped her sell far more earrings and necklaces than the next-best sales-person. She didn't love her job, but it paid the bills. Becca's dream was to marry rich and spend the rest of her life sunbathing and bossing around the help. And while she'd dated plenty of wealthy men in her twenty years, none had been reckless enough to pop the question.

"Carrie?" she said softly. "Please? Let's go, okay?" She picked up Shanna's ankles and nodded at her bat-tered head.

But I balked. "I'm not touching her *head*," I said. I looked away from the pulpy, mottled skin, down over Shanna's chest, covered in the white button-up shirt they wore at the store, the collar smudged with dried blood, a smear of dirt on one side. Her pants were torn at the knee on the same side but were otherwise intact. Somehow her face had sustained the brunt of the impact, managing to hit a bumper no taller than knee-high.

Becca sighed. "God. You're so dramatic. You take her feet then, you baby."

She shouldered me out of the way as she stuck her hands under Shanna and into her armpits, heaving her torso out of the trunk. Shanna's neck stayed askew, her ruined face tilted sharply to the side, like she was sleeping uncomfortably.

Becca was barely perturbed. In fact, she was more irritated by my reluctance than Shanna's dead-ness. She gave me the imperious look she'd given me a million times in my life, and even though my throat tightened and my gag reflex was on high alert, I felt my fingers wrapping around Shanna's shins, careful to touch only the fabric, not her skin, and lift.

She was stiff. Her limbs remained bent and twisted, but she didn't droop or sag, and even through the fabric, I could feel how cold she was. How not-recently-dead she was.

"When did this happen?" I asked, already breathing hard as we trudged toward the mouth of the trail. What we were going to do if we happened upon a stray hiker, I didn't know.

"When I called you," Becca said. I watched her face, but it remained neutral. If anything, she looked merely determined, and we shifted so we walked on opposite sides of the overgrown path, shuffling our feet in time.

"Half an hour ago?"

"About that."

"Where—"

"Jesus, Carrie. I don't want to relive it." She said it as though she were the one having the worst afternoon of her life.

"Well, aren't people going to wonder—" I began, stopping when she gave me a warning look. There wasn't a soul in town who didn't know that look. I'm pretty sure birds have fallen out of the sky after that look.

"Of course they're going to wonder," she said, like she was speaking to a toddler. "And they'll just have to wonder because they're never going to find her, are they?"

"I don't—" I stumbled over an exposed root, its gnarled fingers looking too much like a hand crawling out of the dirt. "I don't know. Where are we going?"

"Not far. You didn't bring your phone, did you?"

"No. Did you?"

"Of course not. Have you ever seen a movie? The police trace your phone, and then you get caught."

"You thought about that?"

She cocked her head, eyeing me patiently. "I thought about you," she said, with emphasis. "That's why I told you not to bring your phone. To help you."

I might have been weak enough to help Becca, but I wasn't stupid enough to believe her. Or argue with her. "Okay."

She either bought the lie or decided to accept it, and

we walked the next fifteen minutes in silence, our foot-steps and my gasping breaths the only sounds as we made the steep climb. I was sweating profusely when we finally stopped at an indiscernible spot on the path, lined by trees on both sides.

"That way," Becca said, nodding toward the trees at my back.

I glanced over my shoulder. "Where?"

"Just go in. Maybe ten, twenty feet. Watch your step."

She didn't give me a choice, just nudged me with Shanna's stiff body, my sweaty left hand slipping in its glove and sliding up to her knee, hard as a rock beneath my palm. I gagged and recoiled, nearly dropping her corpse, muttering to myself as I regained my footing and backed warily into the woods. It was much cooler in there, and even quieter than the trail, nature absorbing our sounds, obscuring our sins.

"Just a little farther," Becca said. "Keep an eye out."

"For what?"

I yelped as the forest abruptly ended and a sheer cliff began. There was no warning. Just a wall of trees, slightly thinner than the rest, and then blue sky and the wide, terrifying expanse of the gully below.

"That."

Unceremoniously, Becca dropped Shanna, who crashed onto the pine-needle carpet, and I squawked and dropped her, too, debris scattering over my shoes. Even through the garden gloves, my hands left sweaty prints on her pants, and as I bent over and heaved for breath or mercy or anything, sweat dripped off my forehead and onto her leg.

"How did—how did you know this was here?"

Becca shifted, and I backed away instinctively, two steps from the cliff, one arm wrapping around a tree. Her mouth quirked, and she gazed out over the emptiness, her toes right at the edge as she peered down. From my position, I guessed it was about a hundred yards to the bottom, and it didn't take much to assume that was where Shanna was going. It would explain her battered face far better than Becca's hit-and-run "misunderstanding."

Becca shrugged. "I just do. Any last words for Shanna?"

I faltered. "Ah, I—"

She laughed. "Just kidding. Bye, bitch." Then she crouched down and hoisted Shanna's body over the edge.

Just like that. One second alive, one second dead, one second gone.

I knew I shouldn't, but I dropped to my knees and watched, seeing something white bounce off the ridge of the cliff, spiraling into the green growth below, then disappearing from sight.

Slowly, I raised my eyes to Becca's.

She gazed down at me, her expression open, expectant.

"You shouldn't have sweated all over her," she said.

I blinked. "What?"

She pulled off her gardening gloves and shook them out, looking for all the world as though she'd just finished pruning a rosebush. She didn't have a drop of sweat or dirt on her.

"You shouldn't have sweated so much," she repeated. "I gave you gloves so you wouldn't leave DNA behind, but you just sweated all over her. You'd better hope they never find her body."

My jaw dropped, like a door easing open, reality easing in. "DNA—" I began, then closed my mouth. I'd been thinking about Becca and Shanna, but nowhere in the scenario had I thought about myself. "But you—*your* DNA—"

Becca shrugged. "Yeah, but we worked together. I lent her my shirt. It would make sense for my DNA to be on her. But you? You didn't even know her."

"They can't—"

"You probably got hair on her, too. You're always shedding like a dog. And if they ask people about who had issues with her, someone's going to remember how you practically stalked her in high school because she dated that loser you liked, then you slashed her tires."

I pulled myself to my feet, sparing half a second to fret over my frizzy brown curls. "I didn't slash—"

"Don't worry, Carrie. I would never tell on you."

"You're the one who—"

"And even if they do find her body—if they trace it back to the day she went missing, and if somebody did suspect you, or if you did get arrested, I mean, technically you're seventeen, right? A minor?"

Her voice rose slightly at the end of each sentence, but they weren't questions. They weren't things occurring to her on the spur of the moment. Just like she hadn't called me immediately after she killed Shanna. Or replaced her bumper. Or bought the gloves. I was her fall guy. Her sister.

"Anyway," Becca said brightly, "we'd better get back before it gets dark out. Who knows what's hiding in the woods?"

I was trembling so violently I could barely walk, my teeth chattering, skin clammy. All the sweat had dried, leaving my skin crusty and itchy and somehow cold. Like the realization that my sister was a murderer wasn't enough, but she had implicated me in it, too. For no reason other than the fact that she could. She had chosen to beckon me into her twisted web, and I had been foolish enough to come.

She sighed sympathetically when we found the trail and reached out to tuck my hair behind my cheek. "C'mon, Carrie. Don't be weird. It happened, and now it's over. Mom and Dad will never know. We're family, and we always have each other's backs."

But reality was setting in too quickly, and the fact that my whole life had just changed was more than my brain was willing or able to handle. My sister was a murderer. And I was an accomplice. I could still go to the police. I could tell them everything. They could probably find the car wash and the body shop where she had the bumper fixed, maybe get video of Becca buying the garden gloves.

But they could also ask people about my history with Shanna, the classmates who'd called me a psycho, and review the records from the interview when I'd been questioned about slashing her tires, a mystery that had gone unsolved until just now. If history tells me anything, it's that Becca will win this war, the way she wins everything else.

"Carrie?" Becca prompted, tipping up my chin with the side of her finger. "Don't panic. It'll be all right. They won't find her. I promise."

"How—how do you—you know?" I stammered.

"Because they never found Missy," she said simply. "And Shanna was skimming from the register and probably took off for Mexico. So there's no reason for anyone to search, is there?"

It was a force of will to meet her eye and shake my head, the gesture leaden and complicit.

Becca beamed at me. "You're the best, Carrie. I knew I could trust you. And you can always trust me, too. Now let's go get something to eat. All this fresh air has made me hungry."

———

Kilduff Park is the largest green space in the town of Brampton, Maine, with nearly two square miles of flat, forested land. There are areas designated for visitors, parks and playgrounds, and trails and lakes, but for the most part it's wild, sprawling forest. In the summer, it bustles with tourists and locals, everyone coming out to enjoy afternoon picnics and sunbathing. But tonight, Friday, October 27, at shortly after six, it's pitch black and a cold wind snaps through the trees, rattling bare branches like a menace.

I can see Becca's car in the corner of the lot. It's a black sedan with a rabbit's foot hanging from the rearview mirror, and she's had it for ten months. Because of her hobby, she trades in her cars almost yearly, always choosing something bland and generic and distinctly forgettable. I once asked where she took the cars she traded in, the ones with smashed front ends and blood and bone buried in the cracks, but Becca just gave me a look. Psychos like Becca have friends in low places. I don't know what she does to repay them, and I imagine that's best for everyone.

The car looks lonely with the engine off, the windows already beginning to frost. Becca must have gotten a head start. I park a few spaces down, leaving the car idling as I zip my coat and yank on a wool hat, mustering up my nerve. It's been ten years since we carried Shanna's body into the woods, ten years since anybody's seen a trace of her. And since then I have helped Becca hide eleven bodies, all of whom had a misunderstanding with the front of her car.

Tonight is lucky thirteen.

I shiver again, and not just from the cold. Taped to the lamppost, framed neatly by my headlights, is a hand-made poster about a missing girl named Fiona McBride. I've seen the signs around town for the past week, an uncomfortable itch starting between my shoulder blades and quickly spreading. I've read the posters, memorized them. Seventeen years old, red hair, blue eyes, average height and build. Last seen wearing a pink hoodie and jeans.

Odds are good I know whose body I'll be burying tonight.

With the exception of Shanna, I haven't known any of Becca's victims. Sometimes because they're random strangers, sometimes because a meeting with Becca's bumper batters their face so far beyond recognition that not even their family would be able to identify them.

I force myself out of the car, wincing at the brittle cold. Almost instantly, the tip of my nose is numb, and my eyes are watering, tears freezing at the corners. I hunch into my coat and yank my hat down farther over my ears, following the narrow footpath that leads into the trees. This isn't one of the main trails that wind through the forest, past pretty points of interest. This lightly worn strip of grass is the route people take when they want to avoid those points of interest. The ones who venture this way are selling drugs or sex, people I'd generally steer clear of. But entering the woods and worrying I might stumble across a drug deal is like jumping into a polar bear pen at the zoo and worrying the water will be cold. I know there are worse things out here.

And she's waiting for me.

I keep my head ducked as I hustle toward the tree line about twenty yards away. In the fading light from the parking lot lamps, I can see flattened strands of grass where something heavy has been dragged into the woods, like prey being pulled into the predator's lair. I shudder, picturing the girl from the poster. Most of the time I don't know who Becca has killed, and I don't ask. It's different when you can put a name to the pale, blank face.

"It's about time."

I nearly jump out of my skin when Becca speaks. She lurks just inside the deepest shadows, her black coat, jeans, and hat making her nearly invisible. All of a sudden, it feels like the modicum of safety provided by the lights from the parking lot is gone, leaving the world a nasty cocoon of Becca's making.

"I came as fast as I could."

"Well, I'm freezing. Let's go."

Even now, a decade later, Becca is the same blond, beautiful psychopath she always was. She crouches in front of a rolled-up carpet and wraps her hands around the end. Since Shanna, she's refined her body disposal methods, and this rug is her favorite choice. She keeps it in her trunk for such occasions, transferring it from vehicle to vehicle as she trades in her cars. Never before has a six-by-eight-foot piece of wool and cotton been so ominous; I can't see the floral pattern without wanting to gag. Becca thinks it's funny.

Unlike my first time, I don't dawdle. I don't protest or ask questions. I just scoop up my end—the feet, always the feet, now—and straighten. Becca walks quickly, our routine well established. She leads; I follow. She kills; I don't. She feels no remorse; I do. But Becca doesn't care about my feelings, because she doesn't care about anybody. She made that clear the few times I tried to protest or tell her I couldn't move a body. *All they have to do is find Shanna*, she'd remind me. *Or maybe they don't have to look for Shanna after all. What if somebody else went missing?* What she was really asking was, What if that somebody was Graham? She knows where he works. Where he lives. It was my boyfriend Alister before Graham, and Jackson before him. It was my occasional friend, my neighbors, anybody I dared care about. So I help move nameless strangers instead of my friends.

The body is light, and the rug is wrapped tightly, molding easily to the slim figure inside. I can feel stiff legs beneath my hands, make out the bump of an ankle bone. The body is female. I don't think Becca has ever killed anyone this young before, but I can't rule it out completely. I only know about the bodies she asks me to help hide.

Becca moves through the trees like a panther, navigating her way in the dark with ease. I follow because I have no choice, the white puffs of her breath like unwelcome smoke signals in the night. We don't hide bodies in the same places. I'm not sure how Becca chooses her sites, and I don't care. I don't want to know. I don't want to be more complicit than I am, if that's even possible at this point.

Right now I know the location of thirteen bodies, have the solution to thirteen families' heartbreak. Answers to the questions that will haunt them until they die. And I say nothing. Not even a whisper. I wouldn't dare.

After we hid Shanna, Becca started leaving something behind with each body to tie me to the death. Maybe a tissue or a few strands of hair; once she told me she put my phone number in somebody's pocket. I can't implicate Becca without implicating myself, and I'm still too selfish to take those last steps.

I wonder how she met Fiona. What Fiona did to make her angry. Sometimes she talks while we hide the bodies, telling me why she did what she did. They cut her off in traffic. Made a rude comment when passing her on the sidewalk. Talked too loudly at the movies. It's impossible to predict what's going to set Becca off, and it's pointless. The only guarantee is that it's inevitable.

"All right," she says eventually. "This is the spot."

I shiver and glance around. We've entered a small pocket in the forest, no more than fifteen feet in diameter, the ground flat and covered with fallen leaves that crunch noisily underfoot. A dense wall of trees surrounds us, their bare branches cracking against one another in the icy wind. The full moon glows overhead like a ghostly spotlight.

I shiver again, and this time Becca smirks.

"Scared?" she asks.

"No," I lie. I'm in a dark forest with a dead body and a serial killer a week before Halloween. Of course I'm scared. I'm not the crazy one.

"Here. Let's dig. You're lucky it hasn't gotten too cold yet; the ground's not that hard." She drops her end of the carpet, the body making a sickening thud as the head smacks the ground, and strides the short distance to the tree where she's propped the two shovels she must have brought in earlier.

My teeth are chattering, and my nose is running. I need to get a tissue, but my hands are still full so I crouch to set down the carpet as gently as I can. The rug unfurls slightly, exposing a pale foot, its toenails painted in dark polish, the color stark against the glowing white skin. Shadows from the clacking branches flicker over her flesh, and that's when I spot it. Right there, on her ankle, a tiny dark shape, a square with a set of wings. I recognize it from the office. A binder clip.

It looks black right now, but in the fluorescent light of Weston Stationery, it's bright red with tiny white polka dots. Angelica boasted nonstop about her tattoo, as though it proved her dedication to the company and erased her negligible sales stats. I'd remarked on this to Becca after a bottle of wine and a particularly teary episode of *The*

Bachelor. I told her about Angelica, how she was kissing up to our boss, trying to steal the promotion for which I'd worked so hard.

I don't always know how Becca picks her victims, but in this case I do know. I picked her.

"Are you going to admire her or bury her?" Becca asks, jamming the shovel into the dirt near my foot like a stake.

"You killed Angelica?" I can't take my eyes off the rest of the carpet, like it'll unroll itself and Angelica will jump out and shout *Surprise!* and this will all be a terrible, morbid joke. Because I know better than to do this. To talk to Becca. To tell her anything I like, anything I dislike. Anything she can use against me.

"*That's* her name!" Becca exclaims, like I've solved the real mystery. "Man, that was driving me nuts. Angela? Angelina? *Angelica*. Right. Angelica." She drops the shovel so it topples over and bangs off my shoulder, then my skull, but I'm too numb to feel it. "Let's bury *Angelica*...right...here."

She chooses a spot near the edge of the circle, where the gnarled tree roots disturb the earth and our fresh grave won't be as noticeable to anyone foolish or crazy enough to venture this deep into the woods, where serial killers and their sisters wait.

I use the shovel as a cane, propping myself up as I stand, my knees weak. "I know her," I say inanely.

"*Knew* her." Becca's busy testing the dirt with the tip

of her shovel, as though if we dig a hole that's an inch away from perfect, something bad will happen. Something worse.

"Becca!" My voice is sharp, and Becca finally looks at me, her bland, beautiful face a porcelain mask in the moonlight.

"What?"

"I know her! People know I know her! *Knew* her," I correct, before Becca can interject. "And we're up for the same promotion! Don't you think people will suspect me? The police will talk to me?"

"Um..." She finds a spot in the earth she likes and digs in with her shovel, using her foot to drive it in extra hard. She's had a lot of practice. "Maybe? But you have an alibi, right? Weren't you at hot yoga or the gym or..." She studies me doubtfully, as though she can see my muffin top through my parka. "Something?"

My heart, rattling like a runaway train in my chest, slows by half a second. I do have an alibi. I was at work, then hot yoga, then the grocery store. I saw Angelica at the office this morning so Becca killed her at some point when people—and cameras—can prove I was somewhere else, not murdering anyone.

"But I knew her," I say. "I can't—I can't bury—"

Becca's brow furrows. "You can," she says. "You're already here, and you have a shovel." She sounds perplexed, like she truly can't relate to my feelings. She does this sometimes. All the time, actually. She's a psychopath, incapable of feeling things the way other people do, unable to register the emotional significance of language or action or literally anything, but she recognizes it. She studies it. She manipulates it, the way a sculptor shapes clay, molding it into whatever she wants.

There's no point in arguing with Becca. Not just because she's likely to kill you, but because if she doesn't win in that moment, she'll circle back when you're least expecting and bring it up. Again. And again. And again. Until she wears you down. Until you're so tired you just give in. And the next time you argue, and the time after, you remember the last time, and then you just don't bother. Becca's focus is singular, and being in Becca's sight line is the worst thing that can happen to a person because she never gets tired and she always gets revenge.

I picture Angelica, her slim figure just a few inches over five feet, and position myself the appropriate distance from Becca to start digging the opposite end of the grave. She was wrong; the ground is hard. There are rocks and roots, and even through my gloves, I can almost immediately feel blisters forming. I'm sweating within minutes, damp curls poking out of my hat and sticking to my cheeks.

"You know," Becca says after ten minutes of silent, sweaty digging, "I've been thinking."

That can't be good. "Oh?"

"I need a trademark. A calling card."

I use the back of my gloved hand to wipe sweat out of my eyes. "What?"

She grins. "A calling card. For the bodies."

"Why? They're never found."

"Yeah, *but if they are*. Like, what if, twenty years from now, they find three of the bodies? If there's no calling card, it's just, like, three dumb bodies. But if I have a signature, they're mine."

"Why would you want people to know they were related?"

She stomps her foot. "Would you stop trying to ruin this?"

"I'm not."

"Anyway. I know what I'm going to do."

I don't encourage her, but she uses her teeth to tug off her glove and reaches into her pocket for something small and cylindrical.

I squint in the dim light. "Is that lipstick?"

She grins. "Yep. I'm going to put it on and kiss their foreheads. If they still have foreheads. Or somewhere. I'll kiss somewhere. Like the kiss of death. Isn't that amazing?"

Obviously it's not amazing, just like it's obvious that telling Becca as much would be a wasted effort.

"It's gross," I say instead. "Kissing a dead body."

She shrugs and applies a generous coat of lipstick. "No worse than kissing Graham."

I don't rise to the bait, ignoring her as I fish a tissue from my pocket and wipe my nose. When I lift my head, I spot movement in the wall of trees behind Becca. It's fast and slight, one shadow shifting among others, two pale white dots blinking, gone just as quickly as they'd appeared. I stiffen and squeak, and Becca pauses in her makeup application.

"What?"

My eyes are locked on the forest behind her, now dark and still. "There was someone there," I say.

She glances over her shoulder. "Where?"

"In the woods. Someone watching."

She snorts and puts away the lipstick. "Really, Carrie?"

"*Really*, Becca."

Becca turns to the trees and gives a pageant-like wave. "Hello!" she calls. "My name is Becca Lawrence, I'm a Virgo, I enjoy short drives at high speeds, and my greatest dream is to eradicate hunger in the whole world!"

"Would you shut up?"

The woods around us, previously dark and dead, now feel alive and watchful. Whoever—whatever—it was could still be there, just out of sight in the shadows. Or they could have circled around, using Becca's voice as cover, approaching from—

I yelp at a loud crash behind me and race into the center of the clearing, gaping at the spot where I'd just stood. Becca is still in the same place, doubled over laughing.

"Your face!" she exclaims, and I see a glint of moonlight on scuffed metal where her shovel lies. She'd tossed it behind me to scare the shit out of me. And it had worked.

"That wasn't funny," I snap, stalking back. "Let's just get out of here."

"Hang on, hang on," she says, lifting a hand as she crouches next to the rolled carpet. "Gotta give Angie the kiss of death."

"Angelica," I correct her.

"Of course," she says, peeling back the carpet so Angelica's body lies exposed and still. "My apologies, *Angelica*."

Where in life Angelica was what an older male co-worker called a "demon spitfire," she is indeed angelic in death. Small and pale, with skin that glows in the moonlight. Her face is not damaged; it looks like she's only asleep. The front of her white blouse is stained dark with blood and dirt, and her skirt is bunched halfway up her thighs, showing scraped knees and smears of dried blood on her calves. Her shoulder-length dark hair is splayed around her head like a fan, and Becca uses her thumb to push a strand off her forehead.

"Ooh," she says. "Chilly." Then she gives a maniacal laugh that only makes this entire, dreadful situation impossibly more dreadful and leans down to press her lips to Angelica's cold forehead. She lingers too long, knowing it makes me sick. She's already messed with Angelica; I'm the only one left for her to amuse herself with.

At least, I'm supposed to be. My eyes skitter around the tree line, but there's nothing there. Not that I can see, anyway. The wind picks up, rattling the branches and the leaves, making my skin feel brittle and cold. Becca's waiting for me to beg her to stop touching the body so we can go, but I won't give her the satisfaction. I dig another tissue out of my pocket and wipe my nose. I don't need Becca to leave clues on the bodies; my DNA is probably everywhere. The only consolation is that if I go to jail, Becca will go, too, and Brampton will finally be serial-killer free.

"Fine, fine," Becca says, shoving herself up from the cold ground and rolling her eyes at my non-drama. "All done." She grabs an edge of the carpet and flips Angelica's stiff form into the grave, the body landing with a muted thunk. I didn't like Angelica in life but I feel bad for her in death, though I know Becca will mock me and do her best to make things worse if I let on that I care. Becca can always find a way to make things worse.

I grab my shovel and start scooping dirt back over the body, ankles disappearing, then shins, then knees. Becca does the same on the other end, obscuring the dark lipstick mark on Angelica's forehead. It takes far less time to fill in the hole than to dig it, and maybe it's because the work is easier or maybe it's because I can't stop the anxious spiders crawling up my spine, telling me someone—or something—is watching from the woods, but I can't get warm. I'm cold, my fingers numb, thighs aching. My eyes keep darting into the trees, searching for something I don't want to find.

"Calm down, Carrie," Becca says, catching me. "There's no one out there. What kind of lunatic would be in the woods right now?" Her lips quirk at her own joke, but I roll my eyes, refusing to smile.

She pats the earth loosely over the grave, and we use fallen leaves and branches to cover it so it doesn't look freshly disturbed. By the time we're done, it's like Angelica was never here.

Becca rolls up the shovels in the carpet and tucks the bundle under her arm. "You know what we should do right now?" she asks, leading the way out of the clearing toward the spot where our unseen watcher may or may not have stood.

"Go home, take a shower and a Valium?"

She laughs. "You're so funny, Carrie."

I wasn't joking, but I don't correct her.

"We should go to the biodome," she continues. "They have that promotion right now where you get special glasses so you can watch all the nighttime animals come out and do their thing."

"Nocturnal animals," I say, eyeballing the suspicious spot. "Not nighttime." It's too dark to see much, but there's nothing to indicate anyone or anything was ever here, besides us.

"And you're smart, too," she trills, grinning at me over her shoulder.

I stick out my tongue.

"Remember how much you loved that place when we were little? You got left behind on that field trip and didn't even care."

I was seven years old and stranded at a biodome, but I didn't mind. Seeing my classmates file out behind the teacher and parent helpers, I'd crouched behind a giant hosta and watched them disappear. I counted as high as I could until they were gone, and then I'd finally explored the biodome on my own, choosing my own path, charting my own course, however briefly.

"It's only eight o'clock," Becca adds, her voice carrying through the dark forest. "And there's that diner across the street with cinnamon buns the size of your head. Maybe we can get one after."

There's no point arguing. She'll just get us lost in the woods and nag me until I agree. I trudge after her. "Okay, Becca. Awesome."

"They have those fishbowl margaritas, too," she calls. "We'll get a couple, to celebrate your new job. My treat. I'm proud of you!"

CHAPTER 2

Weston Stationery occupies the fourth floor of an industrial building in a business park on the outskirts of town. Despite the fact that we design and sell custom and novelty office supplies, our actual work space is drab and beige. The desks are cheap composite, the computers old, the walls bare. Our view is of the parking lot and, if you squint in nice weather, the highway. This was my first job out of college so I have seniority and an arguably good desk, sitting closest to the aisle near the windows, where I can admire the scenery.

There are two interior offices, one of which is occupied by Troy, our boss. The other is being held for either Angelica or me, whoever earns the promotion to Novelty Concept Manager, a verdict that's been outstanding for too long. For the past few weeks I've shown up, tentative and hopeful, and each week Troy has mumbled some excuse about why he hasn't made a decision. Unbeknownst to him, there is no longer a decision to be made.

Weston is supposed to be a creative environment, but everyone except Angelica follows the unwritten office dress code of blandly business casual, which makes her absence on Monday morning particularly noticeable. It's 10:03 a.m. when someone finally says what everybody's thinking: "Where's Angelica?" In an office of fifteen, it's impossible to miss when someone is late.

I can't tell who said it, but as soon as the words are out, everyone's on their feet, peeking over their cubicle walls and peering around as though Angelica's been there all morning and we've just missed her. I stand and imitate the others, doing my best impersonation of Becca impersonating a real, sensitive human.

Troy finally emerges from his office, looking like he got dressed in the dark, as always. A psychedelic-patterned tie does nothing to disguise the fact that today's white short-sleeved dress shirt is the same one he wore Friday, coffee stain and all.

"Troy," someone calls, "is Angelica off today?"

He makes a show of glancing around. "Is she not here?"

"No."

"Let me check my messages." He retreats into his office and reappears again thirty seconds later. "She didn't email to say she was sick. She's not in the vacation calendar. Does someone have her home number?"

"Don't you have it?"

"Um." He returns to his office, and this time he's gone for longer, closer to two minutes. "Straight to voicemail," he announces when he comes back.

There's a long silence as we all ponder what to do. It's too soon to call the police, and no one here is really friends with anyone else, so none of us would volunteer to go to Angelica's house, assuming anyone knows where she lives. And it's only been an hour since we noticed she was missing so it's too early to sound the alarm. Or too late.

After another minute, there's a quiet agreement to return to our tasks and monitor Angelica's absence. If she shows up, Troy will speak to her about tardiness. And if she doesn't…

I get back to work. There's still a promotion up for grabs.

———

I meet Graham for soup and sandwiches at a small café at the opposite end of the business park. We get a small booth in the corner, where we sat on our first unofficial date just over a year ago, when he still worked at Weston. Now he sells medical equipment and wears nice suits every day. He has shiny blond hair, pale-blue eyes, and a perfect smile and passes over his unopened packet of crackers so I can sprinkle extra in my soup, just the way I like it. He doesn't even comment that I don't need the extra calories because, unlike Becca, he doesn't care.

There aren't an abundance of dining options in the business park, and the café is crowded. The air is thick with the smell of wet clothing and minestrone, and sounds of the afternoon lunch rush battle with the two flat-screen televisions hung on the wall above the counter, both showing the same golf tournament.

"Man," Graham says, taking a bite of his sandwich and leaving a crescent of teeth marks in the corner. "I love egg salad. I know that's the lamest thing anyone's ever said, but it's true."

I stir my soup. "That's not even the lamest thing I heard this morning. Today I spent two hours discussing the tension in binder clips."

He smiles, eyes crinkling at the corners. "How'd everything go the other night?"

I choke on a bite of soup and cough into my napkin. I know he's referring to Friday's "work emergency," but my heart still pounds. "Ah, okay."

"Uh-oh. More office antics? What'd Troy do this time? Microwave fish? Buy single-ply toilet paper?"

Anyone who's ever worked in an office knows exactly how atrocious those things are, but they don't come close to the truth.

"Everything's fine," I lie. "I'm sorry again about missing dinner."

He shrugs. "That's okay. We have lots of time."

I hope he's right. Some of my relationships have ended because they weren't meant to be, but some I ended myself because knowing I cared gave Becca too much power over me. Power she knows how to leverage and lacks the emotional competency not to. People are pawns to Becca, pieces to shove around on the chessboard of life, flicking them off the edge when she gets bored or irritated or simply wants to hurt someone.

I had one friend in high school, a girl name Sariah, an awkward loner like me. We met eating our lunch alone in the hallway and became fast friends. My parents were delighted I finally had a friend, unlike Becca, who had so many friends—followers—my parents were often begging her to stay home or hang up the phone or stop having so many parties.

When Becca was in twelfth grade, she wanted an extraordinarily overpriced dress to wear to homecoming. My parents, in a rare show of strength, refused to pay so much, and not even Becca's tantrums would sway them. In hindsight, I remember two of the neighbors' pets disappearing during that time, but there were rumors of a coyote spotted in the area so everyone blamed that. I was no longer keeping my money in my underwear drawer, and I had nothing else of value for Becca to steal. So I thought.

One night, she came to me with an offer. If I paid for her dress, she'd let me go to homecoming with her. I didn't want to go to homecoming. I didn't like dressing up, and no boy had ever noticed me. I turned her down.

Four nights later, she approached me again. She'd been

arrested for attempting to shoplift the dress, flirted her way out of being charged, and promised not to return to the store. So she needed me to steal the dress. "No one will even notice you," she promised. "You're practically invisible anyway."

After my humiliating gum theft attempt, I wasn't about to break the law again, and I told her no. She cajoled and threatened, but at that point, she was my mean older sister, not a serial killer—that I was aware of—and though I was shaking by the time she finally left my room, I'd held my ground. I'd stood up to Becca.

The next day, she passed me and Sariah in the hall. "Hey," she said, flashing us a bright smile. It was weird and blinding because she never so much as acknowledged me in public. There were a lot of people who didn't even believe we were related. I did a double take when I saw Sariah smile back. I'd told her the stories of how wretched Becca was—why would she acknowledge her? "Because she's scary," she whispered.

The following day Becca invited us to join her for lunch. Sariah said yes before I could demand to know what Becca was up to. I was fifteen but still too naive to understand that some people had no moral bottom. Becca was all charm and laughter during the lunch, complimenting Sariah on her kohl eyeliner and heavy black boots. There was lunch again the next day, and the next, and the following Monday, I waited alone in the hall for Sariah, who never came. With a sick twist in my stomach,

I crept to the cafeteria and looked toward Becca's choice table in the corner. There, with her crew of dim-witted minions, sat Becca. And Sariah. Giggling side by side like new best friends.

I'd never really had any friends, and so had never lost one before. It struck me like a blow to the head, making me nauseous and dizzy, my eyes watering before I even thought about crying. And maybe it says something about me, but even more than the loss of Sariah, I was devastated by the theft of her. Becca carved out of my life the one thing that made my miserable school days bearable, and she did it because I wouldn't steal her a dress.

They were friends for the entire week. Lunches, strolling through the hallways. Becca even invited Sariah over one day after school, and they sat in the living room watching movies and eating popcorn while I did homework in the kitchen. If there was an iota of consolation in the entire experience, it was that Sariah couldn't meet my eye. She knew Becca was a monster, and she'd walked into the lair, fully informed.

On Saturday, Becca strutted into the kitchen wearing her expensive new homecoming dress. I was eating dinner with my parents, who stared slack-jawed, beef stroganoff cooling on their forks, as she twirled like the pageant queen she'd never be. "Where did you get that?" one of them demanded. The words were halfhearted since, even if Becca deigned to answer, it'd be a lie anyway.

"I bought it," she replied. "I saved my money."

What money? was the obvious follow up question, but nobody bothered asking it.

My parents exchanged looks and then took the easy way out, as always. "Hmm," my mom said, eating her stroganoff. My dad followed suit.

Becca waited for me to say something, but I just contemplated the egg noodles like I'd never found anything in the world more fascinating. Eventually she harrumphed and stormed out of the kitchen, taking pains to stomp extra loudly up the stairs on her way to her bedroom before slamming her door.

"Well," my dad said after a minute, "it *is* a nice dress."

On Monday, I was eating lunch alone near my locker when Sariah hurried down the hall from the direction of the cafeteria. Her rushed footsteps were preceded by the sound of mocking laughter from a hundred students, reminiscent of the slow-motion footage from a movie, *ha ha ha* bouncing off the tile walls like basketballs, interspersed with Sariah's heartrending sobs. I knew what that soundtrack meant.

She stopped in front of me, shoulders heaving, tears leaving tracks in her too-pale makeup, exposing the acne on her jaw. "Sh-she—" she said, mouth wobbling, too unsteady to shape the words. Not that she needed to. I'd never had a friend for Becca to steal before, but she'd stolen my shoes, jewelry, money. Once a bra that was too big for her but made me feel pretty had gone missing, never to be seen again. She suggested a neighborhood pervert had broken in and taken it. Maybe he had a crush on me.

I'd learned not to form attachments to things, learned to live with the sting of losing whatever I'd been foolish enough to care about. I'd already cried for Sariah and spent a week steeling myself for this moment. The only way Becca would enjoy this more was if she saw that it hurt me, too. Humiliating Sariah was foreplay; now she wanted the payoff.

"Fuck you," I told Sariah, standing up from my spot at the base of the lockers and tossing my half-eaten sandwich in the trash.

I strolled away calmly, in the opposite direction from the cafeteria, but before I rounded the corner, I glanced back. Sariah stood, huddled miserably, her face in her hands. And ducking out of sight behind a classroom door was a too-familiar blond head, the puppeteer admiring her own show.

"You all right?" Graham asks, interrupting the memory. He reaches over and covers my hand with his, and I watch his golden tan against my pale skin, his thumb stroking my knuckles.

"I'm fine," I lie.

Something steals over the café then, a sense of focused urgency, and we follow the invisible tension to the television screens, displaying mirrored news updates and images of a dozen police vehicles, lights flashing, surrounded by a thick wall of trees. The banner text at the bottom reads: BREAKING NEWS—BODIES FOUND AT KILDUFF PARK.

It takes me a second to process what I'm seeing. To recognize the *s* at the end of *bodies*, to understand the plural. *Bodies.* Then to not understand the plural.

A stoic reporter faces the camera, wearing a somber black trench coat, her dark hair whipping into her eyes. "A horrifying discovery has been made at Kilduff Park," she informs us, her tone grave. "Police have not released many details, but this is what we know so far. A body was found early yesterday morning by a visitor to the park. Police determined it was necessary to bring in cadaver dogs to search the area, and instead of finding remnants of the first body, they found another buried nearby. Shortly after, they found another. Then another. The total number is unconfirmed, but we're hearing rumors that at least six bodies have been found buried here at Kilduff Park, though that number could be as high as thirteen. We'll keep you posted."

Time stops. Everyone in the café gapes at the television, half-eaten sandwiches in hand. My astonishment is just as genuine but for an altogether different reason. I've known for a decade that Brampton had a serial killer. But I've only helped hide one body at Kilduff. The other twelve are news to me. My first instinct is to hurl up every bite of soup and sandwich, but I've had a lifetime of experience hiding my feelings, and though it's not easy I force deep breaths in through my mouth and out my nose until the nausea subsides.

"Carrie?"

I'm vaguely aware of the cool press of Graham's fingers on my forehead, slick against my clammy skin.

"I knew something was wrong," he says, coming around to my side of the booth and sliding in next to me. "Maybe it's the chowder." He leans down to sniff the bowl. "I don't know. Does that smell off to you? No, what am I— Here. Can you drink some water?"

The feel of his thigh pressed against mine, the warmth of his body, the realness of him—it makes me even more sick than the images of yellow tape flapping against the tree line at Kilduff. The thought of Graham thinking back on this moment and understanding my reaction makes me feel more guilty than the reason itself.

He pushes away the bowl of chowder and the small plate holding the crust of my sandwich, as though food is the issue. I play along, like it's a bad reaction to the meal and not the news that my sister is a more prolific killer than I knew. Eventually I convince Graham I'm fine to return to work.

"You're sure?" he asks when he drops me off at the door.

I get out of the car too fast, making myself dizzy. "Probably just the flu," I lie, forcing a smile before I hurry inside.

Weston is typically a quiet office. When you come in, people offer a polite smile, and Good mornings are exchanged if you're at the watercooler or coffeemaker at the same time, but otherwise, we're acquaintances, not friends. When I return, however, it's more like a gaggle of schoolkids gossiping at their lockers than a workplace. Even Troy has ventured from the safety of his office to join the group.

They look over when I step off the elevator, and I stumble to a halt. Rudy from Accounting, Gene from Concepts, Laverne from Promotions. I'm expecting the crowd to part and a SWAT team to converge, guns pointed at my head, mean voices ordering me to lie on the floor, demanding to know what I did to Angelica.

But none of that happens. They just stare at me, a sea of sad eyes and worried faces, and finally Troy remembers he's supposed to be the boss and says, "Have you heard about Kilduff?"

I nod stiffly.

"Well, we don't want to jump to conclusions, but we decided to report Angelica's absence to the police. Just…in case."

Someone sniffles loudly, like the report confirms her death, and I force myself to nod again.

"It's too soon," I say, like a good co-worker, holding out hope against all odds. "Maybe she's just—" But I can't finish the sentence. I may be a liar and an accomplice, but I'm not stupid, and I don't want anyone repeating this to the police when they inevitably speak to us and learn that Angelica and I were up for the same promotion. It takes a concerted effort not to glance at that empty corner office, its walls bare, one waiting for the new painting I have tucked away in my closet, bought for a day I thought would come about much sooner and differently than this.

Troy clears his throat. "Right," he says. "Right. Well, we don't know anything for sure. This is all probably a misunderstanding. Let's carry on with our day as best we can, and maybe she'll stroll in and say she forgot to mention her vacation, and she was...out of town."

Last year, Troy was passed over for the position of office fire marshal because he couldn't be reliably trusted to lead everyone to safety during a fire drill, but all eyes are on him now. Everyone wants someone to follow, and it's better for me if that someone is Troy, because then I can pretend to do the same. Then I'm just one of the sheep, blending into the slow, hapless flock.

———

The detectives show up near the end of the day. I'm in the small kitchen at the back of the office, preparing a cup of tea, when the low murmur of office work is replaced by a vacuum of silence. This is the opposite of how I imagined them arriving in the endless, looping reel of possible scenarios for my arrest. I pictured doors exploding open, flash bombs and smoke grenades, big guns and bigger screams. But the reality, I discover, when

I peek my head out of the kitchen and peer toward the elevator, is just two people in winter coats with badges clipped to their hips, speaking to Troy in voices too low for me to hear.

There's a shorter white woman with her hair twisted into a knot, her expression grim, and a taller black man, his expression less easy to read. Her posture is tense; his is relaxed. She's talking; he's quiet. Troy can't decide who to look at.

I jump back into the kitchen, heart pounding, and pour hot water into my waiting mug. I tell myself to stop thinking about Angelica, though thinking about her is probably the most normal thing to be doing right now. All morning there's been a tension in the office, like when the humidity builds outside and a thunderstorm is around the corner, ready to correct the imbalance in the atmosphere. We're divided between two worlds, one in which Angelica is alive and one in which she is not. Only three people in this office know which world we live in now.

"Carrie?"

Troy's voice makes me jump. The tea bag I'm holding flies out of my hands and skitters across the floor. I scrabble on my knees to collect it, my voice too high. "Yes?"

"Could you come out here, please? There's someone who needs to speak with you." His voice gets louder as they approach.

I snatch up the tea bag and straighten as Troy and the

male detective appear in the doorway. I know I look as awkward as I feel as I frantically smooth my bunched skirt, sweat sticking stray curls to my temples.

"Sorry," I manage. "I dropped—"

The detective speaks first. "That's okay," he says, his voice low and relaxed. "We just need a few minutes."

I abandon the tea and follow Troy and the detective to the office that is supposed to be mine. I'm vaguely aware of the female detective leading Gene from Concepts into Troy's office and closing the door. I can't think of any particular reason for them to speak to Gene, but it makes sense they'd speak to everybody. It makes sense that I'm just a box on a checklist, waiting to be marked off. I try to find comfort in this fact, but I don't.

The detective pauses at the door and gestures me in first. Troy mumbles something to excuse himself, though without the refuge of his office, he has nowhere to go and nothing to do, and the detective ignores him anyway.

The room is about ten by ten with a desk tucked into the corner and an empty bookshelf on the wall near the door. The fourth wall is floor-to-ceiling glass that overlooks the entire office, and with the blinds open, it's impossible not to feel every eye on me.

There are two seating options, the leather desk chair and a metal chair someone brought in from the smoking area out back, arranging them across from each other. I hesitate and the detective makes the choice for me, settling into the desk chair and linking his hands over his knees, leaning forward like a friend or a therapist, ready to listen.

I take the other seat, the October chill still clinging to the metal, one leg shorter than the others so I'm immediately off kilter. I tip forward, leaning more into the detective, and then scuttle backward, the chair grunting over the carpet.

"You all right?" the detective asks. He wears a heavy black leather jacket with trim along the collar and dark, well-worn jeans with work boots. He looks to be in his mid-forties, with kind, tired eyes and a reserved smile. I wonder fleetingly why he's talking to me and not Gene. If they've mismatched the genders on purpose.

"Yes," I say, though it's far from true.

"I'm Detective Greaves." He offers something that might be a smile. "Marlon Greaves. Do you know why I'm here?"

I open my mouth to say no and then think better of it. "Our co-worker," I say. "Angelica. She didn't come to work. Troy said he reported her missing."

Greaves nods. "That's right. He did. But she's not missing. I'm sorry to tell you she's dead."

Even though I've known this all along, far longer than Detective Greaves, my stupid, stunned expression is entirely genuine. This is the first time I've ever been told someone I know is dead, the first time I've ever heard someone else talk about Becca's misdeeds. And it finally feels real.

"D-dead?" I stammer. "Like…" I don't finish. There's no other way to be dead. She just is. Plowed into by Becca's car and then wrapped in a murder carpet and buried at the park.

"Have you been watching the news?" Greaves asks. "Kilduff Park?"

I nod.

"Angelica's body is the one found yesterday morning."

My mouth opens and closes uselessly. Because again, though I knew she was there, she was buried. We buried her. The news report said a body was found and others discovered. I assumed Angelica was one of the discoveries, not the original.

"We wanted to talk to her co-workers," Greaves continues, "to get an idea of her activities before she disappeared, her attitude, her behavior. Any plans she may have had. People in her life."

My palms are sweating so badly I have to fight the urge to wipe them on my skirt. "I-I barely knew her. I mean, we worked together, but not closely. We're not a close office."

"Your manager gave us your name when we asked who Angelica was closest to here."

My surprise is again genuine. "Seriously?"

Another mouth quirk. "Seriously."

"We're not. We weren't," I correct. "I trained her, but then we worked separately. I don't know her better than anyone else here. And I didn't notice anything different about her before she—disappeared."

That's true, too, and Detective Greaves is nodding like he believes me. "Let's talk about Friday," he says, the day Angelica was killed. Before I knew she was dead. "Walk me through that day."

Even though it was only three days ago and you'd think helping to hide a body would crystallize the details in your brain, my mind is studiously blank. "It was just a normal day," I say finally, the words sounding lame, even to me. "I came to work, like always."

"What time did you get here?"

"Nine. Maybe a few minutes before."

"And then what?"

"I just worked. I have a design project—specialty binder clips, shaped like monarch butterflies—it's for the conservation society—and I was doing that for most of the day. Then, um, on Fridays I go to hot yoga—"

"Does Angelica go to hot yoga?"

"I-I don't know. Not this class, anyway."

"Okay."

"So I went to the class, then afterward I went to the grocery store." My mouth goes dry, and the words stick in my throat, like that's the end of the story. I wish it were.

"And then?"

My underarms are damp. "Then I went home," I lie. I could tell him what I told Graham, that I had a work emergency and returned to the office, but it would be easy enough to check my computer's log to see if it had been turned on again that evening, which it obviously hadn't.

Greaves jots down something in a notepad I didn't see him produce. "What can you tell me about Angelica?" he asks without looking up.

"About her?"

"Yes."

"Um…She worked here for just under a year. She was really outgoing." My mind races, trying to decide if I should mention the promotion. If I don't, it'll look suspicious. But if I do, it'll look suspicious. "She was a good designer," I say finally. "That's all I know about her."

"Did you see her leave the office early on Friday?"

I shake my head. "I wasn't paying attention. Is that when she—when she—"

Greaves doesn't answer. "Did she ever have any problems at work? Staff she didn't get along with, ex-boyfriends visiting, unhappy clients?"

"Not that I know about. It's a small office. I think we'd know if there were issues."

"Right." He clicks the pen shut, like that's the end of the conversation. Then he says, "Is there anything else you'd like to tell me?"

My whole life I've wanted someone to help me, someone in a position to actually do something about Becca, to step in and confront her, to stop her. But that person has never come along. Those who suspected were too afraid to try, and I've paid the price for their silence. And now my silence is bought, my complicity in her evil too thorough, too enduring.

Greaves is staring at me, his gaze sincere, like he'd march out of this office and arrest Becca right away if I just gave the word.

"No," I say.

—

Becca has a key to my house. I don't know where she got it, because I didn't give it to her. But that doesn't matter because, whether I gave it to her or not, whether or not I ask for it back, she's always going to do whatever she wants, and what she wants is to be annoying. She feeds on other people's grievances the way demons feed on fear.

It's always easy to tell when Becca's there or has been there. Every light is on, the front door is wide open, the television and radio blast like they're in a battle to drown each other out. I have a dishwasher, but she'll leave her dishes in the sink, caked with cheese or egg or whatever she managed to find and microwave. There'll be a tub of ice cream in the refrigerator, half melted, my pitcher of water left on the counter to become luke-warm. Becca might kill strangers with one smash from the front of her car, but for me it's death by a million hurt feelings.

I step inside the home I bought three years ago. It's small and dated, but it's mine—in theory—and I close and lock the door Becca left open. I use my foot to push her sneakers to the side, scoop up her leather jacket from the floor, and hang it in the closet. I'd gone through the motions after the meeting with Greaves, gossiping with my co-workers, eyes wide as we recounted being interviewed by a real-life detective, rehearsing the stories we'd tell later at home, expanding, elaborating. Laverne from Promotions had cried.

I'm still going through the motions, even now that I'm home. I set my laptop on the hall table, take off my shoes, and hang my coat next to Becca's. I spot my brand-new leather gloves sticking out of her pocket and steal them back, stashing them in a pair of rain boots, out of sight. I drop my purse and keys next to the laptop, wondering how many more times I'll repeat these actions, these normal, day-to-day behaviors, in my own home, on my own schedule. How long will it take the police to analyze the DNA from Becca's stupid kiss of death? To find a piece of my hair on Angelica's corpse, to learn of the promotion, to find me?

I peer over the half wall into the living room, at my brand-new couch and love seat, the mismatched ottoman. The coffee tables and thrift store lamps with shades I'd designed and crafted with care. And in stark contrast, a carelessly abandoned bowl of cereal, a beer bottle, and a soda can, courtesy of Becca.

"Oh my God!" she cries, exploding out of the kitchen and barreling down the front hallway toward me. "Can you believe this?" Her cheeks are flushed, and her eyes are bright, hair flying loose from its ponytail, but the time lapse between my entering and her exclaiming is too long to be anything but unconvincing.

"This is amazing!" she trills. "The first time I leave a calling card, and they find it?" She cackles hysterically. "I can't even. It's incredible."

"Incredible?" I echo. "I'm the one who was interviewed by the police today, and it was *not* incredible."

Becca is enthralled. "What did they look like? What did they ask you? Did you mention me?"

Unlike my co-workers, I have no intention of replaying this afternoon's events for Becca's entertainment. She'd like it too much.

"What part of them finding your stupid kiss on her forehead is incredible?" I counter. "And how did they find it?" Though I'd talked to Greaves for twenty minutes, he hadn't mentioned how Angelica's body had come to be unburied; nor had he alluded to any strange findings on the body, like my sister's kiss of death.

She narrows her eyes. "It's not stupid."

"It has your DNA!"

"So? I'm not in any systems. Assuming they can even extract the DNA, they can't match it to anything. And there's no reason to look at me."

"They'll look at me!"

She frowns, like that's the most ludicrous thing she's ever heard. "Why?"

"Because they already did!" I snap. "Because we worked together! Because we were up for the same promotion!"

Becca props her hands on her hips. "You're the only one who even cares about that job, Carrie. Trust me— it's hardly a motive." She does a high-pitched imitation of my voice. "I wanted the interior office so bad I killed for it! Angelica gets all the best paper clips!"

"That's not funny."

She rolls her eyes. "You're ruining this."

"Everything was ruined the second you started killing people and roping me into it."

She's not even offended, just leans against the wall and watches me, deciding how to approach this. What she settles on is, "We bonded, Carrie."

I blink. No matter how I try to predict Becca, there's no way a sane person could possibly guess her next steps. "What? Who? You and Angelica?"

"No. You and me. We were going to go our separate ways, lead separate lives, and not even be sisters anymore. And now, because of all this, we're connected."

"All this" means murder, and being "connected" to Becca is the very last thing any healthy person would want, hence her slew of non-engagements. Hence the fact that my parents decided to start spending winters in Arizona, where Becca finds it too hot to handle. Then, when she refused to visit them, they made the move permanent. The problem is that not being "connected" to Becca is easier said than done because, when Becca decides to sever your "connection," it means you're dead.

"I would rather be connected in a different way," I say, knowing it's never going to matter.

She shrugs. "Well, we're connected in this way. Now come have dinner. I cooked." She flounces off like we weren't just talking about how she wrangled me into a life of crime.

I take two steps toward the kitchen and then pause and sniff. "Is that—"

"Short ribs!" Becca calls. "With parsnip puree! Your favorite. I've been working on it all day. Come eat."

We were solidly middle-class growing up, which means we only went out to eat on special occasions and "dining out" meant chain restaurants, with a glass of water for our drink and never any dessert. One time my dad got a promotion at work and they gave him a hefty gift card for a fancy restaurant in town, and we all went. I got braised short ribs because I'd seen them on television and fell in love. We couldn't afford to return to the restaurant, and my mom refused to invest the time or money to make them, so each year after on my birthday, Becca would save up her money—wherever she'd gotten it—and re-create the meal. It's pretty much the only thing she knows how to cook, and when she puts her mind to something, she excels at it.

But today is not my birthday.

"Why?" I say.

"Why not?"

"Because it's not my birthday."

I step into the kitchen and do a double take when it's not the war zone Becca normally leaves in her wake. It's the small kitchen typically found in old homes, updated once in the 1980s, and I haven't found the time or money to update it again. The counters are chipped square tiles, the backsplash more of the same material, the monotony broken up with an occasional painting of a bunch of grapes or horn of plenty. The cabinets are ugly brown wood with matching uneven drawers, and the floor is the same glaring yellow as the fluorescent lights on the ceiling. But Becca, for once, has not made things worse. The slow cooker is on the counter, the sink is empty, and two plates and wineglasses sit on my small table.

Becca gives an exaggerated sigh and stirs a pot on the stove. "It doesn't have to be your birthday for me to do something nice for you," she says, swiping her finger through the dark sauce on the end of the spoon and tasting it. "Perfect."

"But that's the only time you do anything nice, period."

She sticks out her tongue. "Ha ha. Look, it was really cold out on Friday, and I saw you shivering so I thought maybe a home-cooked meal would be good. And this is all I can make, so voilà."

Not for one second do I believe the answer is that simple, but the only way to guarantee more lies is to ask for the truth. Instead I pick up the opened bottle of red wine on the counter. It's mine, of course. A bottle I picked up on a wine tour with Graham, one I'd been saving for some special, yet-to-be-determined occasion. Or tonight.

I pour two glasses, and Becca fills our plates with food so hot steam rises. She takes the seat opposite me and lifts her glass. "To red wine–braised short ribs," she says. "Because they're delicious."

She'll pout if I don't toast so I clink my glass against hers, knowing she's actually toasting Angelica's murder and our imminent discovery. She once told me that if she was ever on death row she'd ask that her last meal be a burger and fries. I voted for short ribs. And now here we are.

I take my time sipping the wine, waiting for Becca to eat first, just in case there's more to this little charade. But she jumps in, her fork gliding through the tender meat, scooping up short rib and parsnip and braised greens and eating them all in one bite. I'm hesitant but I'm also hungry, and not eating would incur a Becca tantrum that would be infinitely worse than being poisoned.

I take a bite, and it's as wonderful as always. The warmth fills me, leaching more of the tension out of my muscles, and I take another bite. Becca does the same, watching me with a tiny smile.

"What?" I ask warily.

"Nothing. I'm just happy."

"There's nothing to be happy about."

She sighs. "I know you can't understand how I'm feeling, but life is so dull, Carrie. And now, for the first time in, like, forever, I feel…alive." She pauses. "Ironically."

Suddenly the parsnip puree tastes a little gummy, the strings of meat sticking between my teeth. I gulp my wine. Becca feels alive because Angelica is dead. And though I didn't care for Angelica, she's still someone I saw eight hours a day, five days a week, for the past eight months, and will never see again because my sister killed her and I helped bury her.

"How?" I ask, the word lodging in my throat.

Becca frowns. "Same as usual, I guess. You sear the meat—"

"No," I interrupt. "Not dinner. How did it happen? How did you…hurt her?"

She sounds bored, like talking about food prep is infinitely more interesting than murder. "Oh. That."

"You didn't even know her."

"I knew of her. You talk about her."

"I talk about everyone at work."

"Yeah, but she's the only one who was harassing you. Wasn't she?"

She was, but even if every other person in the building was causing me trouble, I'd never admit it. "Yes."

"So, I knew enough about her. And she was in that picture you took at the office party. With her stupid dye job and her cat's-eye glasses? And when I saw her, I just…did it. Hit the gas."

"Where did you see her?"

Becca still works at the jewelry store at the mall. She's a manager now, and as far as I'm aware, no other employees have gone missing. But she has no reason to go anywhere near the industrial park where I work.

Her cheeks flush, and her mouth quirks. Then she waves a hand like a white flag. "Okay, fine, Carrie. I knew who she was from your picture, and one day— totally a coincidence—I saw her when I was getting gas. I complimented her stupid glasses and pretended I recognized her from her work on that three-hole punch design. Remember the one you worked on that she stole credit for?"

Of course I remember. It was Angelica's first month at Weston, and I'd been tasked with training and assessing her. Troy had forgotten to get her station set up, so we'd been working in tandem at mine. I'd had the three-hole punch project saved to my desktop, working on it whenever I wasn't training. And at some point during the week, Angelica had copied the file and used my design as the launching point for her own. When the pitches were due two weeks later, after she'd started working at her own station, she'd secretly emailed Troy to say she'd been struck by inspiration, and would he mind if she threw her hat in the ring for the pitch? And did he know she was so committed to designer office supplies that she had a tattoo of a binder clip on her ankle?

Troy presented both our designs to the client, and they ultimately chose Angelica's, which was a whopping 1 percent different from mine. Everyone knew the truth, but Troy said there was nothing to be done about it. The *client* had picked her design. Angelica swore she hadn't seen mine, independent evolution and all that. Plus, it was just a three-hole punch design—was it really that big a deal?

Troy decided it wasn't.

Becca, apparently, felt otherwise.

"So," she continues, "I pretended I was a head hunter looking for a lead designer for a company so fancy they couldn't be named until she'd signed a confidentiality agreement and asked if she'd be interested in meeting. She said yes, and I gave her the address of that abandoned paint factory—I told her it was being renovated to a state-of-the-art 'creative facility'—and asked her to come by on Friday before lunch."

She scrapes up the last of the parsnip puree with a teeth-aching grind of metal on porcelain. "She showed up late—like, how unprofessional—and I was so mad at her for what she'd done to you, and now trying to steal your promotion, and making me wait, that I just snapped." She drains her wine, apparently completely oblivious that her level of planning doesn't correspond with a sudden snap. "I know you feel bad for people, even when they're mean to you, but if it helps—it only took a second. She didn't even know it was happening."

A loud creak of the floorboards upstairs has us both jumping.

I glare at Becca. "Is there someone here?"

It wouldn't be the first time she'd brought someone to

my place and pretended it was hers so she didn't have to clean up her own messy apartment to play hostess. Her housekeeping skills are almost worse than her social skills.

"Of course not," she says, trying her best to appear hurt.

"Then who's up there?"

We're quiet for a minute, listening, but there's nothing.

"No one," Becca says. "This house is a million years old. It's always making noise. Simmer down."

As always, she's exaggerating, but she's not wrong. The place is nearly a hundred years old, and it moans and groans at inconvenient hours, prompted by gusts of wind, large trucks rumbling by, or a cupboard door closed too hard. The timing of the creak was the scariest thing about it.

Becca gets up and puts her plate in the sink. She comes back with the wine and refills her glass to the brim, red liquid nearly spilling over.

"I hate to tell you this, Carrie, but you're too nice. You never stand up for yourself. You never just say, *Fuck you, world*, and take what you want. That's why you're lucky to have me. I have your back, and you have mine."

That's only because I have no choice, something I know there's no point debating.

"Thanks for dinner." I get up and open the dishwasher to add my plate and freeze. It's a disaster inside. Five pots and nearly every utensil I own with massive amounts of gunk caked onto every item. At the bottom, shards of broken glass reflect the light. Glass Becca knows will jam the machine and force me to call a repairman, racking up hundreds of dollars in charges. Again.

"What the hell is this?"

She watches me over her wineglass, reveling in whatever havoc she hopes will follow. "I cleaned up," she says simply.

"How did you even use this many dishes?"

She drinks every drop of wine in her glass. "I made you dinner," she says, enunciating. "You're welcome."

"I'm not grateful."

She stands, flicking the wineglass with the tips of her fingers so it slides to the edge of the small table, its base hanging half an inch over the edge. "No kidding," she pouts. "You never are."

I turn my back on the performance. Giving Becca an audience is like giving a fire oxygen. It'll just intensify things. I know she'll linger if I start emptying the machine, trying to wring any perverse joy out of watching me clean up the latest mess she's made, so instead I just add my plate to the scene in the dishwasher, close it, and open the cupboard for the box of cookies I'd stashed behind a package of scalloped potatoes. It's still there.

I'm rewarded with Becca's tiny huff. She always takes whatever snacks she can find, eating everything or taking a bite from every cookie and leaving the wasted remains for me to throw away. There are two cookies left in the pack so I take one and bite into it, crumbs sticking to my lips. I throw the plastic sleeve into the garbage and use my nail to carefully separate the glued flaps at the bottom of the box so I can flatten it for recycling.

"Oh, for fuck's sake," Becca mutters, stomping off toward the front door. "You're just so— *Ugh*."

She's the murderer, but I'm the problem.

I say nothing, just wait as I hear the rustle of her putting on her coat and shoes—and probably stealing something of mine in the process—followed by the slam of the front door and an icy wash of October air floating down the hall. A spike of adrenaline rushes through me, making my head pound and my hands shake. I press them down on the counter, something sticky clinging to my palm. Even with Becca gone, traces of her linger everywhere. Her plate in the sink, her glass on the table. The slow cooker, the wine bottle, the mess in the dishwasher.

"Fuck you, world," I mutter, though the world is hardly to blame. My lower lip trembles, and my sinuses sting. I'm not upset about the fight. I'm frustrated. I hate her, and I can't get rid of her. I can't stop her. She just comes and comes and comes, and she never gets tired. Despite her complaints, she never gets bored. I've found ways to sidestep her intensity, but it mostly involves a calm facade that hides the simmering resentment underneath. These surges of adrenaline have no outlet except my shaking hands, clattering dishes together as I yank the mess out of the dishwasher to scrape clean and reorganize. I resent the energy I have to expend in not reacting to every one of Becca's petty stabs at my sanity.

I stalk into the living room to clean Becca's mess there, too. She must have come over early in the day because the cereal has had time to absorb the leftover milk, the pink circles bloated and leaking, one clinging to the side, already crusty and hard. There's an inch of beer left in the bottle, reeking of yeast, but the soda can's empty, some brand I've never heard of with a bright-pink tab. Becca must have brought it over in the hope I'd take the hint and start buying them for her.

I pause on my way back to the kitchen, turning slowly to look at the television tucked into the corner. I'd raced home, fully intending to plant myself on the couch and watch the news, but as always, my plans had taken a back-seat to Becca's. I balance the items in one hand and scoop up the remote with the other, pressing the POWER button. I flip to the local news, still reporting on the discovery at Kilduff. My mind flashes back to that moment in the forest, the movement in the trees. The pale glow of two dots catching the moonlight before flickering away.

Another creak from upstairs has me yelping, dishes flying. The cereal bowl crashes at my feet, soggy loops staining my socks pink. The beer bottle manages to land upside down, murky liquid immediately sliding under the couch, courtesy of my sloping floors. My heart pounds so loudly I almost miss the next creak, quieter than the first, more careful.

My eyes fly to the stairs that climb the wall in the front entry. They're steep and narrow, the wooden rail shaky. It's the only access to the second floor, leading straight down to the front door, the only exit point. If there's someone upstairs, they'll see me trying to flee and be close enough to stop me. The house technically has a back door, but it's so warped from bad weather that it's nearly impossible to open, and even harder to close. I haven't unlocked it in over a year. Again I see those eyes in the trees and imagine them lurking at the top of the steps, watching and waiting.

Another creak, this one familiar. It's the third step from the top of the staircase, and it squeaks like a soul being sucked out of the earthly plane, such a teeth-aching squeal that I always avoid it. I grab one of my lamps, the one with a blue damask shade and a silver trim. I'd spent a fortune on the fabric, but it had been worth it. Its real value, however, is the heavy base. I yank it hard enough to pop the plug out of the socket. My foot slips in the mushy cereal, and I bang my elbow against the wall, advertising my location. I dart a look at the door. Ten feet. Three steps to the hall, around the half wall, five steps to the door. I locked it when I came in, but it's just a dead bolt. Twist, yank, and I'll be in the front yard. If there's someone upstairs, they'll have to—

I run. My socked foot skids as I try to turn, and I smash into the side of the banister, my cheekbone banging hard against one of the spindles. I regain my balance and shove away from the wall, scrabbling for the bronze lock as heavy footsteps thud down the stairs at my back. A scream rips from my throat as my fingers slide uselessly around the metal. Then Becca's cackling laugh pierces my terrified fog.

I turn slowly, slumping against the door as she sprawls on the bottom steps and holds her stomach, laughing hysterically. I'm struggling to catch my breath, my heart in my throat, my knees so weak I'm only standing because I'm propped up.

"Oh my God," she gasps, pointing at me like a circus freak. "Your face! Your—your weapon. It looks like a—a—a penis." She chortles, the sound shrill and grating, and swipes at the tears rolling down her cheeks.

I find enough strength to straighten, pushing off the door and walking back to the living room with as much dignity as I can muster. My shoulders shake with rage, but that's what Becca wants so I busy myself adjusting the lamp and swiping the mess of cereal back into the bowl.

"Just get out, Becca."

"I'm going, I'm going." But she's not.

I grab a handful of tissues from the box on the ottoman and get on my knees to clean the spill from under the couch, spotting another one of Becca's soda cans, its tab glinting in the light.

"Why is this under the couch?" I demand, snatching it up.

She shrugs, zipping her coat. "I don't know. I've never seen it before."

"Of course not. You never know how things get ruined."

"Uh, yes, I do. *You* ruin them, remember? That's why people called you No Fun Carrie."

"No one called me that."

"Well, they should've. Because you're no fun."

"Very clever. Get out, Becca. You're drunk. I hope you're not driving."

"Why? Because I might hit someone?" She laughs again and reaches for the door. I watch her blond hair flounce, the leather of her jacket winking in the light.

"You need to stop letting yourself into my house," I hear myself say.

She lets go of the doorknob and turns to face me, startled. "What? Why?"

There are so many reasons, and she knows them all, and none of them matter. After a lifetime of experience trying and failing to win this war, the mere thought of it exhausts me.

"I need to sleep," I say instead. "Just go."

She takes her time adjusting her coat and fluffing her hair, trying to make me mad. I ignore her and scan the room for any more of the mess she's left for me to clean.

"Carrie," she says.

"What?"

Her eyes are fastened on the muted television, the screen casting flickering shadows across her face. "Look."

I don't want to fall for whatever stupid trick she has planned, but I glance over anyway.

BRAMPTON SERIAL KILLER? reads the scrolling script at the bottom of the screen. They've gone to the newsroom now, two serious anchors frowning at the camera. I grab the remote and turn up the volume.

"...gruesome discoveries at Kilduff Park," the middle-aged male anchor is saying. "Thirteen bodies in total, one deposited there as recently as three days ago, some believed to have been there as long as five years. All of which is incredibly alarming on its own, but now an inside source has told Channel 6 News that all of the recovered bodies have had one foot severed. The investigation is still ongoing, but the signs are clear: Brampton is the hunting ground of a serial killer. Tune in to Channel 6 for continued updates."

I turn slowly to stare at Becca. Suddenly, amid the flickering light and the horrifying news, the monster I thought I knew is the sister I've always known. Becca's expression is, ironically, now some semblance of human. Confusion, surprise, indignation.

"What the fuck?" we whisper at the same time, for very different reasons. I've always made a point not to look at the bodies we hide, and Becca has never mentioned a creepy foot fetish. But I saw Angelica the other night. I saw her ankle with the tattoo, and though I was trying not to look, I'm pretty sure I would have noticed if her other foot was missing. That, however, is not the worst part. The worst part is I thought Becca had killed thirteen people, not twenty-five. She's impossibly more awful than I knew.

"They," she says, eyes locked on the television, a frown on her face, "are *not* talking about me." This, for Becca, is the worst part.

I assume she's referring to the reporter suggesting that a very deranged individual has been frequenting the park, but still I say, "What do you mean?"

"I mean, I've only ever put one body in Kilduff, and she definitely had her fucking foot attached. That's gross."

I cross my arms doubtfully. "You're saying you didn't kill the other twelve people they found?"

"Not those twelve!"

"Then who did?"

"I don't know!"

Becca's not a good actress, but right now she's quite genuinely irritated, like she'd always wondered what it would be like to have her crimes uncovered, and this wasn't nearly as glamorous as what she'd envisioned.

"Becca," I say finally, neither willing nor able to believe the even worse alternative to this scenario, "if you're not the one who put those bodies there, then who did?"

She looks at me like I'm an idiot. "A *serial killer*, Carrie."

CHAPTER 3

By Friday, the police have identified four more bodies. One is from Brampton, the others from surrounding towns and counties. And so far, with the exception of Angelica, they're people who, if they were reported missing at all, were never really looked for: sex workers, homeless people, drug addicts.

For perhaps the first time in history, the rest of the country—and many parts of the world—is interested in Brampton, Maine, population 45,509. And while crime buffs are already speculating on the likelihood of a serial killer stalking New England and using Kilduff as a dumping ground, many are busy pointing out that the "true" horror here is the people whose lives were considered so worthless that it's only once dead that anyone bothered to remember them at all.

I don't care about any of this.

What I care about is the fact that the odd person out in this whole situation is Angelica. Angelica, whom we buried, Becca swears, with both feet. People have already jumped on the fact that Angelica doesn't fit the "pattern." No one has asked if she happened to have been dumped in the park by a different person, but they're certainly making waves that it's the discovery of the body of a middle-class white woman that has prompted an investigation into the others.

I don't know what to believe anymore. My rational mind is certain Angelica had two feet when we dumped her in the shallow grave. My dreams tell me otherwise. That I saw the tattoo and ignored the shadowy stump next to it. That the carpet hadn't unrolled fully, and I saw only what I was able to handle. And each time the sun rises and I wake, I'm more and more confused. I don't want to believe Becca has done this. But I'd be a fool not to.

Over breakfast, I read the article on the front page of the *Brampton Chronicle*. It's more speculation and fearmongering than anything: Keep your doors locked, your children close. It will be awhile before they identify everyone, but so far the youngest body found was twenty-two at the time they disappeared, the oldest sixty-seven. Eight men, five women. A mix of races. The only thing they have in common is that they were all dressed in ill-fitting clothes, and they're all down a foot. Nine right feet; four left. The only thing more horrifying than the story itself is the moniker the press has given the killer: Footloose.

I put my cereal bowl in the dishwasher and finish my cold tea, collecting the recycling bin from under the sink before heading to the front door. Becca's specialty soda cans sit on top, the logo a smug-looking elephant wearing a bowler that makes me grit my teeth. I haven't seen Becca since Monday, and while I asked her to stay away and her absence should be a relief, it's more suspicious than anything. She never respects boundaries. She also never recycles, which makes me even more suspicious.

I pull on a pair of boots and carry the recycling bin down to the curb for pickup, my breath hanging in white gusts in the icy November air. Halloween has come and gone without much fanfare, parents unwilling to let their kids take candy from strangers while somebody's burying bodies in the local park. I have three bags of mini chocolate bars sitting in the kitchen, chanting my name.

I wave to Mr. Myer across the street, also bringing out his trash for collection, and trudge back up the walkway and around the side of the house. The brick-paved path is narrow and uneven, and I run my hand along the wood siding for balance as I walk, keeping my head down to watch my step. There's a larger paved area at the back of the house for the trash cans, and in the colder months, the only reason I come back here is to bring them out front on collection day. The dead grass in the yard is gilded silver, the blades sticking up straight and twinkling in the early-morning sunshine. It's the sunshine that makes the flattened patches of grass stand out stark among the others.

Footprints.

I stumble to a halt and gawk at them, trying to think of the weather over the past week, since the last time I was out here. They could be mine. Maybe I walked over the grass and it's simply stayed so cold that the imprints remained. But I know I only walked on the paving stones, retrieving the garbage cans and dragging them up front. I don't need to step on the grass. And these steps go past the trash and stop at the base of the stairs that lead to my decaying deck. Which accesses the back door.

I glance around cautiously before stepping past the other prints and following them up to the deck. It's gleaming with frost, already melting in the morning sunshine, but there's no mistaking the dirty tread marks in front of the door, the one I haven't been able to open in a year, its wood too warped and misshapen. From three feet away, the door appears the same as I remember it. Peeling white paint, tarnished brass knob, one of those cheap locks you twist from inside. It has no window, no peephole. A piece of wood trim is broken off, but it was always missing.

There are no scratch marks around the lock, nothing to suggest anyone tried to pick it. Even if they did, it would still be nearly impossible to dislodge the door, swollen and stuck as it is. Still, my breath comes shallow as I think about those eyes in the woods, the ones watching us bury Angelica. I reach out a trembling hand and grip the knob, freezing my fingers, and turn. It moves half an inch before the lock catches.

My shoulders sag in relief and embarrassment. It's locked. And coming around back, trying the handle and giving up, is the work of a lazy person. Which means it's Becca, not some mysterious watcher.

I step carefully off the sagging deck and retrace my steps, parallel to the others, like half a rainbow arching to the paving stones. The imprints left by my boots are considerably smaller than the first set, by at least two inches. Becca's feet are bigger than mine, I remind myself. It's one of the few things she didn't have to lord over me when we were growing up. She was taller, thinner, had straighter teeth. And bigger feet.

I drag the trash cans to the curb and park them next to the recycling, telling myself everything is fine. But my breath is coming faster, hanging in the air in desperate, heavy clouds, lingering like an omen.

———

The atmosphere at the office that day is subdued, as it has been since we got the news about Angelica. The detectives haven't come by again, but I'm still too paranoid to relax. Fortunately, that paranoia only helps me blend in, since everyone in Brampton is now living in terror, glancing over their shoulders at every turn, double and triple-checking their doors at night.

I gaze past my computer monitor at the dark office in the corner. There's been no word about the promotion, and I don't know if that's good or bad. I certainly can't ask, not with Troy pacing uselessly back and forth in his own small office, like he might help solve the mystery if he just walks enough.

From my seat, I can see a handful of other monitors, and hardly anyone is working. They're reading every article, every forum, every word they can about serial killers and theories about who and what and why and how. Beyond having identified a few victims and confirming that they were found missing a foot, the police have released little more. No official cause of death. No word if the foot was severed before or after they died. No suggestion that Angelica's death is being treated any differently than the others. The lack of information has created a vacuum, and the world is desperate to fill it with its own unhinged theories.

I take a break from my binder clip design and search *Brampton serial killer,* reasoning that if everyone else is doing it, it will look strange if I don't. The first page is various links to the local paper, all of which I've already scoured, and the second is more forums playing host to crime buffs and theorists. I skimmed those last night, and none of them have come close to identifying Becca or someone like her. They're of the very strong opinion that the killer must be a man, since women don't have the propensity for this level of sustained violence.

Or they're just better at covering it up.

There's a new link on page four, one I haven't seen yet. It's an article in a small paper from the next town over, and it's called "We Love You, Fiona McBride." Automatically, my mind flashes to the posters disintegrating all over town, hanging in tatters from lampposts and bus stops. Her parents—who actually appeared to care that their daughter was missing—have been holding their breath, waiting for that fated phone call from the police, telling them their daughter's body was among those found in the park. But she wasn't.

I skim the rest of the article. Despite the guileless face smiling cheerily in the photograph, her parents describe Fiona as troubled and destructive, headed down a clichéd, dangerous road. They had last seen her three days before they reported her missing because she'd taken to running away or spending nights with friends, both of which meant squatting in local drug dens. A sweep of the known haunts had turned up nothing, with a few rumors that Fiona had been there briefly but not returned. She hasn't been seen since.

To the best of my knowledge, Becca doesn't kill this frequently. If Fiona disappeared two weeks ago, it would be just a week between killing Fiona and Angelica. In my experience, Becca kills about once a year. But the alternative to Becca being the killer is that there's a *second* serial killer in Brampton, and even though I'm alarmingly inured to Becca's hobby, my mind is both unwilling and unable to wrap itself around the possibility of two prolific killers calling our small town home.

I close the article. I know some people say the not knowing is the hardest part, but as someone who knows her sister is a serial killer, I respectfully disagree. I would much rather not know. Knowing opens up too many possibilities in my mind, too many paths to follow, never knowing where they lead, or along which one Becca is lurking. It's the story of my life, and I hate it.

I spot the time on the corner of my monitor: 11:58 a.m. I'm due to meet Graham for lunch at the Thai place in the business park, so I pull on my coat and head for the elevator without making eye contact with anyone. After my interview with Greaves, murmurs started that I didn't seem quite sad enough about Angelica's death. Coupled with the promotion dangling over my head like a sword, the office has banded together like a miniature, ineffective mob, leaving me the odd woman out.

The icy air outside is a slap in the face. It feels colder than it did this morning, the sky more blue, the sun searing my eyes. Even without the buffer of the clouds, the temperature is near freezing, and I shrug deeper into my parka and jam my hands into my pockets. I didn't bring a hat, and now I glance longingly at my car as I walk past, my ears already aching with cold.

I stop.

My car is in its usual parking spot next to the lamp-post, and it's hard to tell in the bright sun, but it looks like the interior light is on. I squint and walk closer, frowning when I realize the driver's-side door is open. Brampton may be small enough that people seldom lock their doors, but we always *close* them. I try to think back to three hours ago when I arrived at work, but it's such a routine trip that I can't decide if what I'm remember-ing is from today or the thousand other days that came before it.

I circle the car, parked innocently in a long line of equally uninspired cars, dirt flecked across bumpers, the windshields smudged with leaky stains left by the salt from the roads. Bending slightly, I squint to look into the driver's-side window, but nothing inside the car is out of order, and when I pull open the door and stick my head in, it looks and smells fine, too. I shiver when a gust of icy air reminds me it's November and give up my inspection. It was probably just me, stressed and careless. If someone was going to steal my car, they could do a lot worse than forget to close the door.

I hustle across the business park, the ten-minute trek increasingly windy. By the time I arrive at Thai Me Up, my curls are a tangled nest, and my cheeks are so cold I can barely smile when I spot Graham at a small table by the window. Wearing a navy suit with a red-and-white-striped tie, he looks like he just stepped off his nonexistent private yacht. After a morning of people avoiding eye contact and whispering behind my back, his genuinely happy-to-see-you smile warms me more than the restaurant's unreliable heating system.

"Hey," he says, wrapping me in a hug and kissing my cheek. "You look pretty."

"I'm freezing." I slip out of my jacket, shivering in my black sweater and trousers, and take a seat, the dim lights of the restaurant glinting off the standard decor of carved wooden wall art, gleaming gold Buddhas, and framed photos of the Thai royal family. A server comes by with a cup of tea, and I gratefully wrap my hands around the porcelain, letting the heat seep in.

"Are people still being weird?" Graham asks. I told him about the awkwardness with my co-workers, and because he used to work at Weston, he understands better than anyone.

"No more than usual."

"And no word on the promotion?"

I shake my head. Graham's the only one who understands how it's possible to feel sad about Angelica and still want the job.

"You'll get it," he says.

I worry the cup between my fingers. "I don't know. Troy's not exactly decisive, and this might be the reason he needs to stall indefinitely."

Graham studies me for a minute, and my heart skips a beat. Not the giddy, excited kind of skip like when we first met, or even ten days ago, but the paranoid kind. The kind that makes me wonder if he sees something in my face, if he secretly believes I had a hand in this.

"It's about that painting, isn't it?" he says finally.

"What?"

"The stapler painting. The one you've had in your bedroom closet for months, waiting to hang in your new office."

My heart thuds painfully against my ribs. "No," I say, my tone unconvincing.

Graham laughs. "Why don't you just hang it at home if you like it so much? I can help you. Then, when you get the job, you can bring it to the office."

"I don't want to hang it at home," I say, too sharply. Defensively. "It's for work," I amend, when Graham lifts an eyebrow. "Like a reward. Hanging it before I get the promotion—*if* I get it—is like popping the champagne before the party. It's premature."

"Okay," he says. "Up to you."

The server chooses that moment to return, interrupting the mild tension. Graham and I don't really fight. It's one of the things I love about him. With Becca, it's the constant, quiet battle to not give in to her petty jabs, the nonstop effort of restraint. Graham rarely takes offense at anything, and he's never hurtful. He's uncommonly kind and self-aware, the polar opposite of my sister. Spending time with Becca is like tiptoeing through a war zone, waiting for the death blow at any second. Being with Graham is like going for a normal walk, anywhere, anytime.

I order the lunch special I always get, and Graham does the same, giving me a questioning look before ordering a plate of spring rolls for us to split.

"Sorry," I say when the server is gone. "I'm really stressed."

He reaches over to touch my hand. "I get it. Everyone is. The stuff that's been going on, it's crazy. Maybe you should spend more nights at my place."

The offer's not even lecherous. He truly thinks he could protect me from Footloose, who I'm 92 percent certain is my sister. Graham and I live on different sides of town, which puts us each closer to our jobs. Driving from Graham's place would add nearly thirty minutes to my commute; same for him if he stays with me. Because of it, we normally spend weekends together, not weeknights, to cut back on morning travel.

"What do you think's going on with all that?" I ask, avoiding the suggestion.

A flicker of hurt crosses his face but is gone just as quickly. "I don't know what to think," he says. "A serial killer? Using Brampton to hide his bodies? It's insane, and it's all anyone at work is talking about. One of my clients was saying that his neighbor's cousin disappeared three years ago, and they never knew what happened. There were rumors about him having money trouble and hiding out from loan sharks or something, but the family never believed it."

I think of the pictures in the paper this morning. "Was he one of the bodies they found?"

Graham shakes his head. "Not yet."

I gulp my lukewarm tea. If it wasn't one of the bodies at Kilduff, it could very well be someone I helped Becca dispose of. I rack my brain, trying to think back three years. I've always made a point not to learn the names of Becca's victims or her reasons for killing them, but sometimes she talks while we're working and I get the information whether I like it or not.

The thirteen bodies I've helped hide have blurred together in a horrible maelstrom, but one of the reasons they haven't been investigated more—or as part of a terrible whole—is because Becca occasionally makes an effort to create a reason for the disappearance, just like Shanna's impromptu Mexican vacation. Gambling, sex trafficking, and mental illness are a few of the stories she's planted. One missing person a year isn't likely to point the police in the direction of a serial killer; thinning the odds with her rumors makes it even less likely.

"What do you think the deal is with the missing feet?" I ask as the server returns with the spring rolls. If she overhears, her expression doesn't change. She's probably heard nothing but serial killer talk for the past few days.

Graham takes a spring roll and dips it into the dish of pale-yellow sauce. "I don't know. I mean, what if this is all a crazy coincidence? What if animals gnawed off the feet and the bodies are a random assortment, not just one guy dumping them there? What if we get everyone worked up and paranoid, and it's all for nothing?"

I stare at him, surprised. "Do you really think that? All those bodies... are a coincidence?"

Honestly, it'd be great if the police took that approach, but the idea is even more mind boggling than the possibility of Brampton playing host to two serial killers.

He shrugs. "I'm just saying, it's too soon to jump to conclusions. And you, living alone in that old house, I don't want you to be afraid."

I think of the creaks and groans I ignore on a daily basis, the ones that have started to sound increasingly ominous since the discovery of Angelica's body. And while I don't agree with the "coincidence" theory, I do agree that it's too soon to jump to conclusions, though I don't know which one's worse: My sister's an even more insane serial killer than I already thought or she has competition?

———

For the third night in a row, I return home to a cold, empty house. The door is locked, the kitchen is clean, and there are no cereal bowls in the living room. No Becca.

I tell myself to relax as I hang my coat. That what I should be feeling is relief, not unease. But like so many Brampton residents, I'm uncomfortable. Even the small chance that the person responsible for the bodies in Kilduff is not my sister has me on edge.

I head for the kitchen, tossing a tray of frozen pasta in the microwave and pacing as I wait for it to heat. My eyes lock on the warped back door, time and weather pushing it inward in a gentle swell, the white paint peeling. The door is about six feet away, but I squint at it anyway, the brass knob gleaming too bright in the fluorescent light. I step closer, bending, and use my hand to shield against the glare.

It's unlocked.

It's one of those tiny locks set into the knob, turned horizontal when locked, vertical when open. And now it's vertical. To be sure, I reach out slowly and turn the knob, waiting for the telltale catch I felt this morning when I did the same thing from the opposite side. This time, there is no catch. The knob turns 180 degrees, popping slightly, the door groaning as it tries unsuccessfully to release from the jamb.

The microwave beeps, and I jump away from the door as though I've been burned. My heart hammers, and I feel flushed and hot, jittery. This has to be Becca. It has to be. She still has keys so she could have let herself in and unlocked the back door in order to retrace her steps into the backyard and...What? Come in through a noisy, stuck door instead of creeping in through the front? She might get a kick out of messing with me this way, but above all she's lazy, and the extra effort isn't her style.

I glance out the window over the sink into the backyard. It's dark outside and too bright inside, and I can't
see anything. I pinch the lock and turn it to horizontal, the tiny piece of metal suddenly feeling small and
insignificant.

I retrieve my dinner from the microwave, the ravioli
still frozen in the center, the white sauce burned to brown
around the edges. I stir it up and chew carefully, eyes on
the window. I never got around to hanging curtains in
here so anyone outside could easily see me and I wouldn't
be able to see them.

I take my meal into the living room and sit on the couch
to eat. I reach automatically for the remote but think of
the nonstop news cycle, *serial killer serial killer serial killer*,
and decide against it. My eyes flicker to the curtains on
the front window, white with yellow stripes, now closed.
For a second, I feel relieved. Then I stiffen in my seat.

The curtains were open when I left this morning.

I glance around for more signs of change, any shift in
my environment to suggest I'm not the only one in it. The
lamps are in place. The couch cushions are in order. The
lonely picture on the coffee table is still upright, me and
Becca, mugging for the camera when we were kids, matching red bathing suits and sandy legs from a day at the beach.

I get up and walk to the curtains. They stop three
inches from the ground and my eyes scan the space between the hem and the carpet, looking for two socked
feet, size nine, belonging to Becca.

There's nobody there.

I reach tentatively for the fabric and pull back one side and then the other, swallowing hard as I peer into my small front yard. I'm not sure what I'm expecting. I parked there half an hour ago, walked up the steps, and opened the door. It's just dead grass and an oak tree that's lost its leaves. My car doors are closed and locked. I triple-checked before coming inside.

I let out a shaky breath.

This is Becca's petty way of getting revenge. She'll probably laugh it off later, whenever we make up, and tell me to be grateful she didn't run me over. *So I left some footprints and closed the curtains! You never told me not to!*

I tell myself to calm down. I know better than to react to this. She doesn't even need to be here to enjoy the results of her stupid pranks. She's probably at home, wrapped in a blanket, watching *The Voice* and smirking when she thinks of me here, finding her little discrepancies. When we were growing up, she used to run up the stairs ahead of me at bedtime, switching off all the lights. The house was old, and the only switch was at the top, meaning I had to climb the dark stairs and enter the even darker hall, lined with yawning doorways, knowing Becca lurked in one, waiting to jump out and terrify me. The anticipation was always scarier than her actual attack. It got to the point where she'd just run up and get in bed, leaving me to tiptoe tearfully up the stairs, waiting for the inevitable, hearing her snickers when it didn't come.

I give up on the cold pasta and take it to the kitchen, tossing the half-full tray in the trash. I have the house on a timer so the heat should come on about thirty minutes before I get home, but it barely works. The one—and only—good thing about Becca letting herself in is that she always blasts the heat so it's warm when I get here. I hear the furnace in the basement, rumbling frantically as it tries to do its job, but it'll be awhile. The sweater I wore to work is too thin, and I blame the cold for my goose bumps, not my overactive imagination.

I head for the stairs, stopping at the bottom, knowing there's a real chance Becca is up there, plotting her ulti-mate scare. Unlike when we were kids, there's a switch down here, so I flip it on and listen. No telltale creaks. No snickers.

I steel myself and start up the stairs, making myself climb at a normal speed, no tentative crawl. I step over the howling third step from the top and pause on the tiny landing. There are two small bedrooms up here and one bathroom. If Becca wanted to scare me, she'd be in my room, since I rarely use the other.

I hum to myself, unconvincingly calm, and flip on the light in my room as I enter. If I'm expecting something terrible, I'm disappointed. It's the same as I left it this morning. Neatly made queen bed and heavy wooden bed-room set inherited from my parents, the wood too dark.

It's an older home so the closet is small, but unlike Becca, I don't have so many clothes that I require my own dressing room. The wooden doors are closed, as always, hiding my jumble of boring sweaters and blouses, work pants and skirts. The stapler painting is in there, too, the one I'm waiting to hang when I get my promotion.

I reach for the door handles—tiny crystal orbs, original to the house—then I hesitate. If Becca's here, this is where she'll be. My bed is too low to the ground for her to hide underneath, as she often did when we were kids, reaching up to grab my foot if it hung over the edge of the mattress.

I prepare myself not to scream and yank open the doors.

No Becca. No monsters skulking in the dark. My clothing waits on the other side, jammed in whatever order the free hangers dictated, the shelf up top holding my favorite Brampton College sweatshirt. I pull it down and drag it on over the top of my work sweater, immediately feeling better.

I step back to close the doors, frowning as something bright on the floor catches my eye. It's the corner of my stapler painting. It's normally jammed all the way against the left wall, held there by a couple of hanging dresses and a pair of tall boots so it can't tip over, but now it's been wedged away from the wall, at an angle.

I slowly lever out the picture, about three feet square, canvas wrapped around a plain wood frame, neon staplers on a bright white background. I hold it up to the light and peer carefully to see if Becca added any special details—her initials, a pornographic drawing, the words

I killed ANGELICA—but there's nothing. I turn it over to check the back. It's bare. I must have bumped it when I was grabbing an outfit this morning and failed to notice. I gather the clothes so I can slip it back into its position flat against the wall, freezing when I see something I never would have thought to look for.

There's a footprint, right where the picture should have been. It's just one, and only half, the imprint large and dark and eerily familiar. If this were a TV show, this is the part where they'd compare impressions of the print from the deck and this one, running them through a database to determine exactly which style of boot this was, and where they're sold, and who last bought one in this town.

This isn't a TV show, but I don't need an expert to tell me it's the same boot. Just like I don't need anyone to tell me the painting wasn't moved to hide the footprint. It was moved to hide whoever was standing behind it, and whoever plans to hide there again.

CHAPTER 4

I spend the night at Graham's. I wasn't supposed to, but there was no way I'd be able to sleep knowing Becca's up to something, and the familiar uneasiness that always creeps in when she's around has built to unbearable levels. After trying unsuccessfully to keep myself busy, I'd broken down around ten o'clock and messaged him. The harmless creaks and groans of the house had turned into ominous footsteps and sneaking breaths, and if Graham hadn't answered, I'd have gone to a hotel. Fortunately, he called back right away from his work party, saying the event was horrible and he was desperate for an excuse to flee. A frightened girlfriend would do the trick.

"At least this serial killer business is good for something, right?" he'd cracked, trying to make me laugh. I was shaking too hard to find anything funny, but I'd mustered up a giggle to reward him for the effort and was halfway to my car before we hung up.

When I wake the next morning, it's after nine, and the sun is fighting its way through the gap in the curtains. Graham's side of the bed is empty, and I stretch out, calm and comfortable, a complete 180 from my near panic attack less than twelve hours ago.

Graham has a one-bedroom condo in a new building on the opposite side of Brampton, with glass-walled towers for neighbors and a park with a human-made pond installed across the street. I get up and tug back the curtain with a finger, admiring the view. I bought my place because it was a cozy, old neighborhood, each house unique and distinct, with established trees and narrow roads. But Graham's development has a guard station at the entrance, two places to swipe your key fob, and an eagle-eyed concierge to stop any random person from wandering in. Until now, I'd found those features unnecessary.

Across the street, a guy in shorts and a running jacket jogs around the park with a pit bull on a leash, and two yoga moms push strollers with one hand while balancing coffee cups in the other. The trees in the park are young and spindly, and the park itself takes up the whole small block. Compared with Kilduff, it's nothing. Compared with Kilduff, it's a relief.

The smell of frying sausages wafts under the door, and my rumbling stomach nags me to get out of bed.

I pull on my Brampton College sweatshirt and wander down the hall to find Graham at the stove, sausage and eggs frying, toast toasting, champagne glasses half full of orange juice.

"Hey," he says, turning as I enter. "Good morning." The kitchen is half the size of mine, but everything about it is shiny and new, infinitely nicer. Granite counters, stainless-steel appliances, cupboard doors that close properly.

I stand on my tiptoes to kiss him. "It smells good in here."

"It's my new body spray."

"Sausage-scented?"

"Dogs love it."

I laugh and take out plates and cutlery. "Can I help?"

"Nope. Everything's ready. Just take a seat, and I'll bring it over."

Even after a year, everything about Graham is foreign to me. His kindness, his consideration. Not just because he's the complete opposite of Becca, but because he's not someone who would tolerate Becca. My parents never made hot breakfast because Becca said the smell nauseated her. If they wanted bacon and eggs, they had to go to the diner in town. We couldn't have sugar cereal because Becca said it would make her fat. No orange juice with pulp. No toaster strudels. No non-organic vegetables. My parents catered to her because it was easier than dealing with her tantrums, and easier to slip me a five-dollar bill once a week and tell me to buy myself something on my way to school. Five dollars, we all knew, could buy nothing.

"Here we go," Graham says, sliding a steaming plate in front of me. He retrieves the glasses and a bottle of champagne from the fridge, pouring it into the waiting orange juice. "I stole this from the party," he confesses. "I thought you needed it more than the doctors."

I take a sip, and it's perfect. "You have no idea."

He smiles and cuts a sausage. "I called a locksmith," he says.

I pause. "Why?"

"So you can change your locks."

Graham had agreed to come over today to help install a floodlight in my backyard and do a thorough run-through of my house in case Becca had prepared any other hiding spots, but we hadn't talked about changing the locks. I'd told him every detail of last night's discoveries, and he'd listened, patient and concerned. At no point had he told me I was being dramatic or ridiculous. He'd listened and then offered to help.

"We were just supposed to install the floodlight."

"I know. But what's the point of shining a light on Becca while she unlocks your door?"

"Well, how much does that cost?" Brampton is not an expensive city but my job only pays so much, and the cost of maintaining an old home is high. I've been tackling projects as finances and enthusiasm allowed—an updated bathroom, insulated windows, new roof. Until now, new locks had not even factored into my thoughts.

"It's not a lot," he answers. "And if it's too much, I'll pay. I'm thrilled you're here, Carrie, but I'd rather you not be here because you're too scared to be at home."

"I'm not—"

He gives me a look that says there's no point finishing the sentence. "You love that place," he says. "And you shouldn't be afraid to live there. Let me help you."

I study my plate. I know he's just being kind. And I have money in the bank, so I can pay for the locksmith. In fact, I should have done it before. There are just so many things I want to do to thwart Becca, but I don't do anything because she always finds a way to circumvent my efforts. And I'm not great at accepting help from people. My parents loved me, but anything they did for me, they had to do double for Becca. I had a scholarship that paid half my college tuition. Becca had no interest in going to school, but when she learned I was going, she applied, too. No scholarship, so my parents had to fork over the whole amount from their retirement savings. If I went on a school trip, Becca demanded the same amount in spending money. If I got a new pair of jeans from Abercrombie, Becca needed two new pairs from Nordstrom's. We don't even have a Nordstrom's, so my parents paid for expedited shipping. Eventually, I stopped asking for help, and they stopped offering. Becca never stopped.

"I'll cancel the locksmith," Graham says when the

silence has stretched on too long. "I'm sorry. I shouldn't have assumed. When you're ready, you can—"

"No," I interrupt. "It's a good idea. I need to change the locks. I'm not sure how much of a defense it will be against Becca, but it's worth a try."

"We'll get a bunch of garlic, too," Graham says. He sometimes jokes that she's a vampire because she's pale and bloodthirsty. "And hang mirrors all over the place."

"Not the mirrors," I tell him, sipping my mimosa. "Then she'll never leave."

———

Graham's dad was a general contractor, and Graham worked with him growing up, which is the only way we're able to get a floodlight installed on a hundred-year-old home without an electrical fire or a four-figure invoice.

When we arrive at my place, we do a quick check of the house, even the creepy basement, and find nothing out of order. Outside, there are no new footprints, and the back door is still locked, both good signs. Or not. If Becca's been back, she's been more careful.

It takes three hours to get the floodlight working, and during that time the locksmith shows up. He inspects the locks on both doors, gives an efficient nod, and gets to work. It takes him less than half an hour, and by the time he's done I'm feeling much better. We head around to the front of the house so I can retrieve my purse from the hall table. The morning is again bright and sunny, the cold air drifting in as the locksmith props open the door with his boot and waits on the steps. Graham disappears into the kitchen to make tea, and I shiver as I fish out my wallet and sort through the myriad cards, hunting for the right one. I don't see it.

I mutter an apology and sift through the cards more carefully, setting them on the table next to my keys. Points card for the grocery store, another for the drugstore, a gift card for a clothing store at the mall, one for the movie theater, one for a coffee shop.

And no credit card.

I seldom use my card unless I'm buying something online. I can't actually recall the last time I looked at it because I have the number memorized. I don't even check the statement. At the end of every month, I glance at the balance online and pay it without verifying the charges. They've never been outlandish enough to concern me.

"I'm sorry," I tell the locksmith, forcing a smile even while my hands shake. I know I'm overreacting. It's just misplaced. Just like I forgot I closed the curtains and didn't shut my car door. I jam the cards back into my wallet as Graham comes into the room.

"Everything okay?" he asks.

"I can't find my credit card," I say, my smile tight. "I might have left it in my other purse."

Graham falters for a second but then smiles back. He

knows I don't have another purse, and he knows I don't use the card. He's always chastising me for paying with debit when I could be racking up travel miles.

"I'll get this," he says, reaching into his pocket and pulling out his wallet. "No harm done."

And while the words are easy enough and the locksmith is entirely unconcerned, the fact that we're changing the locks suggests some type of harm has been done. Or will be done. And the combination of the floodlight and the footprints and the moved picture and the unlocked door and the missing card—on their own, they're insignificant. But taken together? I don't know, but I don't like it. Because as much as I dislike Becca, she's not subtle. She's not patient. She's big scares and mocking laughs and jabs designed to get reactions. This isn't her style.

And that's the scariest thing of all.

The locksmith leaves, and Graham puts away his wallet. He's about to say something when the kettle whistles from the kitchen, making us both jump.

He laughs, breaking the tension. "Forgot about that," he says.

"I'm sorry." I follow him down the hall. "I don't know where my card—"

"I don't care about your card," he says mildly, grabbing two mugs from the cupboard and carefully closing the door that never really closes. "I'm just glad it's done and you'll feel better."

I swallow and watch him pour hot water into each cup

before adding a tea bag. The light, the locks, the boy-friend to check for strangers hiding in closets—it should make me feel better. But it doesn't.

"I'm going to cancel the card," I say, instead of acknowledging my feelings. Or anything else. "I haven't used it in forever. I could have lost it a month ago and not noticed."

"You'd notice it more if you were collecting travel miles," Graham teases as he passes me the steaming mug. "And we were on a beach in Bali."

"I'd definitely notice if we were in Bali."

My laptop is on the kitchen table so I sip my tea as I wait for it to wake up and then log into my bank account. I'm about to click the button to cancel my card when Graham stops me. I hadn't realized he was right over my shoulder.

"Hang on," he says. "Don't cancel until you've looked at the charges. I had to cancel a card once, and they closed the account right away. I couldn't see it again until the new card was activated. You don't want to wait a week to find out if someone's been subscribing to porn sites at your expense."

I force a smile. A porn subscription is the least of my worries. But he makes a good point, and I haven't bought anything I care about him seeing so I click on the account and wait as it loads up the recent transactions. There are only a handful, nothing a credit card company would consider suspicious.

I skim the most recent charges, only six in the last month. A specialty lightbulb I had to order online for an antique fixture in the bathroom; new door handles for the kitchen, to go on the doors I haven't ordered. A bill payment for my cable, my electricity, and something for $38.99 at H-S Loc 49 four days ago. I definitely didn't use my credit card four days ago.

"I don't know what that is," I tell Graham, pointing. "Do you?"

He's shaking his head. "Never heard of it."

I do an internet search for the name but nothing comes up, and I stare at the screen, perturbed. For the most part, my life motors along at a steady, uninterrupted pace. Approximately once a year, Becca calls me to move furniture, but that's the biggest anomaly in my otherwise-boring life. Then it's back to normal. These tiny irritations are like speed bumps that keep popping up without warning, sending me off course, making me uneasy.

"You can dispute the charge," Graham says, patting my shoulder reassuringly. "Just tell the credit card company. It's not much, they'll believe you."

"Right." But my mind is racing, trying desperately to think of any business Becca frequents with 49 in the name and coming up empty.

"Though it seems like a waste of a good credit card," Graham remarks, sitting down across from me. "Forty bucks? At least buy a computer or something, you know?"

Who the hell steals a credit card and buys something for thirty-eight dollars and ninety-nine cents?"

That's exactly what I'm worried about.

—

Detective Greaves comes by the next day. He just knocks on the door like a regular person, calm and unhurried. I, on the other hand, am a nervous wreck. To prove to Graham just how fine I was, I'd insisted on sleeping alone at my place, and had done nothing more than sit bolt upright on the couch in the dark living room, waiting for an attack that never came.

My hair is tangled, I have bags under my eyes, and five cups of coffee between midnight and 9:00 a.m. have left me a twitchy mess. There's a brown stain on the front of my Brampton sweatshirt, and my sweatpants have a hole in the knee. When I open the door and blink in wonder at Greaves, I must look like the most guilty suspect in the world. Especially when my eyes immediately start darting around behind him, waiting for the SWAT team to descend, guns drawn, arrest warrants at the ready.

None of that happens. Greaves is alone. He's wearing the leather jacket and jeans from before, his eyes cool and assessing as he gives me a tiny smile. "Good morning."

It's another beautiful, sunny day, the sky bright and blue, the air crisp and clean. But it's the furthest thing from a good morning, no matter what he says.

"Um, hi." I gulp nervously. I brushed my teeth—thank God—but I had another cup of coffee after and still look like I woke up ten minutes ago.

"I'm Detective Greaves," he reminds me, passing over a business card. I take it, though I still have the first one.

"I know." My eyes flicker to my car, still parked in the driveway. Doors still closed. That's a good sign.

"May I come in?"

I hesitate before stepping back and gesturing him inside. He wipes his feet on the entry mat as he glances around, taking in the surroundings. The closet beside him, the staircase that shares the same wall. The kitchen is visible at the end of the hall, its fake yellow glow clashing with the natural light of the sun spilling through the window.

At least the living room is tidy, now that Becca has stopped coming around. No cereal bowls, soda cans, or stray socks. The television is off, the lamps dark. It looks just like a normal, innocent living room on a normal day.

"New lock?" Greaves asks, making me jump. He's nodding at the door, the shiny new silver knob.

"Huh?"

"You okay?"

I shake my head and swipe a hand over my eyes. "S-sorry," I say, faking a smile. "First cup of coffee always makes me jittery. Um, yes, it's a new lock. I had it installed yesterday."

"Why?"

"Because it was old. Is everything okay?"

"I have a few follow-up questions, if that's all right."

I glance out the front window. We're still alone.

"Where's your partner?"

He smiles. "Asking someone else follow-up questions."

He's already inside so I can't very well say no. I wish I'd let Graham stay the night when he'd offered. He'd know what to do.

"Okay," I say, because I have to. "Do you want coffee?"

"No, I'm all right. Shall we talk in here?"

I think of the kitchen, with its fluorescent lights and coffee smells, like a police interview room on an old television show. It's not flattering at the best of times, which this is not. I wish desperately I was showered and dressed. I look like a car thief.

I lead the way around the short wall and take a seat on the couch. Greaves sits on the matching love seat, kitty corner to me, our knees a couple of feet apart.

"Lived here long?" he asks, taking out his notepad.

"Three years."

"Nice neighborhood."

"I like it."

"Have you ever heard of Soda Jack?"

I frown. "What? Like, Coke and Jack Daniel's?"

"No. Like Soda Jack."

I'm confused. "No."

"Never bought it?"

"I don't even know what it is."

"You sure?"

"Yes."

"Ever shop online at Hartmann's?"

I'm already shaking my head. Hartmann's is a specialty grocer in the center of town. I've visited but never bought anything. It's all overpriced and unnecessary. "No," I say. "It's too expensive."

He smiles. "I agree." Then the smile fades. "You know what they sell?"

I don't bother playing dumb. "Soda Jack?"

"Soda Jack."

"Okay." Because now I *am* dumb. I don't see what this has to do with me.

"Last Tuesday, your credit card was used to buy two twenty-four-can flats of Soda Jack."

"It's a drink?"

"Yeah. A specialty soft drink. Weird flavors, like elder-flower and pine."

"I canceled my credit card."

He glances up. "When?"

"Yesterday."

"Why?"

"I had to pay the locksmith, and I couldn't find my card. I thought I'd lost it so I canceled it." I freeze. "What does Hartmann's show up as on a credit card statement?"

Greaves frowns. "I don't know. Hartmann's, I'd assume."

"Before I canceled the card, I looked at the charges. A few days ago, there was a charge I didn't make."

"You remember the amount?"

"Almost forty dollars. Thirty-eight ninety-nine, I think."

He doesn't need to say anything to confirm that's the price of two flats of Soda Jack. And that's when it finally clicks. The cans in my living room, the ones Becca left behind with her cereal. The ones I'd recycled.

"Do you know who bought it?" Greaves asks.

"Didn't you say they were bought online? Why don't you check to see where they were shipped?"

"I did. They were delivered here."

I falter. "What?"

"Two flats, delivered to this address on Wednesday. Signed for by Carrie."

"I-I didn't sign for them. I didn't order them. They're not here."

"You mind if I look around?"

I've seen enough television to know I should not let the police look around my home if I'm a suspect in thirteen deaths, one of which I actually had a hand in. But I also know I didn't close the curtains or unlock the back door or move the painting or buy forty-eight cans of fucking Soda Jack, so this might actually be a good thing. If someone's in here, messing with me, maybe Greaves can find them.

"Sure," I say.

If Greaves is surprised, it doesn't show. He stands, tucking away his notepad and pen, and gives the room a cursory once-over. After a moment, he walks to the television and peers behind it, opening the doors to the stand and taking in my small collection of dusty DVDs. He nudges the couch away from the wall and puts it back, and while he does it, I have a flashback of the night I fought with Becca and found the can under the couch. I assumed it had fallen, and she'd been too lazy to pick it up, but what if that wasn't the case? What if it was put there on purpose, waiting for just this moment?

And suddenly, belatedly, I don't think it's a good idea to let Greaves search my house. I thought he might find something I didn't want to find myself, but it never occurred to me that he'd find something I didn't want him to find. But now I'm following him down the hall to the kitchen, watching him open the fridge, the crisper drawer, the freezer. I was in here earlier to get milk for my coffee, but I'm suddenly paralyzed by the fear that he'll find four dozen cans of Soda Jack.

He doesn't.

He opens the cupboards, struggles to close them, and gives me an apologetic look.

"Old house," I say, like that's totally fine. I'm totally fine.

He checks the door beneath the sink, where I keep the recycling. I've taken it out since the night I found the cans, but now I know there will be more in there, alongside the empty jar of pasta sauce, the wine bottle, the flattened cereal box. Greaves is blocking the view, but he crouches and uses his pen to sift through the contents. Slowly, he straightens. I wait for him to arrest me, but he just goes to the back door, noting the shiny new knob, and glances at me.

"Why'd you change the locks?" he asks again.

"They were old," I say, my voice wavering. Then I force a tiny smile. "And I'm afraid, with everything going on. My boyfriend thought it was a good idea."

"It is. What's his name?"

"Um. Graham."

"Does he work at Weston Stationery?"

"No. He used to."

"Did he know Angelica?"

"He left before she started."

Greaves nods and watches me. "Well, thank you for your time."

"You're welcome." The words sound hollow, which I suppose they are. In all the times I imagined being arrested for helping Becca, it somehow never occurred to me that I might be implicated in a dozen other murders in which I had no role.

I trail Greaves to the front door and say goodbye, watching as he slowly makes his way down the drive, past my car, and into the black SUV parked at the curb. He sees me watching and lifts a hand so I do the same. I close and lock the door, peering through the peephole as he sits in the car, talking on his phone. My heart hammers in my chest, but I'm not looking at Greaves anymore. I'm looking at my car.

I pull on my winter coat and boots, hovering behind the door until Greaves finally drives away. Then I slip outside. I've driven my car a dozen times since the day I found it with the door open, the day I convinced myself I'd simply been careless. But now I don't think I was.

There's nothing in the front seat or the back, I know. And as I slide the key into the lock for the trunk and pop it open, I know what I'll find here, too.

And I do.

A shiny new case of Soda Jack, twenty-four cans. It's a variety pack, a rainbow of incriminating colors. Someone stole my credit card, ordered the drinks, had them delivered to my house, signed for them, and put a case in the trunk of my car. I don't know what Soda Jack has to do with the investigation, but I know it can't be good, and if there's one criminal enterprise I'm skilled at, it's hiding things.

I get in the car and drive a few blocks to the nearby high school. It's deserted on a Sunday, the back parking lot cold and empty. I stop in front of the dumpsters and grit my teeth as I lift out twenty dollars' worth of soda and heave it above my head. I shove it over the lip of the dumpster, and after a second, I hear it land with a muffled *thump*. I close the trunk, and the slam echoes in the quiet, setting my ears ringing.

I drive home quickly and spend the rest of the day

in the house, anxious and paranoid. Despite having had ten years to prepare for my first-ever police interview, I was completely unprepared, mostly because the things I was questioned about are things about which I knew nothing. Becca has always threatened to frame me, but a small, desperate part of me simply chose to believe the bodies would never come to light, and whatever seeds she'd planted would never manage to grow. And now something is growing, and I don't know how to stop it.

I take my laptop into the living room and sit on the couch, feet propped on the ottoman as I start to search online. I check for any updates on the Kilduff bodies, learning that two more have been identified. But beyond a few family members venturing into the public eye to say belatedly kind words about the loved ones they hadn't really cared were missing, there's nothing new. Forums are teeming with questions and theories, all of which prompt more questions and theories, but none of which generate any real answers. All we know for certain about the serial killer is that the park is their burial ground, and all the victims had a foot missing. If the police have any other information, they're not sharing.

I read a couple of stories from the family members of the identified victims, saying how their loved ones had led hard lives or fallen on troubled times and generally making excuses about why they never realized they were gone. But beyond that, there's no common thread to their story. No place the victims hung out, no mysterious new friends. Just one day there, the next day…not.

My eyelids start to droop, the caffeine and adrenaline draining away as quickly as they'd kicked in. With the doors locked, the curtains wide open, and the sun shining, I finally allow myself to close my eyes.

———

When I wake up, the room is dark and cold, my neck is sore from resting at a weird angle, and my feet have fallen asleep, pins and needles spiking my skin as I wiggle my toes, trying to get the blood moving. I look around slowly, orienting myself. Outside is the dull roar of wind, an unexpected storm.

I reach for the switch on the lamp and stop, my eyes locking on the dark window overlooking the street. The glow of a streetlamp casts shadows on the pavement, and if I turn on the light, anyone outside will be able to see in. Instead, I open the laptop and wait for it to wake up, peering at the time through bleary eyes. Just after five o'clock. Too early to be afraid of things that go bump in the night.

Still, I get up and wind my way around the ottoman, tugging the curtains closed. Doing so cuts out what little light was left in the room, and the piercing cry of a fresh gust of wind outside makes me yelp. Cold radiates from the window, and through it I can hear the rattle of bare branches as they clap together, reminding me too much of the night we buried Angelica.

I shudder as the memory washes over me, but I've had plenty of practice banishing those thoughts, and now I shake my head, jarring them loose. I switch on both lamps and turn up the heat five degrees higher than the preset, even though I know it won't work. I can already hear the furnace protesting through the floorboards.

The wind picks up outside, or maybe it's been that way for a while and I slept through it, I don't know. I can hear it hissing past, more thunks and thuds outside, and then a familiar clatter as one of the lids on my garbage cans is pried free and starts careening around the concrete slab, bouncing off the side of the house, being a general nuisance. I give it a minute to wedge itself into the spot between the deck and the house or blow onto the grass, but it seems content to cause as much hassle as possible.

If my back door opened, it would be less of a headache, but when I check it now, the new lock is still locked, and the wood is still warped. Even if I were inclined to fight to get it open, I know I'd lose the battle to get it closed again, and only compound my troubles. I sigh tiredly. The thing about old neighborhoods is that they play host to two kinds of people: old people and young people with young kids. The kind of people who complain if your car spits too much exhaust or your Christmas lights are too bright—or not bright enough—or your trash cans bang too loudly during a storm. If I'd paid attention to the forecast, I could have brought them inside or maybe braved the shed out back, but I hadn't, and now I'm stuffing my feet into boots and yanking on my parka, just in time for fat drops of rain to start pelting the house. Each sound is stark and accusing, intensifying as the storm gains strength. There's a mournful creak overhead, like the floorboards are crying, and I jerk around to look up the stairs out of habit, but they're dark and empty. It's going to be another long night.

I pull open the front door, holding it tight against the wind that tries to drag it outside against its will and its hinges. I win the brief struggle, angling myself through the gap and onto the steps, tugging the door closed solidly behind me. I pull up my hood, rain smacking my face. My eyes water from the sting and the cold, and I swipe at my skin, my fingers immediately frozen.

I hurry around the front of the house, sparing a quick glance for my car—it's as I left it—before darting around the side. It's pitch black in the space between my house and the neighbor's fence, and I trail my hand along the wood siding, feet slipping on the mossy paving stones. I reach the cans in a few seconds, the new floodlight doing its job too well. It senses my movement and flips on, blinding me, and for a second I'm helpless, eyes aching from the sudden brightness.

I mutter a curse and turn my back, blinking spots from my vision, and when I can see again, I locate the delin-quent trash cans. One's on its side, lid intact; the other is standing upright, collecting rain as its lid continues to rattle. I grit my teeth against the grating slide of metal on concrete and scoop it up, jamming it back on the can. I double-check the other one, but it's secure. Already my thighs are wet from the rain, my teeth chattering, and strands of hair escape my hood and plaster themselves to my cheeks. I glance at the shed I've ignored since I moved in. I checked it once before buying the place, but it was just a cheap and empty structure, hiding no secrets. A rusted lock hangs on the door, open. It's just ten feet from here to the shed, the yard now well lit.

Another gust of wind and the cans clash together like cymbals. I grip each handle, wincing against the cold as I drag them across the slippery grass. At first, I think it's a blessing that they're empty, but the wind has other ideas, using them like sails, lifting and smashing them into my calves and ankles. The cold makes it extra painful, and I slam them into the side of the shed when I arrive, holding one in place with my knee while I fumble to remove the lock. My numb fingers scrape over the rust, but I finally get it off and kick open the flimsy door.

For a long second I just stare at the empty mouth of the door, gaping at me like it can't believe my nerve. But the floodlight illuminates the tiny space, dry and musty and blessedly empty. I shove the cans inside, not caring when one falls, and close the door, replacing the lock and picking my way back over the wet grass. I nod in approval at the floodlight. I'd put off having one installed because I didn't want to deal with it, but facing my fears is empowering. Far better than cowering on the couch all night, flinching from the shadows and my sister.

Back inside, I'm wet and shivering, but somewhat re-vitalized after my errand, though that could be due to my five-hour nap. I hang my wet coat on the banister and kick off my boots. My jeans are stiff with rain and cold, and I peel them off where I stand, tugging down my sweater to cover my ass as I jog up the stairs to grab a warm change of clothes. I flick on the light in my room, the low hum of the radiator beneath the window warring with the rain and wind outside, and open the closet door.

There's a man in my closet.

He's dressed in black, a ski mask covering his face, re-vealing only pale circles of skin around his eyes and mouth. The same shock I'm feeling is reflected in his eyes, a murky gray-green. He was not expecting to be found. Not yet.

He backhands me before I can react. There's the sharp, painful clang of metal hitting my teeth and then the burning tang of blood. I glimpse something shiny on his finger as his hand flies away. A ring. He shoves me, and I stumble a few feet, the back of my knees meeting the edge of the mattress. I sprawl gracelessly, ears ringing from the blow to my face, shock and adrenaline flooding my system. I've never been hit before. Not even by Becca.

And then, while I lie prone and helpless, he runs. He bolts out of the room, and I hear his feet pounding down the steps, the solemn cry of the creaky third stair, the wind rushing in as he wrenches open the door and flees into the street.

For long seconds I lie there, staring at the ceiling light, my mouth throbbing. I touch my tongue to the split in my lip and wince. I trail it over my teeth, stopping when I feel a jagged point where there shouldn't be one. I do it again, then again, and again with my finger, poking at a sore spot to confirm it's still sore.

My tooth is broken. My front tooth. Even more upsetting than finding a strange man hiding in my bedroom closet—the one in which I'd been expecting to find someone—is discovering my broken tooth. It doesn't even hurt, it just feels *wrong*. It feels unfair and brutal. I curl up my knees to my chest as hot tears start to fall, trickling into my ears and making them itch. I want to roll onto my side and sob until I can't breathe, but the sound of the wind and rain filters back in, and I remember the front door is still open.

I get to my feet, expecting to feel more unsteady than I actually am. Everything is too clear, too believable. It's surreal. I know it's shock morphing the lights and the walls, making everything sway and swell, a millimeter this way, a millimeter that way. But I'm still aware enough to skip the third stair as I descend the steps and use my shoulder to force the door closed against the wind, shaking fingers twisting the lock. I glance at the hall table to confirm my purse and keys and laptop are still there.

They are.

He's been here before, I know. Unlocked the back

door, opened the curtains, planted the Soda Jack, stolen my credit card. He's had ample opportunity to do far worse, and he hasn't. Not yet anyway.

My phone sits next to my purse. Becca always complains that I leave it there to charge instead of keeping it with me, because sometimes it takes me twenty minutes to notice her text and she doesn't like to be kept waiting.

It's the last thing I want to do, but it's also my only choice. I pick up the phone and call my sister. Either she'll answer and immediately take a superior tone, expecting me to apologize since I broke down and called first, or she won't answer at all, playing the part of the wounded warrior.

She chooses the first option.

"Hello." It's not a question. Her voice is flat.

"Where are you?" My voice is ragged but firm.

It takes her by surprise. "What?"

"Where are you?"

A pause. "The theater. I'm buying popcorn." Becca goes at least twice a week to buy movie popcorn, her favorite food. She doesn't even see a movie. The staff know her and let her into the concession area without a ticket.

Brampton only has one theater, and it's downtown, a twenty-minute drive from my place. If she had anything to do with the man in my apartment, if she'd sent him in to scare me and lurked nearby to feast on my terror, she couldn't have gotten to the theater this fast. I don't think it's likely she had anything to do with whatever's really going on, but I'm grasping at straws. They're all better than the alternative. Than the reality.

"I want to FaceTime," I say. "Now."

I switch the call, and after a second, so does Becca. She's holding the phone too close to her face, but I can see the familiar red walls, the gold trim of a framed poster. There's the general din of a busy theater on a miserable Sunday night, and in the midst of it all, there's my sister. She's so confused by the tone of the call that she hasn't even put on her smugly righteous face.

Her jaw drops when she sees me. "What the hell happened to you?" she exclaims, her surprise genuine. She's such a shitty actor it'd be easy to tell if she was faking.

"Show me the theater," I say.

"What?"

"Show me!"

She rolls her eyes but turns the camera so I can see the dated interior, the concession stand, the popcorn machines, the passing filmgoers glancing at her strangely. She gives me a 360-degree view, stopping when she's in focus again. "Satisfied?"

I run my tongue over the jagged shard of tooth. "Yes."

"What's wrong with you?"

"Someone was here," I say, the words breaking as they tumble out. "Waiting. In my closet."

Her eyes bulge. "What?"

"He—I—He—"

"Are you hurt? Do you need an ambulance?"

I shake my head. "No. But he—I—"

Becca waits.

"I think it's him," I blurt, recalling the glowing white eyes I'd seen in the dark trees at Kilduff, the ones watching us bury Angelica. They were too far away for me to say for certain it was the same eyes I just encountered in my closet, but it doesn't matter. The signs of someone in my house, the visit from Greaves, and now this. It's all that makes sense.

"Who?" Becca demands.

"The killer," I whisper, my hand shaking so hard the camera can't focus. "Footloose."

She makes a face. "That's such a stupid name."

Tears pour down my cheeks. "I know."

"Do you still have both your feet?"

I rasp out a laugh, though nothing's funny. "Yes."

"Good. I'm coming over, but if you're not bleeding to death, I'm getting popcorn first."

"Okay," I say, the word sounding like a wheeze.

"I'll get you some, too," Becca adds, the most compassion of which she's capable.

She hangs up, and I watch the screen go dark. Greaves's card sits on the table, next to my purse. Under normal circumstances, a person who found an intruder in her closet should call the police, let them investigate, let them protect her. But if I'm right and the person in my closet is Brampton's *other* serial killer, then Becca, unfortunately, is my only hope.

CHAPTER 5

O h. My. God." Becca's in the doorway, gaping at me,
shutting her mouth just long enough to chew the
popcorn she keeps shoveling in. She didn't get me a bag
after all because it was "too expensive." We both know
she ate it on the way over.

"Look at your teeth!" she exclaims, like I knew she
would. When Becca sees a bruise, she has to press on
it. My front tooth is sheared off at an angle, leaving
a dark hole in the center of my smile, and it's visible anytime I open my mouth, no matter how little
I move my lips. I'm upset, clearly, and I know I'll
suffer at the dentist tomorrow, but there's nothing like
a potential serial killer in your closet to put things into
perspective.

Of course, Becca doesn't see it that way. "It looks terrible," she adds when I don't flinch. "It's *super* noticeable."

"Uh-huh. Are you coming in or are you just going to stand there?"

"Oh, am I allowed in now?"

"Temporarily."

She's too lazy to go back out into the rain and drive home so I know she'll stay, even if I don't welcome her with open arms. Not that I ever have.

"Fine." She kicks off her boots, one landing halfway down the hall, and hangs her coat on the doorknob, where it immediately slides off and crumples on the floor. "So," she says, "you think Footloose was in your closet."

"Yes."

"How did he get in?"

"Through the front door. I went out to put the trash cans in the shed and didn't lock the door. He must have come in then and waited upstairs."

Becca frowns, munching on her popcorn as she climbs the steps in tight jeans and a fuzzy pink sweater. She looks like a sorority sister here for a sleepover, not one serial killer investigating another.

I follow her into my room, where she calmly surveys my closet. The painting was moved to the far side to allow for Footloose's escape, and Becca eyeballs the place where he'd stood.

"No," she says finally.

"No, what?"

"No, he didn't come in while you moved the garbage cans."

"How do you know that?"

"Because it's fucking pouring outside, Carrie, and there's no water in here. None on the stairs, none in the hallway. It's dry."

I want to argue with her because Becca becomes impossibly more awful when she's right, but what she's saying is true. Footloose hit me, and his hand was warm. There was no wash of cold clinging to him as he ran past, no wet footsteps on the floor. The clothes in the closet are dry. I was too stunned to notice the obvious: He'd been here all along.

"What?" Becca asks. Her popcorn crunches as she watches me speculatively. She doesn't know how to be sympathetic. A dying animal is just a curiosity, a terrified sister an interesting specimen.

"I was awake all night," I say. "I was in the living room. I couldn't sleep."

She goes to the window and peers into the darkness. Rain splatters against the glass, twinkling in the light. There are no balconies or eaves outside, and the only drainpipe is on the back of the house, too rickety to bear the weight of a grown man. There's no way to enter the house from this level. Only the front door opens on the main floor, plus the kitchen window, which is locked. The unfinished basement has two window wells, both barely big enough for a cat to fit through, never mind an adult.

"Why not?" Becca asks.

"Why not what?"

"Why couldn't you sleep?"

"Because of everything that's been going on!"

"Because of Footloose?" she scoffs. "I mean, I get it. It's alarming to think there could be a serial killer in Brampton, but why would he target you? I've been reading the papers. It sounds like all the people he killed are homeless or addicted or lost—none of them had family who loved them. You do."

I take a breath and tell her everything about the past week—the closed curtains, the moved painting, the credit card—wrapping up with Greaves's visit this morning. At first, she looks bored, like I'm making something out of nothing, but the more pieces I add to the pile, the more interested she becomes. But she's not giddy, the way she gets when she watches one of her horrible plans unfold. She can't take pleasure in other people's success, she can only document the suffering. I'd already come to the same conclusion, but I know now for certain. It's not her.

I should be relieved to know my sister isn't tormenting me, but I'm not. Because Becca's the devil I know. Footloose is the serial killer I do not.

"Well," she says eventually, licking butter off her thumb, "the good news is, he doesn't want to kill you."

"What? He—"

"Obviously, he *could* have killed you. He's been in your house, like, a dozen times, but he hasn't tried to hurt you. I mean, he probably came in here today while you were throwing away the Soda Jack and has just been waiting the whole time, even while you slept." She gestures to my face. "And he only hit you because you surprised him. Oh man." Her eyes light up. "One time, I ran over this girl—she wrote, like, six letters to the store complaining about my 'poor attitude' and, like, lingered in the food court when I was having lunch, bringing her friends and calling me names, saying they'd shop at other stores. Like, whatever, bitch, it's not like you ever bought anything. Anyway, I had enough so I wrote her back and pretended to be from management, and we set up a meeting"—one of Becca's favorite murder techniques—"and I ran her over. Then, when I went to wrap her up in the carpet, she fucking moved, Carrie. It was so scary. I almost peed."

I stare at her. I don't see what this has to do with anything. And I don't like the story.

"Anyway." She shrugs, not getting the sympathy she apparently believes she deserves. "She was mostly dead and in a lot of pain, twitching and stuff, so I smothered her with the carpet. It was probably best for her. Then, you know. The rest is history."

"What is the point of this?" I demand, my early calm evaporated. Hearing a tale of woe from one killer after a close encounter with another isn't exactly helpful.

Becca looks startled. "The point is, he doesn't want you dead yet, Carrie. He had you on the bed, ready to die, and he just left. All those things that have been happening? He's playing with you. So we have some time."

"Time until what?"

"Until he gets tired of this. But that's the wrong question."

I scrape my hands over my face. "Oh my God, Becca. What's the *right* question?"

"Time *for* what."

"Time *for* what?"

"Exactly. Time for us to figure out who this guy is."

"The police are working on that."

Becca lifts a disdainful eyebrow. "The police haven't even noticed two serial killers in the same town for, like, ten years." It's an insane point, but it's fair.

"So how exactly are *we* going to find him?"

She shrugs, the gesture too simple to be anything other than plotting. "I have some ideas."

"And then what?"

"Then what, what?"

"Assuming we find him, what do we do?"

Becca frowns at me. "Then we kill him. What else would we do? Befriend him?"

Cold snakes up my spine as though Footloose is still in the closet, listening to every word.

"We kill a serial killer," I echo, my voice weak and distant.

Becca dumps the last crumbs of popcorn into her mouth, her lips shiny with butter. "Uh-huh," she says. "I mean, look what he did to your tooth. It's hideous."

—

It takes hours, but eventually I fall asleep in my own bed. Becca takes the couch, and when I stumble downstairs the next morning, I half expect to find a serial killer trussed and waiting on the living room floor, Becca standing over him like a game hunter with her trophy.

No such luck.

It's 8:03 a.m., and Becca is sitting cross-legged on the ottoman, eating a bowl of cereal and watching cartoons.

"Hey," she says, glancing up. "How's the tooth?"

"Still broken." I'd emailed Troy last night to say I had to have emergency dental work done today and wouldn't be in. Then I searched online until I found a dental surgeon who takes walk-ins. They open at nine, and I'll be there bright and early to get my smile fixed.

"He didn't come back." Becca trails me into the kitchen, her spoon clinking against the edge of the bowl as she continues to eat.

I flip on the light, wincing against the fluorescent glow, and find the box of cereal sitting on the counter, still open, half a dozen colored fruit flakes sprinkled around it. I shoot Becca a look but don't comment, putting the kettle on the stove and turning the flame up to high.

"Nope," she says, switching it off. "Your tooth is broken. Your root is exposed. If that hot water touches it, you'll die. Or wish you were dead. So to speak."

I carefully probe the tooth with my tongue and decide

it's not worth the risk. Or the argument. I don't especially want my sister here, but there's something calming about her nonchalance. I know her lack of concern has more to do with her inability to process emotions and less to do with the severity of the situation, but it still grounds me. We're here. We're alive. We have a plan.

Sort of.

Becca pours herself more cereal. "Go get dressed," she says. "I'll take you to the dentist. When you look normal again, we'll start our investigation."

I hide a flinch. "I look perfectly normal."

She shrugs.

When I'm finished at the dentist, the plan is to swing by Hartmann's, the store from which I apparently bought forty-eight cans of Soda Jack, and talk to a guy Becca says she knows who works there. I don't know what information we might find that the police haven't already, but I don't have any better ideas so I guess I'm on board.

I ignore my grumbling stomach and go back upstairs, taking a quick shower and gingerly brushing my teeth. The broken tooth tingles, and my split lip stings, the memory of last night coming back like a strike of lightning. I grip the countertop and force myself to breathe, my heart pounding so fast it feels like I'm swaying with it, like the whole room is moving, my world spinning out of control. I'm not just going along with Becca's plan because it's easier than arguing with her. I'm doing it because if I don't, then I'm stuck here, waiting for

Footloose to make his next move. I did that last night and failed spectacularly. At least this way it feels like I have a say in things.

"Hurry up!" Becca hollers.

Slathering on moisturizer, I wince when I touch the invisible bruise at the edge of my mouth. I hastily dry my hair and change into jeans and a sweater before heading downstairs. Despite her urgency, Becca's lounging on the couch, eating what must be her eighth bowl of cereal. I check the kitchen, where the box lies empty on the counter.

"About time," she says behind me, making me jump. She strolls in and sticks her bowl in the dishwasher, half a cup of gray milk sloshing into the machine. "Now let's go get your face fixed."

———

When I climb into Becca's car three hours later, I'm physically and emotionally drained. On the surface, I'm fine. The numbing took care of the root canal, but the nauseating grit of tools on teeth, filing down the shard to do the temporary filling, cotton pads stuck against my gums, has taken its toll. I'm starving, and I'm exhausted, and all I want to do is curl up in bed and never move again.

"Let's see," Becca says.

I turn to face her, not at all wanting to, but knowing it's pointless to fight. Repaired tooth aside, I look terrible.

Dark circles are smudged beneath both eyes, and my split lip reopened and is now bright red and puffy on one side. Still, I shape my mouth into a grimace so Becca can see the results. I brace myself for her insult, but all she does is peer closely and say, "You can hardly tell," and start the car.

I close my eyes in relief and exhaustion, my head dropping back against the seat rest. The light midday traffic makes the trip to Hartmann's a quick one. Becca drives like the psychopath she is, and even without rush-hour obstacles to make things interesting, she still weaves in and out of the handful of cars she finds, veers sharply into the parking lot, and stomps on the brakes. I jolt forward in my seat with a muttered curse.

"You know what your problem is, Carrie?" she asks without prompting.

I'm already shoving open my door, gulping in the frigid November air to quell the nausea curdling in my stomach.

"The serial killer trying to frame me for murder?"

"You don't know how to make an entrance. You're so…" She gestures to me, her lips pulled down in a dramatic frown. "You."

I scoff and start walking toward the entrance.

She hustles along beside me. "If you did this by yourself, you'd tiptoe in there and meekly ask for assistance. And if they told you no, you'd say okay and leave. That's not how things work."

"That's how they work for normal people."

She tugs open the door and gestures me inside. "Normal is boring."

"How would you know?"

She laughs before striding past me into the shop. I've only been to Hartmann's once before, sticker-shock sending me back out as quickly as I'd come in. It's a high-end grocer that caters to home cooks who think they're fancier than they are and people in the neighborhood who are unwilling to make the ten-minute trip to the nearest regular grocery store and have enough money not to care.

The aisles are narrow, the carts small, and classical music wafts out of unseen speakers. There are no national brand items here. Everything is artisanal and organic, imported and important. And expensive. A twenty-two-dollar chocolate bar the size of my thumb. A clear glass jar of truffles, priced by the ounce and guarded by a man with an apron and a scowl. The meat counter offerings include steak and chicken, but also ostrich, alligator, and wild boar. At this time of day, the store is busy with shoppers who don't have to work or who can afford to determine their own hours, and us. A serial killer with a high ponytail and puffy yellow jacket, apparently selected to be the opposite of meek, and offensively normal me.

For whatever reason, Becca weaves her way through the aisles, reading the ingredient list on an eleven-dollar jar of tomato sauce and contemplating a box of gluten-free vegan ladyfingers.

"How long is this going to take?" I mutter when we get to the produce section and she picks up a mangosteen. I know she has no idea what it is, even as she tests its weight and firmness.

"As long as it needs to," she replies.

"I thought you said *I* was boring."

"You are," she confirms. "I'm not. Everyone in this store is talking about me. It won't be much longer until he comes out."

"Who?"

"Nikk with two *k*'s."

"Who?"

She sighs and puts down the mangosteen. "How's it going to look if we just barge in here and demand to talk to Nikk?" she asks reasonably.

"I don't know. What if we just walked in normally and asked normally to talk to him? Normally."

She yawns. "The answer is *suspicious*. If someone's watching this place and they see me ask for Nikk, they'll know we're investigating. But if Nikk just *happens* to be working and we just *happen* to bump into each other, it's a happy coincidence."

There are thirteen people who would argue that "bumping into" Becca is the worst thing that ever happened to them, but they can't say anything because they're dead.

Still, all I say is, "How do you know he's working today?"

"Because I called. Start pretending you're actually going to buy something. You look like a shoplifter."

I open my mouth to argue and then close it, putting two dragon fruit in a compostable plastic bag. "How do you know Nikk with two *k*'s?"

"Promise me you're not going to be this annoying when he gets here."

I roll my eyes. "Promise."

"And act cool when he does."

"I'll aim for normal."

"He beats up his wife," Becca says.

I nearly drop the dragon fruit. "What?"

"Yeah. And then he apologizes with diamonds. I've sold him a *lot* of stuff. We're friendly."

"My God, Becca! Why are we here?"

"Don't judge people, Carrie. It's bad form. Plus, if you really want to know who Footloose is, look closer to home."

"You're Footloose?"

"No, idiot. It's obviously Graham."

I bristle. "It's obviously not."

"I'm too-good-to-be-true Graham!" she says, opting strangely to use a British accent. "I don't kill anyone!"

"He doesn't," I snap. "And he's not British. Why are you saying it like that?"

Becca flips up her fingers one at a time as she makes her points. "He knows me. He knows you. He has access to your house and car. And despite being insane, all the killer's done is make your house a little dirty. That doesn't add up. Why wouldn't a crazy serial killer just kill you?"

The most reasonable response is, *Why haven't you?* but I don't want to know the answer. Instead I say, "He punched me in the face!"

She shrugs, like that's somehow debatable. "Well, maybe he'll buy you a necklace."

My retort is interrupted when a tall, handsome man with shiny dark hair and dimples enters the produce section. Unlike the rest of the staff, he wears a gleaming white button-down shirt and trousers, no apron. A wedding ring glints on his left hand, and his eyes sparkle when they land on Becca. She notices him at the same time, a smile splitting her face. I don't know if her theory is right and everyone in the store was talking about her and word got to Nikk or if terrible people are just drawn together like magnets, but here we are.

"Nikk!" she says, throwing open her arms.

He comes forward and wraps her in a hug. "Becca! What a surprise. How are you?"

"Fantastic, as always. I'm just here with my sister, Carrie. She's hosting a fancy dinner party, and I told her this place has the best food in the city."

Nikk smiles at me and extends a hand to shake. My stomach clenches as I fold my fingers in his.

"Very nice to meet you," he says.

"Same," I lie.

"What are you making with the dragon fruit?" The question is harmless, but I feel pinned to the spot.

"It's a garnish," Becca says, taking Nikk's arm and leading him to the back of the store. "We're so lucky you came along when you did. One of the VIP guests at the party said his favorite drink is Soda Jack. I think you guys carry it?"

Nikk's smile brightens. "Absolutely. Just over here."

We follow him to a narrow aisle with a hundred different kinds of specialty drinks. My stomach somersaults when I spot the Soda Jack. Twelve flavors, each label a different color. It's sold in six-packs, bottles only. The flats of cans must be special order. Not fancy enough for the in-store shoppers.

"Do you know what flavor he likes?" Nikk asks. "We have them all. Lavender, pandan, elderflower—"

"Oh my goodness!" Becca exclaims, clutching her chest. "Is that the price?" She looks like a small-town actress cast in a too-big role, but Nikk seems to be buying it.

He nods solemnly. "It's a little steep," he agrees. "But worth it."

"And people really buy it?"

"They do."

"Who?"

Nikk glances around. "Pretentious people," he says from the corner of his mouth.

Becca's laugh rings out, and this time it's convincing. "People in Brampton?" she asks, disbelieving. As though buying overpriced soda is the biggest crime committed by anyone currently in this store.

"Do you know Spark?" Nikk asks. "The nightclub on West Eleventh?"

"Of course."

"They're the number one buyer. That's why we're the number one stockist."

"Well," Becca says with a sly smile, "I knew I had friends in high places."

A young woman in an apron appears at the end of the aisle. "Nikk?" she calls. "You're needed in the back."

"I'll be right there." He turns to me and Becca. "It was very nice to meet you, Carrie. And Becca, always a pleasure. I'm sure we'll meet again soon."

"I hope so," she says brightly.

Nikk gives a small wave and disappears down the aisle, leaving us alone.

"Meet again soon?" I echo, disgusted.

Becca shrugs. "Every few months."

"W-why don't you kill *him*?" I sputter. "Why, instead of someone who cut you off in traffic or insulted you at work, why don't you kill an actual bad guy?"

She's astonished. "Are you being serious right now?"

"Of course I am!"

"Do you have any idea how much jewelry he buys?" she demands. "That's my commission!"

I scrape my hand through my hair. "I'm going to be sick."

"Stop being so dramatic," she snaps, snatching a bag of parsnip chips off the opposite shelf and shoving it into my chest. "Worse things are happening. Now buy me these. We need an excuse for coming in."

Three minutes later, we're sitting in Becca's car with the dragon fruit forgotten in the backseat, sharing the chips while Becca searches something on her phone.

"Okay," she says around a mouthful of fried parsnip. "Spark opens at eight, so we'll head over around ten to see what we can find."

"Wait. What?" I haven't been to a club in five years. By ten, I'm in my sweats, teeth brushed, face washed. Plus, it's Monday.

"No one's going to be there at eight," Becca says matter-of-factly, putting the car in drive. "So we'll wait a bit."

"What's the point of this? We don't even know how the Soda Jack ties into everything. You think these homeless addicts were buying NINE-DOLLAR bottles of Soda Jack?"

"Nope." She presses on the gas, going twenty above the limit.

"Then what?"

"That's what we're going to find out."

I sigh and stuff two parsnip chips in my mouth. They taste better than I expected. But when I reach for another one, Becca grabs the bag and tosses it into the backseat. I hear chips tumble onto the floor and stare at her in shock.

"Don't stress-eat," she says. "You'll just get fatter."

—

Becca said she'd pick me up at 9:30 p.m., but it's five to ten when she actually pulls up. Though I'm already at the door, she honks obnoxiously, and I see lights come on in the houses across the street. I hustle down the drive and get in the car before Mr. Myer can come out to complain. That's all it takes for Becca to find her next victim, and while I don't know my neighbors that well, I also don't want them to be murdered.

Becca glances over as I fasten my seat belt. "What are you wearing?" she asks, mouth twitching like she's trying not to laugh. I don't react. That's her standard response to any outfit, on any person, at any time. I'm wearing black jeans and boots with a short heel, a sparkly silver shirt, and my parka. Even when I used to go to clubs, I didn't favor short skirts and skimpy tops. A lifetime of Becca pointing out my muffin top and cellulite taught me that dressing sexy was not the thing for me.

We drive in silence, Becca humming along to a song on the radio, one hand on the wheel, her nails freshly painted, appliqué diamonds flashing on the tips.

"Are you going to tell me what the plan is?" I ask when we park a couple of blocks from the club.

"Just follow my lead."

"What is—" But she's already out of the car, heading down the quiet street.

Brampton doesn't have a lively nightlife. Downtown

goes dark after nine, with only the occasional bar or restaurant breaking up the monotony, and West Eleventh is no exception. Spark is the only business currently open on its block, and on a Monday, it's not exactly busy. From two blocks away, I can see a bored bouncer leaning against the brick wall, arms crossed against the cold. Two girls on heels totter down the sidewalk from the opposite direction, and he splits his attention between us and them.

Becca strides down the street, her leather pants and knee-high boots shining in the glow from the streetlamps. Her hair is loose and shiny, hanging halfway down her back, and with a fitted dark jacket and a sway to her hips, she looks like a badass vampire slayer. I hustle behind like her lackey, my toes already hurting in my boots.

A block away from the club, she turns abruptly to her left. I skid to a stop and change course to follow her. "What are we doing?" I demand, my breath coming in frigid white puffs. I jam my hands into my pockets and suppress a shiver. "I thought we were going to the club."

Becca ignores me, and halfway down the street she turns into the alley that runs behind the block of dark buildings. On the right, it's lined with brick walls and barred windows, heavy metal fire doors locked against the night. On the left, it's dumpsters and recycle bins, the smells mercifully faint in the November cold.

A short distance ahead, two women in matching white thigh-high boots hang out behind Spark, the dull thud of bass radiating from inside the club. Because Brampton is so quiet, prostitutes can't solicit business on the street so they hang out behind clubs and bars, waiting for customers to find them.

They turn in unison, overly made-up faces equal parts suspicious, curious, and freezing. One wears a fur coat, but it only comes down as far as her belly button, exposing a band of ghostly pale skin. The other wears a dark trench coat with what appears to be a fox stole wrapped around her neck, two tiny feet dangling on one side. She steps forward as we approach, an intricate tower of braids twisted on top of her head.

"We don't do women," she announces.

"Me either," Becca replies without missing a beat. "Unless you convince me."

She cracks a smile. "How much money you got?"

I hover awkwardly behind Becca. The dim security lights flicker and bounce off the dumpsters and recycling bins like holiday lights.

"Did you guys know Donna-Marie and Jacinda?" Becca asks.

The women visibly stiffen at the mention of two of Footloose's victims, both with arrest records for prostitution, according to the newspapers.

"Shanté, they're cops," the one in the fur coat whispers.

"We're not cops," Becca says, though she kind of looks

like she might play one on TV. "But we're interested in the murders at Kilduff."

Fur Coat looks anxious. "Interested how?"

"I think the guy who hurt your friends might want to hurt my sister."

They peer at me, and I try not to shrink back from their scrutiny.

"Why do you think that?"

"Because he's been leaving clues at her house. Did your friends drink Soda Jack?"

Shanté laughs. "What? No. Ten bucks for soda? We don't pay for drinks."

"But you know what it is?" Becca presses.

"Yeah. Of course. It's right there." She jerks her chin toward the recycle bin, and when I shift forward, I can see a stack of crates, glass gleaming inside. There are a mix of bottles, a few Soda Jack, but more beer than anything else. Which doesn't mean much since the killer had cans delivered to my house, not bottles.

The women and I watch warily as Becca lifts the lid on the recycle bin. Inside is a rainbow assortment of cans, the same ones I found in my trunk. They must use the cans for mixers, the bottles for sale.

Becca reaches in and plucks a can from the top, holding it up so she can read in the dim light, brow furrowed. "Bingo," she says finally.

"Bingo, what?" Fur Coat asks.

Becca grabs three more cans from the bin, each a

different color. Her expression grows more smug and satisfied with each one.

"Did you ever see Donna-Marie and Jacinda leave with the same guy?" she asks, admiring her new finds.

Shanté shrugs. "Depends. They know lots of guys. Maybe you could help me remember."

But Becca has apparently gotten what she came for and is no longer interested in playing.

"Maybe," she says as she strides back down the alley, carrying the cans.

I hesitate before hurrying after her.

"What the fuck was that?" Shanté mutters.

"What the heck was that?" I demand when we exit the alley and return to the car. My lips are frozen, and it's hard to form the words.

"That," Becca says, beeping open her door, "was research." She drops into the driver's seat, and I scurry around and climb in on my side.

"And?" I prompt, because that's what she's waiting for. "What did you find out?"

"Why Greaves was asking you about the cans."

"Okay. Why?"

"Because they're a calling card."

"What?"

"A calling card. Like my kiss of death?"

"You only did that once."

"Regardless, I think Footloose"—she says the name with a sneer—"is using these as his calling card."

I frown. "He's burying a can with each body?"

"Probably just the tab." She snaps one off a pink can—peppercorn—and waves it at me. "Hiiiii, Carrie!"

I snatch it away from her. "What are you talking about?" And then I see. The pink tab has tiny white writing on it, a friendly HI! in bubble letters.

Becca hands me the green can—wintergreen—whose tab reads S'UP? Yellow (sunflower) says YO! and brown (cocoa nib) says HOWDY!

I'm silent for a full minute. I don't know what to say. It's a plausible reason. If these tabs were found on the Kilduff bodies and I recently ordered forty-eight cans, it might appear that I'm planning my next four dozen murders.

I drop the can like it's an admission of guilt. "If the killer's using these as calling cards, why order a specific product from a specific store?" I ask. "As soon as Greaves realizes it's not me, he's going to go through the rest of the buyers and find the guy."

Becca shrugs. "If Footloose actually went into Hartmann's and paid with a credit card, maybe. But he was smart enough to have the order sent to your house and signed with your name so I doubt that's the case. I mean, if you're going to leave a calling card, you don't choose one that can be traced back to you. That lipstick I wore for my kiss of death? Stolen! No one can prove I ever bought Pirate Bride Red. And right now, as far as we know, Footloose has twenty-four cans of Soda Jack you paid for."

"Then what was the point of coming here? We could have looked at the cans online."

"The point is, there's not just one place selling these drinks, but there's only one *buying* them. Footloose doesn't have to go to Hartmann's—he comes here when the club closes, takes a few from the bin, and bam. He has his calling card. And apparently a couple of victims, which means we found one of his hunting grounds. Now, when we get some suspects, we can bring the pictures here and see if anyone recognizes him."

"You have to put those cans back," I say, suddenly panicked. "If we bring them to my house—or yours—and Greaves finds them with your fingerprints, we'll be even bigger suspects. Especially since you actually killed somebody."

Becca frowns as she puts the car in drive and pulls away from the curb. "That's strange, isn't it?" she muses. "That no one has singled out Angelica's death as being any different from the others, apart from the fact that she was actually reported missing?"

"Yes?"

"Think about it, Carrie. Footloose killed twelve people that apparently no one even noticed were missing and buried them so well they weren't found for years. But now he digs up Angelica and leaves her in a place where his work will be discovered?"

"Uh-huh." I don't know where this is going, but I don't like it.

"You know what I always think about?"

"Do I want to hear this?"

She hits the gas, and I press back into my seat. "I wonder, when I die, should I make a deathbed confession? Should I put a list in a safe-deposit box and wear the key on a chain around my neck, and after I pass, someone unlocks the box and discovers my secret?"

"You think about that stuff?"

"All the time. I think Footloose is trying to have it both ways. He wants his crimes discovered, he wants someone to pay for them, but he doesn't want that someone to be him. He wants it to be you."

Icy air puffs out of the heating vent, washing over me like a ghost passing through.

"Which is it?" I say, trying to sound nonchalant but convincing neither of us. "Does he want to kill me, or frame me?"

Becca shrugs and flips on her blinker. "Why not both?"

CHAPTER 6

The next day is Angelica's funeral, and Weston Stationery has closed for the day in her honor. I only found out last night when I got home and saw that Troy had replied to my dental emergency email with the time and location.

I don't want to go to a funeral. I don't want to stand in the cold, mourning someone I never really liked, whom I helped bury and who was then dug up, while my coworkers eyeball me suspiciously. But at nine o'clock the next morning, I'm wearing my best black dress and a long wool coat that's not going to keep me warm enough in the November drizzle. On television, the local news talks about Angelica's funeral and three others set for this week for more of Footloose's victims. With so little else happening in Brampton, it's shaping up to be the event of the season.

The news anchor is joined by Fiona McBride's mother, a pale woman who very closely resembles the missing redheaded girl. It's a last-ditch, desperate effort to return the focus to the handmade posters that are slowly disappearing around town as time passes and hope fades.

I turn off the TV and open the door, yelping when I find Becca on the other side, her hand poised to knock. Her diamond-tipped nails gleam in the glow of my porch light.

"Oh good," she says. "You're ready. Let's go. We can't be late to a funeral. It's tacky!"

My reasons for being sad may be more selfish than sincere, but Becca's cheerfulness is downright unpleasant. And that's when I notice her black dress, boots, and coat. She's even twisted her hair into a prim knot at the nape of her neck, like a princess.

"What are you doing?" I only realize I'm clenching the doorknob when my hand starts to ache.

She gestures to our matching outfits. "What does it look like? I'm going to Angela's funeral."

"Angelica."

"Whatever. We can't miss it."

I'm still gaping at her. "Why?"

She sighs and reaches past me to close the door. "This is good, Carrie," she murmurs, taking the keys from my icy fingers and guiding me down the stairs. "Very convincing."

I glance around, confused, and spot Mr. Myer across the

street, taking down leftover Halloween decorations and doing a poor job of acting like he's not watching us.

"I'm not pretending," I say from the corner of my mouth. "Why are you going to the funeral?"

"Because," Becca replies from the corner of her mouth, "if Footloose is like most bored serial killers, he'll be at the funeral. And maybe we'll spot him."

I slip on a patch of ice, and my voice comes out too high. "How?"

"I don't know. Killer instinct?" She chuckles at her own joke as she opens the car door and ushers me in, before rounding the front and sliding into the driver's seat.

"Becca, that's not funny. What if the police have the same idea? What if they're looking at everyone at the funeral, and they find you?" *Finally* goes unsaid.

"That's not going to happen," Becca says dismissively as she starts to drive down the wet road, headlights flickering across the puddles that dot the street. "And we have bigger issues to deal with. I don't know why, but for whatever reason, you intrigue Footloose." She waves a hand in my general direction, her tone telling me exactly how distasteful she finds the idea that someone could be interested in me, even if that person is a serial killer. "So let's use his weakness to our advantage. He knows you worked with Angelica, and it's safe to assume you'll be at the funeral. If he's going to attend any of these things, it's this one. But everyone in this loser town is going to be there, so we need a way to draw him out. That's why you're the bait."

My mind flashes to a video I saw online where scientists wanted to find elusive crocodiles. They went out on the river at night and put raw chicken on a line, trailing it through the water. Every few seconds, a pair of invisible jaws sprang out, snapped up the rotting meat, and vanished. All they got was a glimpse of their predator, never a full picture. And they lost all the chicken.

"What am I supposed to do?" I ask, not because I want to go along with the plan but because I need to gauge Becca's true intentions.

"Nothing." She takes a right too sharply, and I bang my elbow on the door. "Just be yourself. Apparently you're his type."

"You hear how awful that is, right?" I mutter, rubbing my sore arm. "To be a serial killer's *type*?"

She glances at me. "I guess you have a knack for it."

I shudder, and she laughs.

"Oh, relax, Carrie. You just show up, stand there, and do your usual nothing. I'll do the real work."

"That's what I'm afraid of."

She laughs again, as though we're not driving to a funeral. "God. You're so wound up. Maybe you should take a Valium."

"What? Do you have some?"

"No, do you?"

I huff and glare out the window, refusing to play her game.

"I'm not going to do anything crazy," Becca says, her tone patronizing. "I'm not stupid. How do you think I've gone this long without ever being a suspect? The only time I've even spoken to a police officer was the day I got yelled at for shoplifting. I know how to stay off people's radar when I need to."

I don't bother answering. What Becca wants and what Becca actually needs are two things she's never been able to distinguish between.

Three blocks from the cemetery, the streets are full. The church, enormous by Brampton standards, looms large, its sand-colored stone flat and dull in the gray weather, the stained-glass windows too dark to appreciate. Police officers in neon vests dripping with rainwater stand at the intersections, directing traffic.

"Wow," Becca muses, taking it all in. "This really is the party of the century. I'm glad I got my nails done!" She claims her manicures as a work expense on her income tax returns, saying they help her sell jewelry as she models the rings.

We find parking on a side street several blocks away, huge, leafless trees standing sentry along the sidewalks, showering the car with drops of rain that sound like gunshots when they hit the roof. I open my umbrella and duck out, the heel of my boot immediately sinking into the grass. Freeing myself, I wait on the sidewalk for Becca, who's touching up her lipstick. She must have noticed the news vans.

I shiver in the damp cold and stuff my free hand in my pocket, starting in the direction of the cemetery when Becca is finally ready. The rain increases steadily, pelting our matching black umbrellas, and after two blocks my toes are wet and freezing. My teeth chatter, and I quell my feelings of resentment for Angelica. If she hadn't stolen my work, I wouldn't have hated her and she wouldn't have died. If she'd stayed buried, there'd be no funeral. And if things weren't so suspicious, I wouldn't have to go to pretend I cared. I'd be safe and warm and minding my own business, no new serial killers on the horizon or in my closets.

We reach the end of the third block, and the cemetery and church come back into view. Becca and I halt, taking in the sea of people, an undulating mass of black umbrellas and sad faces. The only color comes from the bright jackets of the reporters lining the street, angling themselves so the church is in the shot. On quick study, I count no fewer than eight news vans, more than Brampton sees in half a year, never mind one morning. Becca turns to me with raised eyebrows, impressed.

The gated entrance to the church is about fifteen feet wide, flanked by heavy wrought-iron doors on either side and now staffed by a dozen police officers, all of whom watch silently as the mourners flow in. It's a bottleneck, and we're soon absorbed into the swarm. Becca grips my elbow so we don't get separated, and we shuffle forward, no option but to go with the crowd.

As we near the doors, a strange feeling washes over me, like I'm being watched. I think immediately of those eyes in the woods and the ones in the closet, and terror grips me. Becca's right. He's here. But when I suck in an icy breath and whip around, the only familiar face I find is Detective Greaves, standing next to two officers in uniform, rain sliding off the shiny brims of their hats.

He holds my stare, unblinking and unsmiling. Just observing. I don't know what to do. If I continue to look terrified, I'll look guilty. And if I smile, I'll look creepy. I jerk my head back to the front as though I hadn't seen him and let myself disappear into the sea of people.

It takes forever, but eventually we're inside the church, the air thick and damp and uncomfortably cloying. It's a huge, cavernous space, but already it's standing room only. People are being funneled to the upper balcony, and I crane my neck to see a row of onlookers gripping the rail.

"Up or down?" I ask Becca when we near the stairs and have to decide to head for the balcony or stand crammed along the walls down here.

"Up," she says, slipping into the line.

I follow her and pick my way up the narrow staircase. Compared with the rest of the church, the balcony is small, only four rows deep, but there are a smattering of random seats still empty, and Becca asks people to move down so we can sit together.

By the time we're seated, I'm sweating, stray curls stuck to the back of my neck, a hot rivulet of sweat trickling over my belly. I shrug out of my jacket and hold it in my lap, and I'm not the only one. Around me and below me, mourners fan themselves with the funeral program, Angelica's smiling face waving at us.

I look down at my own program, and that's when I see Becca. She's got her phone out, and she's recording. Surreptitiously, but she's still recording. At a funeral.

"What are you doing?" I whisper sharply, glancing around for Greaves.

Becca frowns. "What does it look like?" She zooms in on the lower level and scans the rows of faces. "Do you have a photographic memory? No? Me either. And there are a ton of people here. We're going to need something to compare to."

"To compare to what?"

"The other videos from the other funerals."

My eyes bulge. "You plan to go to the other funerals?"

"Of course! Everyone will be there. It'll be weird if we're not. Plus, we need the footage. Someone's going to look familiar, and afterward we can head back to Spark and ask if anyone recognizes the guy."

"What are you even looking for?" I squint at the screen. Because of the dim lighting and everyone's dark clothes, the picture resembles a storm cloud.

"I'm not sure," she admits. I can see her cheek move as she bites it, a tinge of blood on her lower lip. She hasn't chewed her cheek in years, confirming she's not quite as cool as she's pretending to be. "Someone staring at you, maybe? Have you noticed anybody weird?"

"Just you."

"Try harder."

I shift in the chair and try to look around casually, like I'm at a bar, searching for my friends. Except I'm looking for a serial killer who's not seated to my immediate right. Most of the people up here are engrossed in conversation, texting on their phones, or reading their pamphlets. I spot a couple of tears, but for the most part they, like us, are here to be part of something, not because they care.

I turn my attention to the lower level. At the front is a gleaming dark casket, its lid closed, accompanied by an oversized picture of a smiling Angelica, beatific and care-free. The people in the front row are sobbing, and a few others approach tentatively, offering their condolences. Halfway back, I spot a pop of color, and when the man shifts I see that it's Troy and one of his hideous ties. He's with Rudy from Accounting and Gene from Concepts, all of them looking lost and sad.

There's movement in the main aisle, and I watch the top of Greaves's head as he walks in. He wears a dark suit and carries a jacket under his arm, shiny with rain. He's with the female detective with whom he'd visited our office and another, shorter man I assume is also a detective. He doesn't look up.

Somewhere behind me, whispered voices come into

focus, talking about the closed casket. "...other ones I get," a scratchy woman's voice is saying, "but she was only missing for two days—why the closed casket? When my Jenny was buried..."

"I heard the damage to her face was too bad," another woman's voice replies. "It couldn't be fixed."

"And after the business with her foot...," someone else adds, her tone full of meaning that the others all seem to get, murmuring their understanding.

I glance at Becca, who's watching me, her brow furrowed. She swears that when we left Angelica, she was not only buried but fully intact. She had both feet attached, and her face hadn't been damaged from its run-in with Becca's car. The only thing marring her skin was that stupid kiss of death, which the police haven't shared or even asked about. Because her face was too damaged to discover it? Is it possible that Footloose watched us bury Angelica and then dug her up, chopped off her foot, and destroyed her face, thus obliterating the only thing that could possibly connect Becca to Angelica and lump her in with the dozen other bodies in the park?

My heart thumps painfully in my chest as Becca's earlier theory resurfaces. If Footloose wanted to kill me, he's certainly had the opportunity. He's been in my car, my house. He knows where I live, where I work. And yet he hasn't done it. I hate myself for thinking the words, but Becca is right. The only reason for him to mask Angelica's murder in the burials at the park is not for him to take credit for her death but to add one more body to the pile for which I can take the blame.

He's framing me for his killings, making me the scapegoat of not one, but two serial killers. No wonder Becca thinks it's funny.

———

Two days later, I turn into a gas station parking lot on the edge of town and stop next to Becca's car. We'd agreed to meet here at noon to drive together to the funeral for Jacinda Moon, one of Footloose's victims who, according to best estimates, disappeared approximately a year ago and whose friends we'd met in an alley a few nights earlier. She's being buried in her hometown of Newport Village, a quaint oceanside town forty minutes east of Brampton.

I climb out of my car, squinting against the bright November sun. I'd gone into work for a few hours this morning, explained I had to leave early for a follow-up dentist appointment, and then driven here. In an hour, I'll call Troy and tell him my root canal needs to be redone and take off tomorrow as well so I can attend my third funeral of the week.

I step toward Becca's car, frowning as she gets out. Instead of respectful black, she's wearing a bright-red sweater and white jeans, paired with heels I'm pretty sure I last saw in my own closet with the rest of my belongings.

"What are you wearing?" I ask, praying she has a change of clothes in the trunk.

"Work clothes." She snaps her gum and sticks out her hand. "Give me your phone."

I don't. "Why?"

"Because I was checking the film I took at Angela's funeral—"

"Angelica."

"—and most of the people were too far away to get a good look at them. The lighting in the church was terrible and even the ones I did manage to zoom in on are still hard to identify. I found an app that will help."

"Why didn't you install it on your phone?"

"I did. But I can't come to the funeral today so I need to put it on yours so you can get some good footage."

My jaw drops. "What do you mean you can't come? It was your idea!"

"It's still my idea," Becca points out, flicking her fingers impatiently. "And *you* can still go. Some of us have a job we can't just skip out on whenever we feel like it. Now give me your phone, Carrie. You can't be late to a funeral. It's bad form."

"Everything about this is bad form," I protest, even as I hand over the phone.

"Do you want to go to jail for killing a dozen people?"

"Of course not." Though I've lived with the possibility of exactly that lurking in the back of my brain for nearly a decade, this is the first time it's truly seemed possible.

"Then be grateful I'm helping you and stop complaining about everything. This app will help you zoom in on people's faces and analyze their features. I downloaded the other part onto my laptop so later we can use the program to compare faces and see what matches we come up with."

"There'll be a ton," I argue halfheartedly. "Everyone within a hundred miles will be attending the funerals, just to feel like they're part of the action."

"They'll lose interest." Becca covers her mouth as she yawns, underscoring her point. Angelica's funeral had lasted nearly an hour, tearful speeches and tributes and a particularly bad original song sung by a second cousin. If Jacinda's funeral is anything like it, only half the audience will bother to attend the next.

"Okay, all done." Becca passes back my phone and wipes her hands, like she's accomplished something more than abandoning me in my time of need. "It's pretty straightforward. Zoom in as best you can, make sure there's nothing too bright in the background to ruin the focus, and hold the camera steady. No shaky hands."

I look at my shaky hands.

"Email me the footage, and I'll add it to my file," she continues. "You'll get more at tomorrow's funeral, and then the fun part begins."

"None of this is fun."

She pulls open her car door. "Not with that attitude.

Bye. Good luck." She drops into the seat, slams the door, and drives off with a half-assed wave.

I get into my own car and make the trip to Newport, the radio playing quietly. I change the channel whenever the news comes on because all anyone can talk about is Footloose and the funerals. Even though I had nothing to do with Jacinda's murder, I can't shake the queasy feeling that I'm just as bad as all the other busybodies, sticking their noses in now when they wouldn't have given her the time of day when she was alive.

The Newport paper had posted an article online advising of Jacinda's funeral, including a short piece on her life. She'd been thirty when she disappeared, only two years older than I am now, a high school graduate with a 3.8 GPA and plans for college. A car accident a week after graduation left her with back pain and a prescription for oxycodone that turned into an addiction. She'd spent the next ten years stealing and selling whatever she could to pay for her habit, eventually resorting to selling the only thing she had left. Unnamed "friends" said she'd been working the streets for a year but had plans to get clean and start over somewhere new. When she disappeared, they hoped she'd taken off for greener pastures.

She hadn't.

The Catholic church in Newport is a fraction of the size of the church in Brampton, and the police presence is sized down considerably. The parking lot is full but I find street parking just a block away, and there's no bottleneck at the doors, just a small cluster of weeping family members handing out pamphlets to those who enter. I take one and murmur my sympathies, feeling like a hypocrite. Like most people here, I never even knew Jacinda.

Becca had advised me that the best place to sit was near the back, at the end of the pew closest to the aisle so I could surreptitiously film people as they came in and linger at the end of service to film them again as they exited. The church is about three-quarters full, crowded mostly at the front, and I easily find a spot at the back. I sit on the hard wood, feeling immediately guilty and suspect. These two funerals are the only times I've set foot in a church in twenty years. I glance around for Greaves but don't spot him. Apart from the officers directing traffic out front, I see no one in uniform.

At the front of the church is a long white casket, its lid closed. Next to it is a large picture of Jacinda, the quality grainy, suggesting the original image had been too small when they blew it up. She's young, wearing a basketball jersey and grinning at the camera, a strand of hair flying across her forehead, like she was in motion when it was taken. I stare down at my hands, clutching the pamphlet so hard it's crumpled nearly in half. I haven't even touched my phone. I'm doing a terrible job of spying. But instead of trying harder, I smooth the pamphlet, expecting to see a schedule of the funeral plan like they had for Angelica. Instead it's a listing of local treatment centers and resources for substance abusers and family members impacted by addiction. At the end, there's a link to an existing GoFundMe campaign to help the family pay for the burial.

I fold the brochure and put it in my pocket, willing myself to relax. The doors are propped open behind me, allowing the cool November air to flood in, and I take a deep breath. When my nerves have calmed a bit, I wipe my sweaty palms on my dress and pull my phone from my pocket. I'm in the last pew, and there's about five feet between me and the family on the other end of the bench, their heads bowed. I turn on the camera and rest my phone on my lap, angled slightly so it can see the doors. Immediately the plan fails. The bright sun outside makes everyone coming in a dark shadow, impossible to identify.

The sound of a throat clearing echoes throughout the space, and everyone abruptly sits up straighter and faces forward. I stuff my phone back in my pocket as the priest or pastor or whoever, a tall, hearty man in white and purple robes, stands at the dais and says a few words about Jacinda, calling her things like "our lost sister" and "the Lord's newest angel," and around me I hear strangers weeping.

When he finishes, an older, stooped woman takes his place. She talks about Jacinda in the present tense, like she's still with us. Anyone who wasn't crying is bawling by the time she's done, and I have tears in my eyes, too.

We stand to sing a few songs to which I know none of the words, but everyone's lost in their grief, and no one notices. They say when a person goes missing not knowing is the hardest part, but this knowledge doesn't seem to have helped.

The entire ceremony lasts twenty minutes, a fraction as long as the celebration of Angelica's life, and there's talk of a reception at the family's home nearby. I'm suddenly incredibly grateful Becca isn't here because, like the psycho she is, she'd insist we go. It's bad enough that I linger in my seat, wiping my tears and doing my best to film people's faces as they file past. The line is long, and they move at a snail's pace, age and grief slowing them down. I watch on the screen as the app Becca downloaded traces green grids over their faces, sharpening their features for later analysis. I half expect to see the eyes from my closet glaring out at me, but none of these people are familiar. No one looks like a serial killer. Then again, neither does Becca.

When there are only a few people remaining huddled at the front, I stand and pull on my coat, squinting against the sun as I step outside. There's a man on the steps in a suit and tie, solemnly thanking everyone for coming, and a guilty lump lodges itself in my throat at his words. I keep my head down and nod quickly, scurrying down the steps in the direction of my car.

"Hey," someone says.

I keep walking.

"Hey," they say again. The voice is female, raspy, vaguely familiar.

I'm nearly at the sidewalk when I stop and glance around, freezing when I spot two familiar faces. It's the women we met behind Spark, Shanté and Fur Coat, dressed in their funeral finest. Shanté's dark braids are twisted into an elaborate knot on the top of her head, a strand of pearls peeking out in the open vee of her dark jacket. Fur Coat now wears a different fur coat, long and shiny, too heavy for the day's weather. Her skin is deathly pale and caked with cheap makeup, tear tracks cutting a swath through the powder. I expect them to be outraged to see me here, but their eyes are sad, not angry.

"Um." I shuffle closer so we don't have to raise our voices to be heard. People are looking, but they're looking at them, not me. "Hi. How—how are you?"

Fur Coat sniffles and shrugs. "Not good."

"I'm sorry for your loss," I say, because I can't think of anything original.

"How you doing?" Shanté scans me from head to toe, making me grateful again that Becca didn't come along.

"Sad," I say, because that seems right. "Like everyone else. I didn't know you'd be here."

"Why wouldn't we be? She was our friend."

"That's not—" I stop myself, hearing the defensive note in my voice. As soon as Becca gets you on the defensive, she pounces. "That's not what I meant," I say, more calmly. "It's a long way from Brampton."

"We hitchhiked," Fur Coat offers. "It took two hours to get here, and they wouldn't even let us in."

That's why I didn't see them during my reconnaissance. And why they didn't see me, thank God.

"It was a nice ceremony," I say. "She was really loved."

Shanté scoffs. "Yeah. That's why they didn't notice she was gone. Didn't even look!" She raises her voice on the last point, and a few more heads turn.

"Did you?" I ask. "Look?"

She plants her hands on her hips. "Of course we did! But that lunatic got her! We couldn't find a thing."

"Where did you look?" I press, channeling my inner Becca. If the footage I got in the church doesn't turn out to be useful, maybe I can get something here. What, I don't know, but anything is better than nothing.

Fur Coat purses her lips. "Around."

"The guys she was...with?"

"Yeah. Mostly. I don't know who she saw last, but most of the men we meet are nice guys. A little sad, but harmless. They like to talk, they like us. I thought maybe she mentioned something to one of them, someone who seemed a little...unusual...but they all said the same thing. Nothing."

"What about you guys? Did you ever have any 'unusual' customers?"

"Of course," Shanté answers. "We all do. But not *that* unusual. Not chop-off-your-foot-and-bury-you-in-a-park unusual."

Fur Coat nods her agreement, eyes darting around uncomfortably. Used to being judged, maybe, but not in broad daylight.

Then it strikes me. "Are they here?" I ask, my head swiveling. "Any of the guys?"

Shanté snorts. "Yeah. They're here. I recognize a few."

"Where?"

"All over. It's not like they're wearing signs."

I slide my phone out of my pocket as covertly as possible, though no one is watching me. I turn on the camera and aim it at my two new friends. Shanté is about to balk, but I channel Becca again. "Smile," I order. They falter, but do it. "One more." I pretend to take another picture, but I'm filming the crowd over their shoulders, letting the app zoom in on faces, triangulate, analyze, whatever the hell it's supposed to do. The service is over, but dozens of people still linger on the church lawn, all manner of age, race, and gender. Just like I couldn't pick out a serial killer from the crowd, I couldn't finger any of these men for availing themselves of my new friends' services, but apparently it's more common than I know.

"Let me make sure I got some good ones," I say, turning the phone away from the women and aiming it at a new group of people, squinting at the screen as though scrutinizing the picture.

"What are you doing?" Fur Coat asks suspiciously.

"Getting some video," I answer. "Just play along."

Shanté hesitates before getting her own phone from her bag and snapping a few selfies. After a second, Fur Coat does the same. All the people who weren't looking at me before are scowling at me now, thinking the three of us are Jacinda's friends and co-workers, using the funeral to beef up the content on our social media pages. It's not ideal, but it's better than them knowing what I'm really doing.

Shanté and Fur Coat ham it up for the crowd, and when I think I've filmed everyone in the vicinity, I upload the videos to a file transfer site and send Becca a link. I plaster on a smile and put away my phone. "That's good," I say. "Thanks for your help."

"Anytime," Shanté says, though I can't imagine there'll be a second time. Their other missing friend, Donna-Marie, was from Boston, her body flown home. I don't think anybody's making the trip to Massachusetts.

I fish my car keys out of my pocket, noticing clusters of people talking angrily, hands flapping in our direction. I turn to the women. "You guys need a ride?"

———

Graham is quiet that night, sitting at his kitchen table, cartons of takeout scattered between us. I chew a mouthful of pad Thai, still in my dress, my mind racing. As distasteful as my undercover funeral activities may be, there's something exhilarating about the experience. A change from my dull day-to-day, work and home and work, repeat. For once, I'm being active, not reactive. I'm the one in charge.

"I'm worried about you," Graham says finally.

I pause, mid-chew. "Why?"

He gestures at me, eyes wide. "Why? Because of this! You're going to strangers' funerals."

"I knew Angelica."

"And the girl today? The sex worker? Did you know her?"

My eyes skitter away. *The sex worker.* That's kind of formal. Or maybe it's just politically correct. Or maybe it's how Footloose thinks of his victims.

I swallow past the guilty lump in my throat. Graham has never been anything but great to me. I can't let Becca—of all people—be the one to make me doubt him. She's the murderer, not him.

"No," I say finally. "I didn't know her." I didn't know Jacinda, but I spent an hour with her friends on the drive home, and I liked them. They were nice, smart, funny, and grieving. With the exception of Graham, the only person I really spend any time with outside of work is Becca. For so long, I've been afraid of what she might do to any friends I manage to make that I've managed not to make very many at all. And while Shanté and Laurel and I might not have made brunch plans, today still felt like more of a human connection than I've had in a long time.

He arches an eyebrow, doubtful and judging.

"A lot of people are stressed about what's been going on," I insist when he doesn't speak. "And there's safety in numbers. They feel comfortable at the funerals. It's how they grieve. They're not being weird, they're being human."

"You work in an office," Graham points out. "And you have me. And your sister. You're not exactly alone."

"It's hard to explain."

He grunts and drags his fork along the edge of his plate, scooping up a stray piece of papaya. "No kidding."

The food that tasted amazing a minute ago now tastes like dust. "I'm going to another funeral tomorrow," I say, a bit defiantly. I stand and take my plate, scraping it into the compost bin.

Graham looks at me in surprise. "What?"

"It's in Paige. For one of the homeless men."

"What the fuck, Carrie?"

I want to flinch, but I hide it. Graham seldom gets mad and never curses at me, but a lifetime with Becca has taught me how to hide my feelings anyway.

I turn and stick my plate in the dishwasher. "I want to."

"Why?"

"Because it helps   "

"What the hell are you grieving?" He's standing now. "You didn't even like Angelica. She stole your design, and she was trying to steal your promotion!"

I stare at him, my whole body going numb, hiding

the stress bubbling beneath the surface, even as my heart pounds.

"Why aren't you grieving?" I hear myself say, deploying Becca's familiar turn-the-tables tactic. "Why aren't you scared? There's a serial killer in our town, and you—"

"And I what?" Graham snaps. "I'm not homeless? I'm not addicted? I'm not a sex worker? I'm not saying anyone deserves what happened, but I'm not afraid because I'm not his type, and I'm not grieving because I didn't know those people! What you're doing is—is—unwell. You're taking part in someone else's pain and pretending it's your own, and I don't know what you get out of it, but it's—"

"Unwell?" I finish.

"It's something your sister would do."

The words land like a physical blow. I knew people in school who loathed being compared with their siblings because they couldn't measure up—their sister was so popular, their brother so athletic. But I've always feared that any comparison to Becca meant I was soulless, like her. That deep down, buried beneath years of propriety and cautiousness, is someone dangerous, festering in the shadows, waiting for the slightest crack to slip through and wreak havoc.

My hands are trembling, tears stinging my eyes. "I can't believe you just said that."

But Graham doesn't back down at the sign of my tears. "I can't believe you can't see it. You're the one who told me how, when you had your appendix removed, she faked kidney stones and got herself hospitalized beside you, ordering flowers for herself so your side looked empty. How when your friend's father died, she spread the rumor that he'd tried to molest her. She gets off on the attention, Carrie. She does these things because she gets something out of it."

"What am I getting out of this?"

"I don't know! You tell me."

But I can't. I can't tell him anything. I can't tell anyone anything because the whole situation has been so fucked-up for so long that the truth is beyond comprehension. He's not the one with a serial killer in his closet and his family tree. And even though Graham doesn't know the half of it, the way he's looking at me now still threatens to break my heart.

———

The funeral for Ron Anderson is a fraction of the size of Jacinda's and not a tenth of the spectacle they set up for Angelica. The church is small but even then it's not full, half the parking spaces are available, and there are no police officers directing traffic or anywhere in sight.

The sun is absent, thunderstorms promised in the low, dark clouds, and I clutch my coat to my chest as I hurry toward the church door, propped open with a rock. There's no one on the steps to greet us, no funeral program, no enlarged photo in a gilt frame at the front. The church is dim, and flecks of dust float down from the rafters, captured in the weak light spilling through the windows. A dozen pews line either side of the narrow aisle, just the first few rows dotted with people, and a closed casket waits at the front, small and brown. No one is crying.

A few heads turn as I enter, my heels making too much noise. My plan was to sit in the back pew as before, but now that there are witnesses, my feet carry me toward the casket to pay my respects. I'd seen Ron Anderson's picture in the paper, gap-toothed grin and wild eyes, untreated mental illness the excuse given to explain his lifestyle. Propped on the casket is a small photo in a plastic frame, taken years earlier. His hair is combed, pale-orange freckles dotting his cheeks and nose. The paper said he was nearly sixty at the time of his death, but he can't be any older than thirty in this picture.

I turn, my eyes downcast, intending to retreat to the back of the church, but something compels me to raise my head, and when I do, I spot Greaves in the fourth row, alone in the pew. Watching me.

I hurry past, feeling his eyes on me as I go. But I can't leave, not just because it will look bad but because I still need to film. Becca was right about the rapidly dwindling interest. There are only twenty or thirty people here, and if Footloose is among them, it will be easy to cross-reference this group against the larger number at Jacinda's and Angelica's funerals.

Still, I can't sit at the very back without looking like an interloper so I sit in the sixth row, far enough away that Greaves can't watch me without openly turning his head and staring, which he doesn't seem opposed to doing, since he's doing it now. He lifts an eyebrow in inquiry, and I scramble to think of an appropriate response. A smile seems horrible, a glare confrontational, tears insincere. In the end, I settle on a helpless shrug, a tiny gesture that says, *I don't know either*. He watches me for a moment longer and then turns back to face the front, his expression never changing.

I pull out my phone and text Becca. The detective is here. The one from my office. He thinks I'm nuts.

Her reply is immediate. The best defense is an insanity plea.

Shut up.

I'm off Thursday and Friday, she writes. I'll go to the next few. You go to work and act normal.

For some reason, I type, Thanks.

How is it? she asks.

The funeral?

What else?

Sad.

An eye roll emoji.

I put the phone away.

The funeral is brief, paid for by an anonymous uncle who's not even in attendance. The only speaker is the priest, who offers a few stock phrases about lost sheep being welcomed back into the flock, and everyone who leaves looks more disappointed than mournful.

I linger in my seat, filming as best I can while Greaves remains in his pew, two rows ahead. He hasn't looked at me again but I felt him the whole time, like he knows exactly what I'm doing, if not exactly why. When I've filmed enough, I hurry out, sending Becca the link to the video, grateful to have no more funerals on the agenda for the week.

It's only four o'clock when I get home, but it's already dark. The skies opened up on the two-hour drive back, heavy raindrops battering the windshield, bright slices of lightning severing the black clouds with whiplash precision.

I drive past my house twice, slowing so I can study it for strange signs, any sense of evil. I'd left the living room curtains open and a light on when I left earlier, and they're both as they were, the house looking warm and lived in.

I park and climb out, hustling up the dark driveway to my front stairs, splashing in an unseen puddle that drenches my calf in ice water. I shiver and pull my keys from my pocket but stop before inserting the key in the lock, crouching to check my new welcome mat. Becca bought it for me as a safety precaution, even as she'd laughed at the irony of me setting out a welcome mat for a serial killer. We'd marked the landing with two tiny dots and positioned the mat just so. If it's moved, someone may have been here. If it's still in line, maybe not.

It's not the best plan.

Thunder rolls in the distance, snapping at me to stop putting off the inevitable. The mat is in place, and I straighten, feeling moderately more secure. I let myself in and listen carefully, eyes scanning the living room, the stairs, as far back as the dark kitchen. There's nothing out of place.

I close and lock the door behind me, the smell of ozone still hanging in the air, and take off my coat and boots. I peel off my pantyhose where I stand, my left foot drenched, toes red from the cold and the damp. I'm two steps in when I smell it.

I stop immediately, one hand on the banister, and sniff again. Ahead of me, the kitchen looms dark, and I think of Becca and her tricks. I wouldn't put it past her to have lied about work, sent me to a stranger's funeral, and come here to make a mess. Graham gave me a baseball bat to keep in the house, and I left it by the front door as a security measure. Even without any obvious warning signs, it makes me feel better to have it in my hand as I call, "Becca? I have a bat, and I'm going to hit you with it."

No answer. No sound at all. I move past the staircase and take two quiet steps, my bare feet growing even colder. I'd forgotten to change the thermostat, and it's not programmed to kick in until five o'clock. I don't want to turn it on now, knowing the sounds it will make will drown out anything I need to hear.

The smell is stronger now that the front door is closed. Something vaguely rotten and mineral-like. I recall the one and only time that I'd ever called Becca a psycho to her face. The next day, I'd found a skinned rabbit sitting in a pot on my stove. Becca doesn't know how to hunt things that know they're prey so she hadn't killed it herself, just bought it from a specialty butcher and then later complained about the price. Still. Message received.

The entrance to the kitchen looms large and dark. Without a light in the backyard, there's nothing to reflect into the room, to distinguish the inert shapes and shadows from something human peeling away from the wall, leaping for my throat, claws and fangs bared. I jab the end of the bat into the room, moving fast so if Becca leaps out, I'll hit her first. But nothing happens. I hear only my own breathing, my damp foot sticking to the linoleum, fingers scrabbling along the wall for the switch, finding and flicking it on.

The fluorescent light whines as it flickers to life, casting the room in its eerie yellow glow. I study the room. The stove—empty. The cupboards—closed. The back door—still locked.

I whirl around, but there's no one behind me. I consider marching right out the front door, getting into my car, and driving to Graham's, but after last night, I don't want to see him. I don't want to hear him say how going to these funerals is making me paranoid, that there's nothing to be afraid of. And maybe he's right. Maybe it's nothing. Maybe there's no smell at all. Maybe I'm just imagining the scent of Ron Anderson's body, my mind conjuring the whole thing.

Except I know I'm not. After a life with Becca, I don't need to use my imagination to dream up horrible scenarios. And while the floor upstairs is silent, no haunting creaks and groans to amplify my fear, my legs are still weak as I force myself to the bottom of the staircase, gazing up into the dark.

I make it two steps before bile rises in my throat. My palms are slick with sweat, and the bat shakes in my fingers. I'm more likely to drop it on somebody's foot than hit them with it. I clutch the rail with one hand and try to control my breathing, but it's impossible. I'm desperate for air, but also desperate not to breathe. The odor is too strong here, too unmistakable. It smells like iron, the tang on your tongue when you prick your finger and suck away the pain.

It's blood.

A lot of it.

I think of Becca and her stupid game, lurking in the shadows, waiting to pounce. I could do what I did all those times as a child, climb the stairs, sniveling and afraid, giving her power she didn't earn. Or I could spend another sleepless night on the couch, afraid of the dark.

But this is more than just darkness, and I don't want to be afraid of it, even though I should be.

I grip the bat with both hands and charge up the stairs without warning, making the creaky third step howl, swinging the bat in a wide, deadly arc when I reach the landing. It cuts a swath through the dark, the force and momentum taking me with it as I spin too hard to my left, the bat crunching through drywall.

For a second, my own cry rings in my ears, and then the house is deathly silent. The metallic stink of blood is mixed with the powdered spray of drywall, and my nose twitches. I sneeze as I reach for the switch at the top of the steps and turn on the lights, the overhead fixtures too bright after the impenetrable dark.

The hallway is empty. The doors are open, as I left them. The only thing different is the new hole in the wall.

Sweat runs in rivulets under my arms, over my rib cage, catching in the elastic waistband of my underwear. My skin is flushed but I'm cold all over, my fingers numb as they pry the bat free, barely feeling its weight in my hand. I swivel my head, trying to discern the source of the smell, but it's impossible to tell. There are only three options: my bedroom, the bathroom, or the guest room.

Tears sting my eyes, sorrow for whatever or whomever I'm about to find. I move to my left, to my bedroom, since that's where I last encountered Footloose. I hold my breath as I reach in a hand and find the switch, flicking it on.

There's nothing. My neatly made bed, the closet doors open, the curtains drawn. It looks safe, though I know it's an illusion.

I turn back to the hallway, the guest room at the end, the bathroom in between. As soon as I near the bathroom, I know I've found the source. It's a small space, a single vanity, a toilet, an ancient tub and showerhead, and an ornamental grate in the ceiling that was the 1930s equivalent of a ceiling fan. It doesn't do anything to help with the smell, the sickening reek of congealing blood, the sting of metal clinging to the back of my throat and making my stomach seize.

I find the light and force myself to turn it on.

Then I scream.

CHAPTER 7

I stand next to Becca and survey the gory scene in my bathroom. The white of the tub is stained with bright-red blood, dark at the edges where it's dried and congealed, carving itself into the porcelain like the outline of a map. The tiled walls, faded yellow with age, are now mottled with pink, the aftermath of someone taking buckets of blood and hurling them into the shower, letting the rancid mess drip down the walls and pool in the basin below. There's approximately an inch of blood, red and black and clotting, with small, unidentifiable globs floating on the top. The smell is horrific.

They put the tub's plug in, whoever did this. Footloose, most likely. But possibly Becca, my brain whispers. It's the kind of thing she would do. And guiltily, reluctantly, I think of Graham, who knew I'd be at the funeral and was unhappy with my decision to go. This seems a step too far for someone so kind and even-keeled, but right now no one is innocent, and no one is safe.

Becca takes it all in, hands on hips. With her hair in a ponytail and a bright-green T-shirt with a teddy bear on the front, she looks like neither a serial killer nor a person who might know how to capture one.

"It's only in the tub," she says finally, her brows tugged together in contemplation. I'm still on the fence about her guilt, but so far she's done a fairly convincing job of appearing innocent and unaware. I'd woken her from a nap when I called, shrieking about a bloodbath, and when she'd finally dragged herself off the couch and driven over, she'd given me credit for my literal interpretation of things. Unlike me, she hadn't screamed until nearly fainting, dropped a baseball bat on her foot, and gagged hysterically as she limped downstairs for her phone.

I'd waited in the living room until Becca arrived, yanking the curtains closed in case he was out there, enjoying the show. Then I paced, a nervous, trembling mess with a throbbing toe, jumping a mile when the furnace kicked in with a low growl and heat squeaked out the ancient vents.

"It's only in the tub," Becca repeats now, stepping into the room and plucking my toothbrush from the cup on the sink. She crouches and dips it into the bloody bath, snagging the plug and straightening as the gory mess swirls down the drain. It only takes a minute, the old pipes groaning as they swallow the mess, but the porcelain, its finish long since worn off, is porous, and even with the blood gone, it's just as red empty as it was full.

"So?" I say finally, unable to look away.

Becca tosses my toothbrush into the sink, the bloody bristles leaving red scratches down the side of the basin. "So," she says, "if you chopped up a body in the tub, naturally, that's where the blood would be. Splashing blood all over the room would have been overkill. So to speak."

"Tell me you have a point."

She sighs, meeting my eye in the mirror. "Nobody died here, is my point." She sounds like a bored teacher, reciting the alphabet for the thousandth time. "He's framing you again. Messing with you, too, obviously, but framing you. If the police think you're chopping off people's feet, maybe they check the tub for blood. Ta-da. They found it. That's definitely worse than the Soda Jack cans."

"No kidding!"

She shrugs, and the shaking I'd thought had passed comes back, a shudder racking me so hard that my teeth snap together and I have to clutch the doorframe for balance. Becca reaches into the tub and twists the hot-water tap, using the handheld showerhead to spray it down. Bright-pink water runs in rivulets over the tiles, carving tracks through the basin and disappearing down the drain. She does this until the worst of the mess is gone, until the room is foggy with steam and my hair is sticking to my neck.

"Bleach should work," she offers, surveying the scene

when she finally runs out of hot water. "It's only been a few hours, probably not long enough to stain."

"How do you know that?"

"Bleach always works."

"How do you know it's only been a few hours?"

She stares at me for a second, eyes widening as the implication sinks in. Then her dramatic, unconvincing side takes over, and she presses a hand to her chest. "Do you think *I* did this?"

"Did you?"

Her eyes narrow, and she drops the act. "No, you moron. And I know it's only been here a few hours because you were only gone a few hours. Unless you're even stupider than you seem right now and failed to notice a lunatic dumping blood in your bathroom while you were at home."

She storms past me, taking care to elbow me in the ribs. I wince, rubbing the sore spot before following.

"Sorry," I say, just as she stomps on the creaky step and it lets out an otherworldly yowl. I don't even know why I'm apologizing. She's done far worse than pour blood in a bathtub.

Becca stalks into the kitchen, and there's a popping sound as she uncorks the bottle of wine I was saving for my Saturday-night date with Graham.

"Do you know what your problem is, Carrie?" she asks, not for the first time. Then she drinks straight from the bottle of my expensive wine, also not for the first time.

I grab a glass from the cupboard and extend it for her to fill. "It's the two serial killers in my life."

After a second, Becca smirks, her teeth stained pink, and pours an inch into my glass. "You're too negative," she says. "You never look on the bright side."

"Educate me, Becca. What's the bright side?"

"If Footloose was here, dumping blood in your bathroom"—she gestures to the ceiling with the bottle, wine sloshing perilously close to its mouth—"then it means he wasn't at the funeral."

"And that's great because he was in my home, instead of watching me somewhere else?"

"No, genius. Because we can use today's footage to eliminate the creepers who've attended all three funerals. If he was at your house, he wasn't at the funeral today, ergo, anyone on today's tape can't be Footloose. Ta-da! Bright side." She toasts herself and drinks deeply, a tiny rivulet of wine running down her chin like an overfed vampire.

I slump, burdened by my terrible consolation prize. "That's something, I guess."

"Do you know how hard it is to chop up a body?" Becca asks after a minute. "It's, like, incredibly difficult. That's probably why Footloose only takes a foot."

"How do you know this?"

"I tried it once. I didn't tell you because it didn't work out. This is when I lived in that apartment with the blue door. I couldn't do it now. Actually, I couldn't do it then either." She laughs at her own joke. "Anyway, I got him into the tub and tried to saw off his arm, but it was hard. I had a knife, a cleaver, a saw—I could barely get through the bone. So I gave up on the idea. It was the guy we buried at the golf course, remember? By the tenth hole?"

"I remember the hole. Not the arm."

"That's because it was still attached. He was wearing a sweater so I just put it back on. You could hardly tell the difference."

I finish my wine. "That's reassuring."

"There you go, being negative again. I'm just saying, Footloose didn't chop up the body here either. He probably never has. That might not even be human blood, we'll never know. It's just a message."

"What's the message? Fuck you?"

Becca chuckles. "You're funny, Carrie."

I put my glass in the dishwasher. I'm tired, terrified, and not at all cheered by Becca's positive outlook. "I'm not trying to be."

"He's just having fun with you. Sometimes the hunter likes to play with his prey. But don't worry. Not for much longer. You go back to work, business as usual. I'll hit up the next few funerals and start comparing the footage. We'll find something."

"And then what?"

Becca grins and uses the tip of a manicured finger to collect a drop of wine near the corner of her mouth. "Then we kill him."

—

In my six years at Weston Stationery, I have never taken as many sick days as I did last week. Guilt propels me out of bed, no matter how ill I am. Sniffling, sneezing, dizzy—I show up. So it's more out of obligation than desire that I go to work on Monday. When I arrive, I feel like the black sheep of a dysfunctional family, showing her face at Sunday dinner. My co-workers— never really my friends but at least my acquaintances— are torn between glaring at me and avoiding me. Their judgment and contempt are palpable, if not entirely unjustified.

I've barely made it to my desk when Troy ventures from his office, blinking like a mole emerging from its burrow. Today's tie is a threadbare yellow satin, and even from a distance, it makes my head ache, my eyes tired and gritty from another poor night's sleep.

Becca spent the night on the couch, baseball bat at the ready, but Footloose did not return. Not that it helped much. This morning, I'd opened a new toothbrush and freshened up in the kitchen sink.

"Carrie," Troy calls, his voice too loud in the quiet space, "may I see you please?" After a second, he adds, "In my office?"

I hang my coat on the back of my chair and walk toward the corner, feeling every eye in the office tracking my progress. I've been through too much recently to feel properly nervous about whatever this is, but something oily still curls in my belly, a sense of foreboding.

Troy closes the door behind us and gestures to one of the two chairs closest, while he rounds the desk. Vertical blinds cover the glass wall that looks over the rest of the floor, and as usual they're closed, for which I'm grateful. I know how to hide my feelings, but I'd still rather not have an audience if I'm being fired.

"So," Troy says, folding his hands on the desk and using his thumb to flick at a hangnail. "Congratulations."

He says the word so somberly it takes three full seconds for it to register.

I stare dumbly. "What?"

He smiles, pleased to have fooled me. "Congratulations, Carrie. You've been promoted to Novelty Concept Manager. The team at Amari loved your work on the three-hole punch and have placed an order for five thousand, as well as a request for a concept sketch for a whole product line. Well done."

My mouth falls open, but no words come out. For so long, all I've wanted was this promotion, and with everything that's been going on, I've barely been able to think about it. And now, after a week of terror and funerals and bloody bathtubs and serial killers — something good.

A smile stretches my face, far bigger than the occasion warrants, but I can't hide it. "That's amazing!" I say, relief in every syllable.

"You deserve it," Troy says. "The inside office is now yours, and you can move in today."

Tears prick my eyes, too many emotions swirling inside me. I think of my stapler picture, finally ready to move out of the closet. "Okay," I say, still beaming. "Okay. I will."

Troy stands, and we awkwardly shake hands. I'm elated. I barely feel the hateful glares when I float back to my desk and pick up my purse and my coat, taking them to my new office. I admire the shiny desk, the leather chair with its high back, the blank space on the wall for which I have the perfect piece of art. It's not quite as easy moving the rest of my things—two computer monitors, the tower, my printer, the contents of the drawers—but I do it, unassisted. Troy still has his blinds closed and likely hasn't thought about the logistics of this, and no one else offers to help.

Still, I don't care, and when I have everything moved over, I shut the door and text my sister: I got the promotion!

She writes back right away: That's fantastic!

I have an office now.

How are your co-workers dealing with it?

Great! I type. Very supportive! I type the words too fast and make myself count to twenty before pressing SEND, so they seem convincing. If I tell Becca the truth, she might kill someone else, and I want to enjoy my promotion without worrying about murder for a few minutes.

—

It's dark when I leave the office. I get as far as my drive-way before my earlier confidence gives way to fear and common sense. I'd forgotten to leave a light on so, even though the curtains are open, the living room window merely reflects back the night, obscuring whatever fresh horrors wait inside.

Becca hadn't offered to stay over again, and I'm too proud to ask her, even as I squirm in my seat, hands grip-ping the wheel, ready to reverse out of here at the first sign of trouble. I'm still mad at Graham—and apparently he's still mad at me because he hasn't called—and even if I weren't, I couldn't ask him to come over, since my bathroom's out of service. As soon as I have the thought, my bladder gives a squeak of annoyance. Technically, the toilet still works, but I'd gagged at the mere thought of using it this morning, skipped the coffee, and peed at the office.

I can't do that again.

Nothing moves in the house, but it still looms, large and dark and unknown. The creaky floors and groaning walls, the furnace sounds and flickering lights—all the things I'd thought made it charming and mine—they're all too much. I back out of the driveway and drive down the street, like maybe anyone watching will think I just forgot to pick up milk and am heading to the grocery store.

In reality, I drive into the city center with its bright lights and pedestrians braving the cold, restaurants and shops still open and glowing, alive. I drive in circles for a while before pulling into the underground parking for a large chain hotel. I park and grab my purse and laptop, hurry into the elevator, and jab the button for the ground level. The doors glide open, revealing a large lobby with a water feature burbling happily behind the front desk. A chandelier sparkles overhead, and a handful of guests wait in the seating area, next to a roaring fire.

Already I feel better.

I haven't stayed in a hotel in years, and the price for a room with a queen bed and no view makes me rethink my plan, but the thought of going home has me handing over my brand-new credit card. I take the elevator to my room on the eighth floor, a small cube with a scratchy green bedspread and a clean bathroom. The nightstand has a Bible and a room service menu, and I stand at the window and look down at the twinkling city, safe and anonymous.

As much as I'd like to pretend I'm someone exciting who spends nights in hotels and does crazy things, the truth is I'm tired. Before I get too lazy, I drag myself back downstairs and visit a few of the nearby shops, picking up a new dress to wear to work tomorrow and a toothbrush. I grab a pizza for dinner and take it all back upstairs, check the closet and under the bed, lock the door, hook the chain, and drag the nightstand in front of the door. I briefly consider opening my laptop but eschew the idea of work in favor of eating and watching TV until I fall asleep at ten, waking up only when the sun streams through the curtains I forgot to close. After my first decent night's sleep in a week, it takes me thirty seconds to remember I'm in a hotel and another thirty to find the alarm clock, the digital display telling me it's after eight. I fling myself out of bed, take a much-needed shower, and drive to work with damp hair. I'm hustling toward the building, the sunny November day somehow feeling ten degrees colder than normal, when I hear my name. It's too bright, and I shield my eyes, shivering in the wind as I try to find the source.

"Carrie!"

I hear it again and turn back toward the parking lot, freezing when I see Graham jump out of his car and hurry toward me, a bouquet of flowers in his arms.

"I—What are you doing here?" I ask, still squinting against the sun.

Graham stops a few feet away, uncharacteristically uncertain. And, when he shifts so he's blocking the sun and I can see him better, unshaven. He's always clean-cut and tidy, his hair trimmed at the barber every six weeks, his shirts ironed, suits dry-cleaned, socks thrown away at the first sign of a hole. Now he looks how I feel, like he's coming apart.

"I wanted to make sure you were okay," he says, his voice tense and awkward. "I called you a dozen times last night, and you never answered. I even called Becca."

My eyebrows shoot up. Saying he called Becca is the equivalent of saying he kicked a puppy. Graham would never do that.

"My phone—" I begin. I'd turned it off last night, halfway through the bottle of wine and paranoid that Becca or Footloose could somehow use it to track me.

"I drove to your house," he adds. "I rang the bell. I knocked. I went inside."

My stomach plummets. Graham has a key, and he's usually welcome at my place whenever he wants. But not right now.

"It—"

"I was worried about you!" he exclaims, dragging his fingers through his normally perfect hair and leaving it tousled. "I felt bad about our fight, and when I couldn't reach you, I thought about Footloose and how I said I wasn't his type. Then I started thinking how Angelica *was* his type, and you knew her, and—" He breaks off and shakes his head.

"I'm sorry," I say, reaching out to touch his arm.

But he moves away. "Where were you? I mean, I'm glad you're okay, but…" He gestures to me, the wet hair, the late arrival. "That's a new dress, right?"

For a second, I'm too stunned to speak. Graham thinks I was cheating on him. I'm the least likely person in the world to cheat on someone. I barely even have one option, never mind several. The worst part is that I'm relieved that's his biggest fear. Because it means he didn't see the bathroom and he doesn't know the truth, which is far worse than anything his imagination could conjure.

"I stayed in a hotel," I say. "Alone. I was paranoid about Footloose, and I didn't want to go home, and we…" I'm not faking it when I let the sentence trail off, unsure how to identify exactly what we are right now. But I've also seen Becca do this too many times, leaving the other person to fill in the blanks, letting them determine the course of the conversation and then decide if she likes the direction it's heading.

Graham is stricken. "Carrie. You stayed in a hotel because you were afraid?"

I shrug, embarrassed, since it's true. For most people it would be an overreaction, but in my case it's fully justified. "I haven't been sleeping," I admit. "So I turned off my phone and just crashed."

He studies me, but he's no longer suspicious. He trusts me. He's checking to make sure I'm okay, that I'm well rested. "Do you feel better?"

"Yes. I'm sorry I scared you."

"You don't have to apologize. I'm sorry I said you were like your sister. You're not. You're nothing like her."

I force a smile. "That's good to hear."

"And she told me about your promotion. Congratulations. It's about time."

The smile becomes more real. "Thank you."

He extends the flowers, slightly wilted. "These are for

you. Sorry, they're half dead. I left them in the car last night when I couldn't find you."

I accept the bouquet, my nose running too much to actually smell the roses. "They're perfect. I'll put them in my new office."

"Have you hung your painting?"

"No. I'll do it tomorrow."

"I can help you, if you like. I can drive over to your place and—"

"No," I say too quickly. Graham flinches, like maybe I'm still mad. I hesitate when Rudy from Accounting passes by, giving me a wide berth, like I might brain him with my bouquet. I wait until he's inside, the doors closed behind him. "They still think I had something to do with Angelica's disappearance," I say, my voice low, even though Rudy's gone. "I don't want to rub it in their faces."

Graham sighs. "They know you didn't have anything to do with what happened to Angelica. They just want someone to blame. They feel powerless, and this is their way of feeling like they're in control of something."

I think of the funerals I've attended, the video I've taken. The funerals Becca will attend and record. The one thing we have a say in, in this whole, horrible mess.

"You're right," I say, though he's not. "They'll get over it. But in the meantime, I'm going to keep a low profile."

Graham arches an eyebrow and looks me over, the

appreciation in his gaze making me blush. "In that dress?"

I hadn't bothered trying it on at the store yesterday, and though I'm wearing it with dark tights, there's no missing the fact that the dress stops a few inches above my knee, much shorter than anything I'd normally wear.

"I bought it yesterday," I admit.

Graham smiles, glancing around as he steps close. "Well, I'm glad you did. Can I see you later? Do you want to have dinner?"

"Yeah," I say. "Absolutely."

"Good. Wear the dress."

My lips are frozen from the cold when he kisses me, and so are his, but we're both smiling when we step apart.

———

It's a quarter to three in the morning, and I'm wide awake, crouched on the floor in Graham's guest bathroom. Like everything in his apartment, it's small but nice. Fancy vanity, shower with marble tile, gleaming fixtures. He even has a picture on the wall. But while I normally spare a moment of envy for these things, tonight I can't. Tonight I'm listening to the tinny sound of Becca's voicemail greeting when she doesn't answer—again—and I'm asked to leave a message—again.

She'd texted me that afternoon to say she'd gotten some good video at the latest funeral and was heading home to start comparing the images. She'd uploaded the link so I could download it, too, if I wanted to help. I'd been in a meeting with Troy when she'd called later, leaving me a rambling, excited message. I play it again now, for the tenth time, though I already know it by heart.

"Carrie!" she exclaims, sounding triumphant and exasperated. "I found him! I can't believe this fucking worked, but I found him. He's on your tape and my tape, and I bet he'll be at tomorrow's funeral as well. I bought a tracking device on my way home, and I'm going to follow him to his car and put it on his bumper, and then we'll know where this fucker lives. We'll destroy him, Carrie. Promise." There's a pause, like she's distracted by something, and then, "Graham called me last night, by the way. He wanted to know where you were. He didn't even know you got a promotion, and when I told him about it, he didn't sound very happy for you. What a dick. I don't know what you see—"

A shrill beep cuts her off, signaling the end of the message.

My heartbeat is so loud I can hear it thrumming in my ears, nearly drowning out the recorded voice asking if I want to save the message or delete it.

I'm equal parts excited and terrified by the news that we might have a lead on Footloose, but I know Becca too well to take her at her word. If she's lying—or just plain wrong—about finding him, I don't want to get my hopes up. And I really don't want to have a hand in helping her torment another innocent person.

In tenth grade, I had my sights set on being student council treasurer, something only my family knew. There was another kid at school, a scrap of a girl named Thindi Gill, and one day Becca and I arrived at school to see that Thindi had made posters. They were beautiful. Full-sized poster board with glitter and sequins and even a slogan: GILL FITS THE BILL! She must have spent hours on them.

I was devastated, seeing my silly dream slip away before I'd even made a single effort toward achieving it. But Becca was irate. In her mind, Thindi's efforts were a personal attack. That night, while I went to the art store and overspent on supplies, staying up well past my bedtime to make my own posters—CARRIE THE ONE!— Thindi's house was burning to the ground. Everyone except the family's pet rabbit got out safely, but because the fire was deemed suspicious, they endured a lengthy legal battle with the insurance company and had to move out of our area and into a new school district. I was student council treasurer for the next three years.

I watch the video Becca uploaded—again—trying to find a face in the crowd that looks like a serial killer. But none of them do. I'd even watched the clumsy videos I'd taken at Jacinda's and Ron's funerals and didn't find a match.

My eyes start to blur, weariness and worry battling

for dominance. After Becca's message, I'd tried to reach her all afternoon, but she'd been pretty pissed that I'd shut off my phone during my hotel stay and is holding a grudge. She's probably just ignoring me to hold on to her purported insight just a little bit longer, but I can't stop the invisible fingers of fear slowly tightening their grip on my spine, telling me that's not the case.

———

I can't concentrate.

I'm in my new office, staring at the blank spot on the wall where my stapler picture will hang if it's ever safe to go home again, and I can't do anything but think of the one person I'm constantly hoping to forget.

I called Becca when I woke up this morning, but the call went straight to voicemail. I've called three more times with the same result. Becca can be petty and wretched, but she's not one to pass up the opportunity to gloat about finding Footloose, and since I'm the only person who could give her an audience, her silence is frightening. It's more frightening than finding a man in my closet or having Greaves knock on my door or discovering a bathtub full of blood. Those things have happened. They're horrible, but they're known. This is not. I can't just climb the stairs with a baseball bat and get answers. I can't do anything.

But I can't stay here either.

It's eleven o'clock, and the funeral Becca is supposed to attend today is in nearby Marlo, just a twenty-minute drive. According to the newspaper website, it's supposed to start in half an hour. It occurs to me that, if Becca found yesterday's funeral boring, this would be the perfect way to ensure that I attend today's. She has to know I'll try to find her, and the most likely scenario is that I'll sit through another awkward service, an interloper with a phone in her hand, and she'll be laughing in the parking lot when I come out, boasting about how she got me to do her work.

The mere thought makes resentment burn in my chest, but it doesn't do enough to replace the fear nestled alongside it. Not once in my life have I been afraid for my sister. She's always been the biggest predator in the room, the one sitting at the top of the food chain, picking and choosing her next meal. But that was before Footloose.

I stand up and grab my coat, pulling it on as I cross the floor to Troy's office. I'm aware of heads turning as I walk, but I ignore them. No one has congratulated me on my promotion.

I knock on Troy's door, and he looks up from a sudoku puzzle, hastily shoving it under the desk with the same panic he'd display if he were hiding a copy of *Hustler*.

"I have to go," I say.

He's still fumbling with the paper. "Oh. Um. When?"

"Now."

"Will you be back?"

A slideshow of possible scenarios flashes through my head. Becca at the funeral. Becca not at the funeral. Becca dead in my house, me too afraid to go inside. Becca hiding in my house, laughing as I linger in the driveway, too afraid to go inside.

I hoist my purse onto my shoulder. "I don't know."

I don't wait for his answer, just head for the elevator. Rudy from Accounting is already there, waiting, and he scurries off to the side when I stand next to him, like I might strangle him on the ride down. When the car arrives, I step on, and Rudy does not. I shrug and let the doors close.

When I get to my car, I do a quick lap, peering in all the windows for anything strange and checking the trunk, which is empty. I get in and twist the key in the ignition, the engine whining as it turns over, cold and unhappy. I know the feeling.

I look up the address for the Baptist church in Marlo on my phone before navigating my way out of the parking lot and onto the highway. The skies are gray and low, promising rain and worse, but I don't care. I thought Becca's plan to stick a tracking device on Footloose's car was stupid, but I'll go along with it, just as long as she's there.

Marlo is a small town, considerably more shabby than Brampton. Single-story bungalows line the quiet streets, lawns flat and yellow, the houses in not much better shape. The sidewalks are empty, the occasional piece of trash marring the gray landscape, and it's only when I make the turn for the church that I see any people at all.

The church is small, the tiny wooden cross perched at the top glowing stark white against the darkening sky. The double doors are propped open, and a man in a suit stands next to them, shivering. Getting out of my car, I quickly scan the few vehicles in the lot, none of which are Becca's. I hustle toward the church as the wind picks up, cutting through my winter coat like a knife.

"Hello," the man at the door says. He's pale with dark eyebrows, drawn low in grief as he passes me half a sheet of paper. The funeral program. I don't even remember whose funeral I'm attending, I'd just memorized the date and time.

"Thank you," I murmur, taking the page and stepping inside. The church is so dim it takes my eyes a moment to adjust, even with the low light outside. There are only eight rows of pews here, all of the benches short, holding no more than six or eight people comfortably. There's a closed casket at the front, a blown-up photograph of a middle-aged woman next to it. She wears a white blouse and a strand of pearls, her hair nicely cut as she smiles for the camera. She looks like the mother of the few friends I ever had.

The front three rows are full, but the rest are empty. I don't see Greaves. I slip into the sixth row, by myself, and ignore the curious stares as I read the short program.

Marcy Lennox, fifty-one. Mother of three, former banker. A drinking problem turned into a meth problem, and one day she left rehab and never returned. No one saw her again until the police unearthed her decomposed body in Kilduff. The family is asking for donations to be made to the local homeless shelter.

I put away the program and skim the heads in the front rows. No Becca. I wouldn't put it past her to be hiding, to have something horrible planned. It wouldn't be totally out of the realm of possibility for her to step up front to say a few words about the deceased. At this point, I'd welcome it.

But it's the man with the dark eyebrows who says a few words about Marcy, the mother he hasn't seen since he was sixteen. His words are kind and softly spoken, and people are sobbing by the time he finishes. A younger girl gets up and tries to speak but cries too hard to get out more than a few words. Someone hugs her and says it's okay, a song plays, and then we're done. For the last time. I'm not attending another funeral, no matter what. Graham accused me of coming here to take part in someone else's grief, but he couldn't have been further from the truth. I didn't know these people, but I have been part of keeping other people from knowing the truth about their loved ones' fates, people who hadn't been homeless or addicted, people whose families *did* look for them, and are still looking. I may not have caused this family pain, but I have done the same to others, done worse.

I don't bother filming. If Becca knows who Footloose is, then we have enough footage, and I don't want to record this anyway. I get up and escape as soon as possible, keeping my head ducked in case anyone tries to speak to me. I gulp in the cold air when I'm outside, icy drops of rain already starting to spit down, hitting me in the forehead, making my brain hurt. I stand on the steps and survey the parking lot, but there's no one there. No Becca.

I hurry to my car as the rain picks up, dropping into the driver's seat and wiping my face with my hands. I only intend to wipe away the rain, but tears are coming, too, hot on my cold cheeks, and I rest my forehead on the steering wheel and let them fall, grief and stress and fear erupting in a torrent.

It's hard to believe in the concepts of heaven and hell when you've done what I've done. But even though it'd be better for the world—or at least the residents of Brampton and the surrounding towns—if Footloose has indeed gotten to Becca, I'm still praying to anyone who's listening that she's okay. I promise not to help bury any more bodies, to anonymously reveal the locations of the others, to get her to stop killing. I'll do anything.

The parking lot is empty when I recover. I haven't been here long, but the other attendees wanted to be here even less. The sky is now nearly black, the rain washing over the windshield in sheets, obscuring me from any curious passersby. I start up the car and shiver as cold air whooshes out of the vents, turning on the wipers and making the return trip to Brampton.

I drive on autopilot, and it's only when I reach the turn for my house that I realize again that I really do not want to be there. Instead of making a right, I flip my blinker to turn left and wind my way through the rainy streets to Becca's apartment building. She lives just a ten-minute walk from the mall but insists on driving to work each day "just in case." It's her favorite joke. I'm the only one who's in on it.

Her building is about twenty years old, three stories of white stucco and Juliet balconies. It's not fancy, but it's spacious and affordable, and the neighbors are old and unfriendly, which suits Becca, who's only really nice to people intending to buy jewelry. They require a permit for street parking, and Becca always has a prime spot in front of the building. The spaces aren't reserved, but a longtime elderly tenant had unofficially claimed one of the spots for his 1959 Mustang, acting, in Becca's opinion, "like a smug asshole" about the whole thing. Until the otherwise-quiet street became a haven for vandals with a particular penchant for vintage Mustangs. His car was hit four times in two weeks—slashed tire, scratch in the paint, smashed taillight, stolen gas cap—until he finally sought out a private garage to keep his baby safe. Now it's Becca's spot.

And today it's empty.

Just like she has—had—a key to my place, I have a key

to hers, though unlike Becca I never use it. I can't even remember the last time I was here. Either Becca's at my place or I don't want to see her. I run through the pouring rain, my new dress soaking through and sticking to my thighs, holding a hand over my head in a futile effort to stay dry. By the time I'm under the awning at the front door, I'm dripping wet, hair plastered to my skull.

I fumble with my key ring, the keys slipping through my wet fingers until I find the right one and stick it in the lock. I don't bother with the buzzer. If Becca knows I'm coming, she'll just hide and try to scare me when I get there. There's no elevator so I take the stairs to Becca's door, 301 nailed on in cheap brass numbers. I hesitate, key extended.

Standing here is like standing on the high dive at the local pool when we were kids, staring at the water miles below, too afraid to move. I'd stand there forever, the other kids in line starting to shout, the lifeguard patiently offering to come up and guide me back down. But as frightening as jumping was, going backward was even worse. Because Becca was waiting at the bottom of the ladder, and being mocked for backing down was infinitely worse than jumping.

I twist the key in the lock and open the door, as normally as I possibly can. If Becca's inside watching a movie, I already know she'll tell me she didn't go to the funeral because she saw the forecast, and look how wet I am, my hair looks terrible. But she's not here.

Her apartment opens into a wide living room with a couch beneath the window on the far wall, the murky light from outside spilling in. There's a kitchen off to the left, a bedroom on the right. Though she takes pains with her personal appearance, she's never been one for decorating or cleanliness, and the white walls are bare, no artwork, not even a clock to break up the bland expanse. The clean walls are in stark contrast with the rest of the space, discarded clothing, pizza boxes, wine bottles, and cereal bowls littering every surface. There's a film of dust on the dining table, the garbage can is overflowing and starting to smell, and when I peer into her bedroom, the bed is unmade. The closet doors open to reveal a colorful tornado of clothing and shoes, half of which are probably stolen.

I call out "Becca?" as I approach the bathroom, even though I already know she's not here. The door is ajar, and there's no smell of death, but I still use my foot to push open the door and jump back in case someone leaps out.

But no one does. The room is empty, and the tub is not full of blood. Becca's toothbrush and toiletries litter the countertop, a pair of lacy underwear forgotten on the floor. It would be difficult to tell if Becca left town, because this is exactly what her apartment would look like if she had. Likewise, it would be difficult to tell if someone had ransacked her apartment, because it would also look like this.

I keep replaying her voice message, that moment when

she paused as though she'd heard something. I'm assuming she was home when she left the message, that she was sitting on her couch, laptop on her knees as she toasted her genius plan for finding Footloose.

Now I walk back to the couch, one of its cushions askew, two throw pillows stacked on one end, another two on the floor, and study it. The TV is on the opposite wall, and this is where Becca spends most of her time when she's here. She doesn't cook, and she doesn't clean, so if she's not watching something on television, she's online, watching videos of dog rescues and movie trailers. I frown at the coffee table. Three mugs, two cereal bowls, and a copy of the book Graham gave her for her birthday, never opened. No laptop.

In my mental image of Becca phoning me, she had her laptop open, the software program running, the still images of Footloose matched on the screen, one from my video, the other from hers. Peeking out on the floor by the edge of the couch is the cord from her laptop. I trace it back to the wall, where it's still plugged in.

The slick, icy feeling that's been crawling along my spine returns, intensifying. I whirl around and scan the apartment, but I'm still alone. The front door is closed and locked, how I left it. I stride into the kitchen and scan the counters for the laptop, but it's not there. The dining table is bare, save for the dust. In Becca's bedroom, the night tables are cluttered, but no laptop. I shake the blankets on the bed, but it's not there.

I search everywhere I possibly can, but I can't find it. I've never seen Becca leave home with her laptop. I can't picture her sitting in a coffee shop, working on a novel. I can't picture her anywhere. Just as abruptly as I could envision her laughing at me, the visions are gone. When I try to think, I get a blank screen in my mind. Static. Like the connection is lost.

Becca and I do not operate on the same frequency. Becca is on a wavelength blessedly unknown to most humans. But a lifetime of fearing her, dreading her, and preparing for her has given me a sixth sense about her. And suddenly that sense has fled.

—

It is clear when I report Becca missing the next morning that the police do not care. That they have been inundated with hysterical reports of missing family members, all possible victims of Footloose, girls who turned out to have merely snuck off to be with their boyfriends and crept back in too late or husbands who went to the bar after work and passed out on a friend's couch instead of going home to face their wives.

I've never been in a police station before, and even when I imagined it, it was always while I was wearing cuffs, being escorted in through a shower of jeers and slurs, wronged family members getting in their punches while they still could. The reality is far less dramatic.

The Brampton police station is a squat, single-story brick building with the same yellow lighting as my kitchen and tile floors scuffed beyond repair. A bulletin board by the front doors is covered with posters providing the phone numbers for emergency services, an ad for a local private investigator, and several missing persons posters.

A bored police officer sits behind a desk and a plastic barricade, staring dispassionately as I do my best to explain why my fears are legitimate and more pressing than everybody else's, why I think my sister may actually be a victim of Footloose. The woman stares at me balefully and repeats in the same flat tone as an operator: Your sister is an adult. She has not been missing for forty-eight hours. You cannot file a report. She probably met somebody, her phone died, and she'll be back tomorrow. There's no need to panic.

But I can't stop the panic welling up inside me, not only because Becca is my sister and she might be dead, but because, unfortunate as it is, Becca is my *ally*. Becca is the only one who knows the whole truth, a truth I can't tell anyone else without implicating myself. Becca, the town serial killer, is my safety net.

"Please," I try again, hands trembling as I press them flat on the counter, attempting to compose myself. "Please just let me— My co-worker was one of the people found in the park and—"

"Ma'am." The police officer eyeballs my hands like

they're weapons. "If you have not heard from your sister after forty-eight hours—"

"Ms. Lawrence?"

A deep voice has me turning to find Greaves behind me, still in the dark jacket and jeans, his expression politely concerned. I haven't seen him since the last funeral, and I don't know what his presence means now, only that he's the one person in this building who might actually take me seriously.

"My sister is missing," I tell him, my voice breaking on the last word. "It hasn't been forty-eight hours, but she's—I just know—"

Greaves shoots a small smile at the officer who was not helping me and places a hand on my elbow, swiping his card over a sensor for a set of sliding doors that open into the squad room. It smells like coffee and paper, and a series of desks and cubicles fills the space, not terribly dissimilar to the setup at Weston. Only here, no one is looking at me.

"We can talk over there," Greaves says, leading me to a set of desks tucked into the far corner, beneath a window covered with bars. The desks abut each other, computer monitors in the center, the equivalent of a digital wall between the two stations. The other seat is unoccupied, and Greaves wheels it next to his desk, waits for me to sit down, and then does the same.

"You want some water?" he offers. "Coffee?"

I shake my head. "My sister is missing," I repeat.

"She's—I know she needs help. She's not okay. Something's wrong."

Greaves folds his hands on the desk. "Why do you think that?"

I gave this a lot of thought last night, trying to figure out what I could say without implicating either one of us.

"Becca is really fascinated with the Footloose story," I begin, though *fascinated* is hardly the word. "After Angelica's d-death, we—I—she's been going to some of the funerals. Me too. She thought she might see him there and figure out who he was."

Greaves arches an eyebrow but doesn't seem particularly impressed. Probably because he's been doing the same thing. "Did she have any luck?"

"She seemed to think so. Two days ago, she left me a message and said she'd found him. She was going to go to a funeral yesterday—for Marcy Lennox, in Marlo—and find his car and put a tracking device on it."

Greaves's other eyebrow goes up. "Where did she get a tracking device?"

"I have no idea. She said she bought one. But after that, I never heard from her again. I've been calling, and no answer. I went to her apartment, and she's not there."

"What about her car?"

"She parks on the street, and I didn't see it."

Greaves pulls a notepad out of a drawer and finally jots something down. He's left-handed, his wrist blocking whatever he writes from view. "Does she work?"

"Yes, at Robson Jewelry in the mall. She was off the past two days so they haven't noticed anything."

Another note. "Does your sister have a boyfriend?"

"No. I don't think so."

"Any friends?"

"I—" I think of wife beater Nikk. "Not really. Not that I know of."

"What about your parents? Where are they?"

"Phoenix. I called them. They haven't heard from her."

Another note. "Are they concerned?"

"I didn't give them a reason to be."

Greaves puts down the pen. "Can I listen to the voice message?"

My heart rate kicks into overdrive, but I'd anticipated this, and now I take my phone out of my purse, call up the voicemail, and put it on speakerphone. There's a low murmur in the office, but not enough to drown out Becca's voice. I set the phone on the desk and play the message.

"Carrie!" Becca crows, sounding elated and proud. "I found him! I can't believe this fucking worked, but I found him! He's on your tape and my tape, and I bet he'll be at tomorrow's funeral, as well. I bought a tracking device on my way home, and I'm going to follow him…"

My eyes well up as the rest of the message plays, the pause, the bit about Graham. I use my thumb to wipe away a tear and look at Greaves, who's looking at me.

"You haven't heard from her since?"

"No." I show him the call log, the two missed calls from Becca the same day, and all of my unanswered calls to her since.

"When did you go to her apartment?"

"Yesterday. In the afternoon. I went to the funeral first to see if she was there. When she wasn't, I went to her place."

"How did it look?"

"It looked…okay. She's messy, and that's how it was. I stayed there all night to wait for her, but she didn't come home." I also stayed because I was afraid of my own house and its bloody bathroom, but I don't mention that.

"All right." Greaves makes another note and puts down the pen. "I'll have someone look into it."

"You're not going to?"

"No," he says. "I have my hands full. But Detective Schroeder will be in touch."

I glance around the busy room as though I might spot Detective Schroeder and be able to convince him to start working right away. Greaves stands, giving me my cue to leave. Now I can see the notepad, just four scant words scrawled across the yellow paper: *Becca, missing, one day.*

"While I have you here," Greaves adds, too casually, "do you know a Shanté Williams?"

My circle of friends, loved ones, and co-workers is small. "No."

"You sure?"

"I think so."

He types on his keyboard, a painstaking, two-finger approach, and then turns the monitor so I can see it. It's a mug shot, familiar dark skin, pretty eyes. This time her hair is loose and curly, no braids, no pearls around her neck.

"Oh," I say as Greaves nods, like he knew all along. "I do know her. Well, sort of. I met her at a funeral."

"You just met her there?"

I think of the night Becca and I approached Shanté in the alley behind Spark. I'm not going to try to explain. "Yes."

"And then what?"

"Then I drove her back here, to Brampton. Her and her friend Laurel. Why?"

Greaves hits a few keys, and the screen goes dark. "Because she's missing, too," he says.

CHAPTER 8

I go home. It hardly seems like the safe thing to do, but if Becca was right and Footloose gets his kicks from toying with me, then the blood in the bath and making my sister disappear and watching me flounder should provide entertainment for a while. At least, that's what I'm hoping as I crouch on my front step and study the welcome mat, now decidedly out of line with its dots. It's hardly a foolproof method to determine if someone's entered the house; the mailman could have moved it or a door-to-door salesman or a neighborhood kid asking for donations for a school fundraiser.

Or a serial killer.

I turn the key in the lock and slowly open the door, letting my senses kick in. My eyes scan the dim interior, grateful for the smidgen of sun filtering through the window, confirming everything inside looks the way it should. A bit sad and shabby, but in order. I sniff, but this time it doesn't smell like blood. It smells like...bleach. And it's cold.

The baseball bat is where I left it, propped against the closet door, so I step inside and kick off my boots, leaving the door unlocked in case I need to make a quick exit. I hang my coat on the banister and scoop up the bat, creeping down the hall in my funeral dress and stockings. I don't know why I'm creeping. If Footloose is here, he's already heard me come in. Same for Becca. And if there's another morbid disaster waiting for me in the bathroom, there's nothing a baseball bat will do to help.

Still, I swing it in a careful arc as I enter the kitchen, which doesn't matter at all because it's empty. There are no creaks and groans from upstairs, the back door is locked, there are no cereal bowls on the counter. There's no sign anyone has been here since I last left, but I don't feel safe. I'm not sure I ever will.

I head back toward the stairs, the cold and the odor of bleach wafting down the steps. "Becca?" I call as I start up. I don't actually think she'll answer me, but maybe my voice will mask the sound of my footsteps and give me a split-second advantage over anyone lurking.

I reach the landing and swing the bat again, this time careful not to whack the wall. The hole is still there from last time, but the dusting of plaster on the ground is gone. And the smell of bleach is much stronger up here.

I do a quick scan of my bedroom, but it's as I left it, the closet empty. Now, however, the window is wide open, icy wind whipping in, the curtains flapping. I return to the hall, approaching the bathroom. The door is open, the smell of bleach strong enough to make my eyes water. I hold my breath and flip the light switch, expecting the worst.

But it's not worse. It's…better. The bathtub is a gleaming white, the tiles polished, the silver fixtures shining. *It's clean.*

For a moment, I wonder if I imagined the whole bloody tub thing in the first place. Because less likely than a serial killer filling my bathtub with blood is Becca *cleaning* the tub. And she's the only one who could have because she's the only one—besides Footloose—who knew it was dirty. I hadn't given her a new key to my house, but she was still pretending to be asleep when I left the other day so she could have done it anytime between then and leaving me the voice message about finding Footloose. And then…

Wiping away tears at the unknown horror waiting at the end of that unfinished sentence, I force myself to keep moving, anything to not think of what I believe to be true. I change out of my dress and into a pair of sweats, splash cold water on my face and comb my hair, but it doesn't hold the nagging thoughts at bay. Much like Becca, they keep resurfacing, circling the perimeter, looking for weaknesses in my defenses. I try to tell myself I've done what I could, I filed a report with the police, but I hear the emptiness in that excuse. For all her wretchedness, if Footloose had captured me, Becca would turn over every stone in this town to find me, if only to get a better look at my corpse.

My laptop is on the bed, and now I stare at it, an idea forming. If the police aren't going to help me find my sister, I'll have to do it myself. And the only clue I have to Footloose's identity is Becca's voice message. *I found him! I can't believe this fucking worked, but I found him! He's on your tape and my tape…*

I have access to all the funeral footage, and the name of the program—FaceKnown—Becca was using to compare the faces. I grab the laptop and jog downstairs, snagging the baseball bat and heading into the kitchen. Sitting with my back to the jammed door so I can see the entrance to the living room, I hunt online for FaceKnown and download it. Becca had texted me her account details so I log in and navigate to the folder she'd named Funeral Fun.

I'd sent Becca my videos from Ron Anderson's and Marcy Lennox's funerals, and she'd uploaded both of ours to the site. The footage from Angelica's funeral is too dark and distant, so I select the film Becca got at the funeral a couple of days ago and run it through the program to identify the faces. It takes about fifteen minutes to analyze everything, and the screen fills with a collage of strangers, all with little yellow markers mapping their facial features.

I connect my phone and upload the film I took at Jacinda's funeral and scan it next. Twenty minutes later, it's done, and I have another page of faces ready to analyze. It takes a few minutes for me to figure out how to get the software to compare the pictures, but I eventually get it working, watching a little hourglass rotate on the screen as it goes through the motions. Soon after, a green checkmark appears, confirming the process is done. A dialog box pops up and informs me I have six matches.

All at once, I'm flushed and anxious. I'm not sure exactly what I'm looking for, but I don't expect this will be as easy as simply spotting the same murderous face making an appearance at every funeral. I know there will be familiar faces from the police, as well as interlopers like me and Becca, cluttering up the results. But something Becca saw convinced her she knew Footloose when she saw him, and while I lack her killer instinct, I'm hoping I can see it, too.

I click on the results, and the screen populates with six sets of photos, the analytical data displayed next to each. Immediately, I see Greaves and delete him. Next is the female detective I recognize from her visit to our office the day Greaves questioned us about Angelica; I delete her, too. There are two elderly women, pictured together in each shot, and I figure they're just busybodies too old for murder and eliminate them. That leaves me with a middle-aged Asian man who doesn't have the same dead, hazel eyes I saw in my closet, and a red-headed woman it takes me a moment to identify as the mother of the missing girl, Fiona McBride. I keep them on the list of possible suspects, if only so it has something on it.

Next I view the video I took at Ron Anderson's funeral, a considerably shorter clip with considerably fewer people. Again, Greaves is there, but he's the only match. I eliminate him and, just to be sure, download the second video, the film Becca took at Angelica's funeral. It's much longer than the others, and the hourglass spins interminably as FaceKnown scans and analyzes, comparing it with the others. Zero matches. Despite the fact that I know Greaves was there, the footage is too dark to provide an accurate result.

I contemplate the images of the unknown Asian man and Fiona McBride's mother. We attended five funerals, took video of four, with only three clips being useful. This is the only footage we have. Assuming Becca wasn't lying in her message, what did she see that made her think she'd identified Footloose?

Again when I think of Becca, my mind goes blank. My brain has unplugged from whatever data source it used to predict and prepare for the behavior of a psychopath. Somewhere deep down I've already accepted that Becca is dead, and my mind has started deleting a lifetime of self-preservation strategies.

The sound of the front door easing open makes me

jump out of my chair. I fumble for the baseball bat, knocking it over and out of reach. I'd forgotten to lock the door when I came back down, and—

"Hello? Carrie?"

I slump into my seat, gripping the edge of the table and trying to catch my breath. Graham. It's just Graham.

"Carrie?" he calls again. I hear his footsteps coming down the hall, toward the light.

"In here," I say as he reaches the kitchen and spots me.

Relief washes over his handsome features, even as he smiles to cover his nerves. "There you are. Troy called me and said you didn't show up for work, and I just…got in my car."

I finally remember I have a job. It hadn't even occurred to me. I'd slept on Becca's couch and gone straight to the police station, forgetting I actually have a life of my own to lead.

"I totally forgot," I say, shaking my head. "I—I just—"

"Are you okay?" Graham pulls the other chair closer and sits down. "You're really pale, and it smells weird in here. What were you doing?"

"Um…" I definitely don't want to go into detail about the bathtub, and it's hardly the most important thing right now. "I think Becca's missing," I say finally. "I went to the police, and they—" My voice breaks. "They didn't take me seriously because everyone is so paranoid." Tears spill over before I know it's happening. I've been to four funerals and barely shed a tear. My sister is the bane of my existence and she's not even definitely dead, and I can't stop crying.

"Hey," Graham says, wrapping an arm around my shoulders and pressing a kiss to my temple. "Everything's going to be okay. It's been a really stressful few weeks, but Becca disappears all the time, you know that. Remember the night she was supposed to host your birthday party and you all got to the restaurant and she wasn't there because she'd gone to Bangor? And she hadn't even made a reservation so you ended up at Burger King?"

I sniffle and nod against his chest. There are a lot of times Becca disappeared because it suited her, but this time is different. This time we were investigating a serial killer who knows who we are, and probably what we're doing. But of course I can't say this to Graham. He hugs me, his head turned away from the laptop, and I carefully reach over and minimize FaceKnown so he can't see what I'm up to.

"It just feels wrong," I say finally, because I want someone to listen to me even if they can't help. "In my gut. I know something happened."

Graham pulls back, his concern sincere. "You think that something is Footloose?"

I shrug helplessly. "I know everyone is saying that right now, but—but I *know* it is."

Graham stands and takes two glasses out of the cupboard, filling each with water from the tap. He sits back down and passes me one, the cup warm in my hand. "What did the police say?" he asks. "When you told them."

Relief floods me. I know Graham can't help me find Becca, but without her, there's no one in my life I can talk to about any of this. Or parts of it. My co-workers, the police, my parents. I'm alone without Graham. "They said it hasn't been forty-eight hours, and she's an adult, and her phone probably died, and she'll show up soon enough." I swipe at a tear. "But I went to her apartment and her car wasn't there, and it—"

"It looked like something had happened?"

I shake my head. "It looked normal. Too normal."

Graham purses his lips, and I know he's trying not to dismiss me the way the police did. "Did you tell the police that?"

"Yes. I told Detective Greaves, the one investigating Angelica's murder. And he said he'd pass it on to some-one, Detective—" I rack my brain. "Detective Schroeder. But they're not going to do anything. I could tell from the way he said it." Mostly I could tell from the way he mentioned Shanté's disappearance and my connection to three missing-possibly-dead women. The only thing he's likely to do next is issue an arrest warrant.

"Okay," Graham says decisively. "You know what?"

I sit up a bit straighter at his authoritative tone. "What?"

"I'm going to take the day off work and spend it with you. And we're going to make posters and hang them on every available surface in this town. Then we're going to drive around until we find Becca's car. Brampton's not that big, and Becca doesn't exactly have a lot of friends. If she's passed out on a couch somewhere, we'll find her. If she's on a shopping spree, we'll find her. And if she's on a crazy bender, we'll find her."

I laugh through my tears. "You really think so?"

He uses a thumb to wipe my cheek. "I know so. I'm going to run upstairs to use the bathroom. You find a good picture of Becca for the poster, and we'll make one and head out to get it copied. Sound good?"

I nod gratefully. "Yes."

He jogs up the stairs, dodging the third howling step, and I hear the bathroom door close. I sip my lukewarm water and frown; I hate warm water. Graham knows this but says cold water is bad for digestion. I get up to grab ice, pulling open the freezer door and screeching. I fling it closed and leap back, water sloshing out of the glass and drenching my leg.

There's a severed foot in my freezer.

There's a severed foot in my fucking freezer.

I don't know whether to scream or gag or laugh hysterically, and the only person who would know what to do is missing.

Upstairs, the toilet flushes, and I scramble to clean up the water on the floor, sticking my glass in the dishwasher, no longer thirsty. I look around in a panic like I might find a better spot to store a severed foot, but nothing presents itself. For most people, this would be cause for hysterics, but I've buried thirteen bodies. I've seen worse. I've done worse. And I do now as I did all those other times: absolutely nothing.

I hear water running as Graham washes his hands in a room that, just two days ago, held a basin of blood. I gag a little, thinking of my life, and then sit down, close FaceKnown, and scan my phone until Graham returns.

"What'd you find?" he asks, dropping into his chair.

For half a horrible second, I think he's talking about the foot. Then I realize he's referring to the photo I was supposed to choose.

"Oh. Um. I haven't decided yet." I scroll through the photos I have of Becca. My hands shake, and the screen struggles to decide which way is up, the pictures blurring. I try to focus, seeing the severed foot when I should be seeing my sister.

I don't have many pictures of her because our most memorable moments together are better left undocumented, but eventually I find a couple of usable pictures. There's one from Christmas when she'd spent the night and we'd worn silly pajamas and watched *Bridget Jones's Diary*. There's one of her trying and failing to catch a goose, her hair and arms twisting in the wind, laughing hysterically as the bird darted back to the safety of the pond. She'd been pretending to avenge my honor after I'd told her one had hissed at me the day before, but fortunately she never caught it.

Ultimately, I settle on a shot of Becca that I'd captured

accidentally when she was watching an airplane in the sky, its smoke trailing like a sea serpent. I'd meant to take a picture of the clouds, but at the last moment Becca had turned her head and stared straight into the camera, her blue eyes wide and unguarded, her mouth slightly curved in amusement. For that one tiny second, she'd looked...human.

"How about this one?" I ask, showing Graham the picture on my phone.

He barely glances at it. "It's perfect. What should we say in the description?" He turns the computer and starts typing as I email myself the photo so we can insert it into the poster. MISSING, he types at the top in a huge font, highlighting the text and coloring it bloodred.

My stomach turns, and my eyes slide unwillingly toward the refrigerator, to the foot inside, toenails painted bright pink, dark skin gray with cold. I was telling Greaves the truth this morning when I said I didn't know what happened to Shanté.

But I know now.

———

We print three hundred posters, buy two heavy-duty staplers, and spend the first hour plastering the posters around town. Every telephone pole, every streetlamp, several trees, shop windows, and car windshields. We put a poster on every available bulletin board: the library, the grocery store, the bowling alley. At nearly every turn, there's a faded, tattered poster of Fiona McBride staring back, the same red text, the same hopeful smile, the same desperate plea: any information, please call.

We spend the next two hours driving in circles, eyeballing every black car that could be Becca's and coming up empty. We return home three hours later with nothing more than a bucket of fried chicken and a bottle of wine for dinner. Graham is intending to stay the night, but for the first time ever I really don't want him to. Now that I've had three hours to process the fact that there's a severed foot in my freezer and that Footloose has taken his love of toying with me to a gory new level, I need space to think. I'm angry and I'm worried, but mostly I'm terrified, and without Becca I don't know what to do. For my whole life, Becca has been the opposite of my moral compass. Whatever she did, I'd do the opposite. But in this, dealing with someone on her same psychotic wavelength, she was the one pointing me in the right direction.

And now she's not.

My driveway is only big enough for one car so Graham parks on the opposite side of the street, and we cross over to my place. It's late afternoon and the sun has poked out its head for the final hour of daylight, making the house appear charming and historical instead of daunting and deadly.

"Hello?" calls a voice behind us just as we reach the steps.

Graham and I turn together to see a man in a beige trench coat getting out of a car. He's short, barely my height, and slim, with thick glasses that make his eyes look overlarge and concerned. He offers a smile as he approaches.

"Carrie Lawrence?" he asks, and when I nod he extends a hand. "I'm Harry Schroeder. I work with Detective Greaves at the Brampton Police Department." He shakes my limp fingers and reaches inside his coat to show us the badge hanging around his neck before passing us each a business card. I'm so stunned I can barely read it.

"Detective Greaves said you stopped by this morning to file a report about your sister, is that right?" Schroeder blinks, his eyes owlish behind the thick glass.

"Um, yes," I manage. "I didn't—I didn't think—" I didn't think Greaves had taken me seriously or had any intention of doing anything more with my message than balling it up and throwing it in the trash.

Schroeder waits patiently.

"Um…" I shake my head to clear it, to remember the story I'd told Greaves. "I didn't think you would look for her," I say. "Since it hasn't been forty-eight hours."

His smile is terse, official. "Given your connection to one of the people found at Kilduff and another missing person, we thought it was a good idea to talk to you sooner rather than later."

Beside me, Graham stiffens. "Another missing person?"

Two of my neighbors have come out to sweep their

steps, no doubt searching for entertainment now that their afternoon programs are over. Graham notices them watching and rests a hand on the small of my back. "Maybe we could talk inside," he suggests.

I want to balk—I do, after all, have a foot in my kitchen—but it's freezing, and Mr. Myer is slowly sweeping his way down his driveway, heading in this direction.

Schroeder smiles politely. "Sure. If now's a good time."

I lead the way up the steps, glancing automatically at the welcome mat, seeing that it is again askew. When Graham and I left, I'd made sure to check it, ensuring the corners were lined up with the dots. And now they're not. Maybe Schroeder knocked on the door first and then waited in his car for us to return. But maybe not.

I unlock the door and turn the knob just as Mr. Myer calls out. "Hello? Excuse me?"

I see Schroeder wince and force another smile, like he's used to being accosted by citizens asking him to solve their problems. We all turn to see Mr. Myer hovering at the end of the short driveway.

"Is that Graham?" he asks, though there's nothing wrong with his vision. Graham once helped him rake the leaves on his front lawn, and he interpreted this to mean Graham was the new neighborhood handyman. "I wondered," he continues, voice deliberately wobbly, "could you help me with something? Really quickly?"

It's clear Graham doesn't want to go, but he's too well mannered to say no.

"Of course," he replies, starting back down the steps. "Leave the door open," he says, lips barely moving. "I want him to know I can't stay."

I try not to laugh. "Of course."

Schroeder and I watch Graham jog over to meet Mr. Myer, his hand on the older man's elbow as he guides him back across the street. I push open the door and step inside, using a shoe to stop it from closing. Schroeder spots the baseball bat propped against the closet and gives an acknowledging nod. Apparently I'm not the first person in Brampton to arm themselves, however inadequately.

With the cold winter air slipping in, I keep my coat and shoes on, setting Schroeder's business card on the table alongside the card from Greaves.

"So," Schroeder says, hands in his pockets as he glances across the street where Graham is using a rake to help Mr. Myer knock old Halloween decorations out of his tree, "you're worried about your sister?"

"Yes." I nod too quickly. "She hasn't— What did Detective Greaves tell you?"

"Why don't you tell me what you told him?"

I recap my conversation with Greaves, and, like him, Schroeder asks to hear Becca's voice message. I keep an eye on Graham, still preoccupied, and play the message. It's not great that Graham thinks our funeral visits were morbid, but if he learns they were a means to catch a serial killer, he'll lose it.

An icy gust of wind whips in, making us both shiver and shift farther down the hall, away from the cold. I stop after a couple of steps. I pretend it's so I can watch for Graham, but I don't want Schroeder in my kitchen.

Unlike Greaves, Schroeder takes copious notes. He jots down Becca's address and phone number, the make and model of her car, the license plate. He asks about her job, her friends, any boyfriends. I tell him as much as I can, but I know that's not enough. Without the truth—without disclosing the real reason I think Footloose is involved—it's clear Schroeder doesn't think this is urgent.

"Detective Greaves mentioned you also know Shanté Williams," Schroeder says, watching me carefully. "And that she's been reported missing."

"I don't *know* her, know her," I tell him. "I *met* her. But that was just one day. I haven't seen her again since."

"What day was that?"

I count back to Jacinda's funeral. It already feels like a lifetime ago, like too many more worse things have happened. "Thursday. I met her at a funeral."

"And you drove her home?"

"I drove her back to Brampton," I correct him. "With her friend Laurel. I dropped them at the mall. They asked me to."

Schroeder makes a note, pursing his lips, like he's thinking. Then he says, "She was reported missing on Wednesday. But she was last seen on Monday night."

I stare blankly, the words slotting into place, forming

the wrong picture. That I was one of the last people to see another missing person. But I wasn't. "Her friend," I say, "Laurel. I dropped them off together. Greaves said she's the one who filed the report. She knows Shanté was okay when I left."

"And you didn't come back after, for any reason? Didn't meet her again?"

"No!" I try to keep the panic out of my voice. Not just because I'm being suspected of harming someone I didn't, and not just because that person's foot is in my freezer, but because every second they spend investigating me, they're not looking for Becca.

"Is everything okay?"

We turn at the sound of Graham's voice, see him at the base of the steps, one hand on the railing. He looks like a handsome football player, tall and strong. When he climbs the stairs and stands in the door, he dwarfs Schroeder, his shadow casting the smaller man in darkness.

Schroeder takes his cue. "We have your phone number," he says. "We'll be in touch if we have more questions. And we'll keep an eye out for your sister."

I don't answer. I know I'll cry if I try to speak. There's a sick knot lodged in my throat as I watch Schroeder leave, and the tears spill over as soon as he's in his car. Graham closes the door and wraps me in a hug, murmuring comforting nonsense into my hair.

"They won't help," I sob. "She's missing and they— they just keep asking the wrong questions."

Graham snags me a tissue from a box on the hall table, though there are too many tears for it to help. "I'll make us some tea," he says, leading the way to the kitchen. "Then we can talk about what to do next."

I slump into the chair at the kitchen table and bury my face in my hands. "I met this woman at one of the funerals," I say, before he can ask about the other missing person Schroeder mentioned. "Her name was—is—Shanté. She was friends with the dead girl. And now she's missing, and they think because I—I'm—connected—" I hiccup and moan miserably. "I didn't have anything to do with this," I say. "I swear. I would never—"

Graham turns from setting the kettle on the stove, his expression one of astonishment. If this moment weren't so awful, it would be funny. "Carrie!" he exclaims. "Of course I know you don't have anything to do with this! My God. I know you. The police are—are— They're just doing their job."

"They're wasting time. Every second—"

"But," he says, something about his cautious tone giving me pause. He pulls out a chair and drags it close, sitting so near our knees almost touch. "What about...Becca?"

I blink at him, my lashes still damp. "What do you mean?"

"Well..." He studies his hands, knotted in his lap. "She knew Angelica. And she knew she was trying to steal your promotion."

My eyes widen involuntarily. Graham thinks it's

because of what he's suggesting, but it's the *accuracy* of it. Growing up, there were a handful of people who thought maybe Becca was behind some of the strange happenings in our neighborhood, missing pets, stolen items, awful rumors. But even fewer dared point the finger, because the ones who did inevitably suffered some terrible fate.

It's been years since I've heard someone suggest Becca in relation to anything bad, but murder? Even though his theory is entirely correct, it still feels wrong. Her absence is the first crack in the foundation of my idea of my sister as an indestructible monster. This accusation is the chisel sliding in, wedging open the concept even wider. It makes her a fraction more human. More fragile.

Still, because I have to, I say, "Becca would never—"

"And she was going to the funerals," Graham adds. "I know you went, too, but you were grieving. Becca wasn't. She was just…feeding off the situation. And I know she's your sister, but Carrie, she's always been a little bit…different. Unsettled."

"She wouldn't—"

He plows on, clearly having given this some thought. "Remember when you told me about the time you fell down the stairs in your prom dress?" he asks. "And how she filmed it and posted it online? The way she always brought up the story about your failed birthday party, just so she could laugh at it? Becca gets off on hurting you, Carrie. On watching you suffer. So maybe she didn't hurt these people—I'm not saying she's a *serial killer*—

but I wouldn't put it past her to be hiding in the shadows somewhere, laughing as you get caught up more and more in this mess. Don't give her the satisfaction of seeing you suffer. Just...don't."

My chest is tight. Graham is saying the words I've kept bottled up for so long, the ones I wanted my parents to say, the ones I needed to hear from some authority figure, someone who could actually stop Becca. Because knowing this is one thing; doing something about it is quite another.

And while the thought of Becca being dead leaves me numb with horror, if I'm right and Footloose has indeed gotten to her—then this could all be over. Becca started it, after all. She killed Angelica and forced me to help bury the body. Introduced herself to our unseen watcher in the woods. Came up with the plan to attend the funerals and catch Footloose. It was all her.

I know from a lifetime of experience that what Graham says is true. When a tormenter like Footloose gets off on the game, they keep playing. But if I withdraw from the competition—if I stop searching—he'll get bored and move on. Maybe I've already played my part. Hung the posters, alerted the police. Maybe it's time for me to bow out and let someone else clean up Becca's mess this time.

I can see Graham watching, feel him gauging my reaction as though he can hear the wheels turning in my brain. One time when we were kids, we'd gotten balloons at the fair, and Becca promised to hold mine while I ate my ice cream. Almost immediately she let them go, the strings slipping through her little fingers while she made no move to grab them. I'd cried, and my parents said it was an accident. But I knew better.

I can't give up on Becca too obviously. I have to try to hold on. Pretend, at least. And then maybe, hopefully, this game will run its course, peter out, all its horrible pieces turning to tiny specks in the sky, disappearing into the clouds. And then I can move on, too.

——

It feels wrong to buy groceries while your sister is missing. It feels wrong to grab just one box of cereal instead of two so I can hide one while she scarfs the other. Half a carton of eggs instead of the full dozen because she won't be there to accidentally drop six on the floor and then claim she has somewhere to be instead of cleaning them up. An expensive chocolate bar I'll leave on the counter instead of tucked inside my underwear drawer where there's only a 50 percent chance she'll find it. A million little things that should feel normal but don't.

I can't shake the guilt. I imagine Greaves watching me on the security cameras, my spine too straight, my shoulders stiff. Reading the labels on packages before placing them neatly in my basket, like a first-time criminal trying to look unsuspicious and failing horribly. I picture him accosting me as I enter the dairy aisle, flashing his badge, everybody staring as he shouts at me for shopping while my sister is missing. *What's wrong with you?* he demands. *What did you do? What do you know?*

Nothing, I'd tell him. *Nothing and everything.*

My hand shakes so badly I drop the jar of tomato sauce I'm holding, thick red goo exploding across the floor and spattering my shoes and jeans. An older woman at the opposite end of the aisle jumps at the sound, narrowing her eyes in my direction before disappearing around the corner, hand raised to catch someone's attention. I stand frozen in place, fat shards of glass gleaming in the fluorescent lights, reflecting the growing red pool, reminding me of too many other messes I've cleaned up.

A skinny young kid in a green apron and white shirt materializes with a mop bucket and a dust pan, smiling stiffly.

"I'm sorry," I say. "It slipped."

"No problem." He lifts the mop, gray water sluicing off its head before he drops it into the murky red smear and smudges it across the floor. "Did you need another jar?"

"No. I changed my mind." It's getting hard to breathe. My winter coat feels like it's weighted down, too hot and too heavy.

"No problem," he says again, not looking up as he mops, getting everything back to normal. The old woman resumes her hunt for the perfect pasta, and I back away, the metal bars of the basket handle digging into my hand where I hold it too tightly, afraid I'll lose my grip on everything.

I hurry out of the aisle and into the next, frozen foods, opening a door and staring at a wall of TV dinners, gulping in the stale, cold air. This is what I've wanted my whole life. Becca gone, disappeared. My life my own, not monitoring the shadows, nervously wondering which one she'll emerge from and what she'll have done or intended to do. I wanted mundane and boring. I wanted normal. Becca may have been other people's idea of sick and twisted, but she was my normal, and now life feels like a boat ride on choppy waters that's suddenly veered into a sheltered inlet, and all I can do is cling to the rail, waiting for the next bad thing.

I give up on groceries and head toward the exit, the red and blue lights above the cash registers too bright, the shoppers too slow, the smells from the fish counter too strong. The floors are slick with tracked-in slush and snow, and my dirty shoes tinge the puddles orange-pink with tomato sauce. My stomach lurches.

Outside, the sun is too bright, and I shield my eyes. *Don't give her the satisfaction of seeing you suffer*, I hear Graham say. *Just don't.*

I look around anyway, but Becca's not lingering next to the shopping carts, flashing her inane grin, a casual *Did you miss me?* as she stares too intently, memorizing the worry on my face, the lines around my eyes. Feeding off the panic.

She's not here because she's missing.

I stride back to my car, keys in hand. It's midafternoon, and the lot is full of vehicles and shoppers, carts rattling over the pocked pavement, someone calling out holiday greetings though it's not even December. As I near my car, backed neatly into its spot, I see white papers pinned beneath the windshield wipers of half a dozen cars on either side. They flutter in the light breeze, folded in half, but one corner lifts just high enough for me to recognize the red font we'd chosen for the posters yesterday, the word MISSING waving at me.

I stop, turning in a full circle, looking for the distributor. We'd hung every copy we'd made yesterday, but I wouldn't put it past Graham to print more and hand them out again. But he's not here. I don't see anyone suspicious, no one moving from car to car, no one with a stack of paper in their arms. Only about a dozen cars have them, all on my side of the aisle. Some concerned citizen, redistributing flyers they'd found floating around? A teenager ripping them off lampposts and shoving them on random cars, not knowing one was mine? Becca, tormenting me yet again? I swivel, peering for her face behind a window, ducked behind a car, giggling as she watches me suffer. But she's not there.

I snatch the paper from my windshield, the wiper hitting the glass with a sharp crack. I want to crumple the poster and throw it away, but then I think of Greaves. Watching me. If he was following me in the store, my awkward behavior had certainly failed the test, and throwing away my sister's missing poster won't help my case. I take a breath and get in the car, tossing the paper on the passenger seat and twisting the key in the ignition. Cold air hacks out of the vents but I don't wait for it to warm up, putting on a pair of sunglasses and pulling out of the spot. The poster crinkles as it shifts on the seat, trying to get my attention. I ignore it. Becca doesn't even need to be here to be annoying.

I drive past her apartment, parking in the spot she stole from the old man, the space still empty. Her unit looks over the street, and from here her windows appear dark, no blond head strutting past, laughing at her latest successful effort to make me crazy.

I close my eyes and let out a breath. She's missing, I remind myself. And while I have to keep up the pretense of looking for her in normal places, I can't keep looking for her over my shoulder.

We'd plastered every electrical pole and streetlamp on this road with the missing posters, and the one in front of me is already hanging on by a single staple, threatening to slip away, like yet another lost soul. I don't have the staple gun so I grab a piece of gum from my purse and chew it quickly. When I get out of the car, the icy breeze immediately makes my temples ache.

I pry up one prong of an old staple and use it to pin down the corner of my new poster. Pulling half the gum from my mouth, I wad it up to stick down the opposite corner. The mint makes my teeth ache in the cold, and I wince as I reach for the remaining gum to finish my work. I'm frozen in that grimace when I finally see what I'm hanging.

It's not the same poster.

I know what I saw in the parking lot. I'd seen the lettering on someone else's car, MISSING. I saw it.

But my poster doesn't say missing. It says FOUND.

The picture beneath those bold red letters isn't Becca looking as normal as she can, smiling in the sunshine. It's Becca, looking dead. She lies crumpled in a way that makes my stomach turn, the eerie glow of an overhead light casting a halo around her body, deeper shadows sliding away into the edge of the photo. A thick, dark gash slices across her forehead, disappearing into her hairline, pointing like an arrow to the large pool of blood beneath her left ear. It glints in the overhead light, giving it life and movement, as though it continued to grow long after this picture was taken. Long after there was any life or movement left in its owner.

There's nothing else on the page. No taunting message, no threat, no clue. Just a picture of my sister with a distinct smudge on her right cheek, darker than the blood, the red stark against her eerily pale skin. Not just any red, I know. Pirate Bride Red, the color she'd chosen for Angelica's kiss of death that night in the woods when she'd announced her new calling card and Footloose had watched us from the shadows.

Slowly, I peel the new poster off the pole and straighten the original, Becca smiling back at me, her blue eyes watching me cover up yet another crime. I use my last piece of gum, telling the world the same story, but a new lie. MISSING.

I take the new poster halfway down the block to a sewer grate and crouch before it, glancing up and down the street. It's empty. Quickly, I tear the paper in half one way, then the other, then again, and again, and again. I break FOUND into five pieces, feeding each letter between the metal grate. Finally, I slip Becca's bloody face and its kiss of death through the slats, watching her puffy yellow jacket disappear, a dark smudge on the left side. Her jeans, tattered on one leg. I know those marks. I know what caused them. I've seen them so many times that I know even in death, Becca would appreciate the irony of dying by her own preferred method of killing. Somehow, somewhere, he got her. Mowed her down with her stolen car, took her picture, and gave it to me. The image stops at her knees, so I don't know if Footloose took his trophy, but I don't care. Becca was his real opponent, and now she's dead. He won. The game is over.

I stand and wipe my hands on my pants before returning to my car. The missing poster waves to me from the electrical pole, trying to get my attention. But I refuse. Soon enough it will be scraped off by a city worker, disintegrate in the rain, or blow away with a strong gust of wind. Soon enough, it, like Becca and her victims, will be gone, too.

—

The next few days are a blur. I call my parents in Arizona. I call the jewelry store. I tell everyone Becca is missing and I don't know if she'll be back, but the police are looking into it. I give them Detective Schroeder's name, in case they have a clue. My parents aren't terribly concerned, not yet. They know Becca likes attention, and this is just as likely another petty ploy. The people at the jewelry store sound relieved, but I pretend not to notice, just as I pretend to be alarmed.

Despite the fact that my world has been upended, I haven't noticed a single thing out of place. No strange sounds in my home, no objects where they shouldn't be, my car just how I left it. I bounce among the five stages of grief—denial, anger, bargaining, depression, acceptance—trying to find the one that fits, but the way I'm feeling is not there. *Relief.*

I've known in my gut for days that Becca was dead. I'm angry at her for getting us into this mess, for putting us on Footloose's radar, for choosing to play our hand instead of folding. There's no one to bargain with, no god that would save Becca's soul. I wouldn't trade her life for anyone else's; she's already done that.

I don't know if I'm depressed or just numb, that shock someone feels when they lose a job, stepping out of the office and into the world, the future stretching out interminably. What do you do when you have nothing to do? And acceptance. Accepting that I won't get any more late-night phone calls to move furniture, no one else pointing out the spare ten pounds I carry, using me as their voodoo doll just because they like sticking pins into something.

It's over.

I tell myself this again and again as I brush my teeth and change my clothes, eat breakfast, take out the trash, and sit silently with Graham while he keeps me company, just being there, because he can.

On Wednesday evening, I'm packing a suitcase. I have a flight to Phoenix at eight because I'm going to see my parents. I'll stay a week. Maybe two. We'll wait out Becca's supposed game, and when enough time has passed, we'll say maybe she's not missing after all. And we'll never say she's dead, but we'll all think it, and we'll all agree maybe that's not such a bad thing. Like me, they'll stop looking over their shoulders, checking the locks on their doors for scratches, kneeling to peer under their beds. They'll breathe.

I'll never be grateful to Footloose, but the police are hunting for him for all the bodies at the start, so he'll get what's coming to him. There's been no discovery of a body in a bright-yellow jacket, so wherever he killed her, he's likely moved the body, hacked off its foot, and made her the first resident of his newest burial ground, just another mystery that will go unsolved.

I snuck out the night after I got the news, drove to the

edge of town, and threw Shanté's foot off a bridge, into the Brampton River. If it's found, the police will know in which direction to point the blame. And if not, it's not like it changes anything. She's still dead. Becca's still dead. They're all still dead.

I zip up my suitcase and sit next to it on the bed, staring into my closet. The stapler painting is there, peeking out like a promise. I'll hang it when I get back. It'll be a fresh start. A new job, a new life.

I sniffle and wipe away a stray, conflicted tear. Even though Becca was a monster, she was still my sister, the one constant in my life. And I'm reminded of her every time I pour a bowl of cereal and the box isn't empty; when I reach for my favorite pair of shoes and they're still in the closet; when I drive through town and her face gazes back from every lamppost, bulletin board, and shop window. I think she'd like the idea of people believing she's missing, searching for a girl who'll never be found. It's what she enjoyed while living. Wasting everybody's time and taunting them forever, knowing death is the only answer.

A knock at the front door interrupts my mourning. I frown and go downstairs, opening the door to find Detective Schroeder on the other side. He's wearing the same beige trench, hanging open to reveal a shirt and tie beneath, his badge clipped to his belt. His eyes are solemn and overlarge behind his thick glasses, and he gives me a small nod when he says, "Good evening, Ms. Lawrence."

I don't move to let him in. "Hi."

The night sky is dark and low, a storm waiting to unleash. It's the perfect time to leave town for Arizona's sun and anonymity. In Brampton, I've become the lost girl's sister, joining the ranks of the other grieving family members, the closest thing we've got to local celebrities.

Schroeder tucks his hands into his pockets. "Do you have a moment to speak?"

"Do you have an update?" I ask, though of course he doesn't. "Where's Detective Greaves?" I peer past him but can't see his car. Can't see if he has backup, waiting to arrest me for not reporting that Becca has, after all, been found. And myriad other awful things I've done.

"No update," he says. "We're still looking into it. I wanted to check in with you, see how you're doing."

Unlike Greaves, Schroeder doesn't look like he's waiting for me to mess up, to say the wrong thing, to implicate myself. Maybe it's just the glasses, but he looks naive and young, like he'll try his very best to get justice for Becca, even if there's none to be found. He looks like he cares.

"Fine," I say when the cold gets to be too much. "Come in. But I don't have anything to add. I told you everything I could, and I don't have much time."

He steps inside. "Why's that?"

"I'm going to Arizona. My parents are there."

"Ah. Hopefully a change of scenery will be nice for you. The weather will be better, definitely."

"I think so."

He takes a notepad and pen from his pocket and shoots me an apologetic smile. "I'll make this quick. We're still searching for Becca's car. You're certain it didn't have GPS?"

It takes everything I have not to laugh. "No GPS."

"And there's nowhere else she might have left it? No boyfriend? No places she likes to party?"

"No. She always parks in front of her apartment. She would have told me if she had a boyfriend. She'd have called by now."

"Is there anyone you can think of who might have wanted to hurt your sister?"

I freeze. "What?"

"Is there anyone—"

"Why would you ask that?"

"We need to investigate all angles."

I shake my head. "No. There's no one. She didn't— She wasn't—" I'm lying, obviously. But the truth is, I don't know. I don't know what her co-workers might tell the police. That she was one of their top salespeople for ten years running? That a woman who complained about Becca to management later mysteriously disappeared? I don't want to say she had no enemies if everyone else is saying the opposite.

"What about Footloose?" I blurt out.

Schroeder, spinning his pen in his hand, stops. "There's no reason to believe your sister is dead."

I fight to keep my expression neutral. "But what if…What if she is?"

He clicks open his pen but doesn't make a note, glancing at the baseball bat propped against the closet beside me. "Everyone is on high alert right now. It's natural to assume the worst. But that's premature."

"Are you considering it?"

"We'll consider all options. Do you have a particular reason to believe your sister might have encountered Footloose?"

Yes! I want to scream. *Because she was searching for him!*

But even if I did somehow manage to convince them Footloose was responsible, and even if they did investigate and find him, what would he say? That he first met us at Kilduff, burying Angelica?

"I mean, you heard the voice message," I say finally. "She thought she'd found him. But I don't really think she did. I guess I'm just…scared."

Schroeder gives me a small, reassuring smile. "That's understandable. I'm sure the time away will help." He tucks his notepad back into his pocket and gives a decisive nod, like that's it. There's nothing to investigate. They'll keep the file open for a while, and eventually it will go cold. The posters I hung will disintegrate in the rain and snow, and in the spring the world will come back to life, fresh and new, with one less serial killer.

"I won't keep you," he says, reaching for the door. "If we have any questions, we'll be in touch."

"Keep me posted," I say. "If you find anything."

"Absolutely." He glances around, wringing his hands, like he needs to do something to help since the Brampton PD has been fucking useless so far. "Do you—do you have a suitcase? For your trip?"

"It's upstairs. I— "

"Let me help you with it," he says. "It's the least I can do." *Since I probably won't do anything else* goes unsaid.

"You don't have to," I try, but he's already heading toward the stairs, brushing past me.

"Which room?" he asks over his shoulder.

I follow awkwardly. "To the left. With the light on."

"Got it." He steps deftly over the noisy third stair from the top and reaches the landing, turning toward my room. Half of my brain appreciates the lack of the mournful yowl of the stair, while the other half most definitely does not. I go cold, my hand stuck on the banister.

Schroeder realizes his mistake at the same moment and turns, his pen still in his hand. This time when he clicks it, I see that it's not a pen, it's a syringe. I scramble back, my socked feet sliding on the wood, throwing myself down the stairs, toward the baseball bat, the front door, safety.

Something pierces my hip, hot and agonizing, and I stumble down the steps as my limbs go weak. The world narrows to a pinprick, and I try to scream, to say something, to do something. But as ever, I do nothing at all.

CHAPTER 9

I'm moving.

The lingering effects of whatever drug Footloose injected me with have left me groggy and disoriented, and all I can tell for certain is that I'm lying on my side, wrapped in something that smells incredibly bad, and I'm moving. Rough fabric scratches my cheek, and each panicked breath makes me gag on the thick odor of must and decay.

It's dark. It's so, so dark, sharpening all my other senses to a nauseating edge and making everything that's already terrible even worse. I squeeze my eyes shut and will myself to wake up, the way you do in a nightmare when you get to the point of no return and your brain opts to spare you the horror of whatever's about to come. But when I open my eyes, I'm still in the nightmare.

There's a loud smack, and I bounce two inches before

thudding back down. Chilly air snakes around my bare feet, and a metallic growling sound cuts through the cocoon of drugs and rough fabric. My senses continue to sharpen until the cold air feels like winter and the growling sounds like an engine and the fabric feels like...

I gag and try to shove it away, the way you'd bat at a spiderweb, but my wrists squeal as something sharp digs into the soft skin, tightening with each frantic attempt. Breathing becomes difficult, my lungs refusing to expand as though my body would rather smother than inhale the horror. I'm not in my bed because I'm not sleeping, and this is not a dream. I'm in a car. The trunk of a car, to be specific. And I'm wrapped in Becca's murder carpet.

Visions of all the bodies I've seen wrapped in this thing flash through my mind like a gory movie trailer. Limp feet poking out the end, clad in sneakers, sandals, heels. Sometimes one foot would be bare where the blow from the car had knocked a shoe free, sometimes the exposed toes would be painted, and sometimes there was too much blood to tell.

"Do you ever wash this thing?" I ask Becca, covering my mouth and nose with my sleeve as the sickening odor of congealed blood seeps from her trunk.

She frowns. "Why would I?"

"Because it stinks."

"Well, yeah. It's got a dead body in it. That's not my fault."

Another bump and bang and my temple smacks the floor. I moan, nausea roiling through me. I'd always thought the carpet was on the small side, the kind you'd use in an entryway for people to wipe their feet or store their shoes. And now that I'm inside it, it feels even smaller. That dark-red stain where someone's brains had leaked out, that tiny hole where a broken bone had stabbed through—they could be pressing against my cheek, my chin. The reminder of Becca's murderous hobby and my guilty conscience, literally rubbed in my face.

Panic sets in, sweat beading on my temples despite the chill. I writhe desperately, trying to ignore the rotten smell, and eventually succeed in flopping onto my back, breathing hard and trying not to throw up. The carpet gives way a little when I bend my knees a few times, loosening just enough for me to hear the rush of icy November wind outside and the faint roar of a passing car. We hit another pothole, and again my head smacks the floor, my teeth snapping down on the inside of my cheek. The motion jostles the carpet, and it falls open around me, and immediately I realize that the murder carpet, for all its horrible history, was, ironically, keeping me alive. It's freezing in here.

I shiver and try to focus. The trunk is low and wide, and I'm lying sideways across it with my legs bent relatively comfortably, all things considered. The metal frame rattles above and below, the rumble of the muffler close to my head. I wiggle my feet, moving them apart one inch and then another. They're unbound, albeit shoeless and freezing.

I feel around with my toes until I find indentations in the car frame for the taillight to slot in, its back ridged with wires and strange protrusions. I roll onto my side, facing away, to give myself leverage, and take a few practice swings. When I'm ready, I kick back with my heel, missing entirely and whacking my foot on something sharp. I curse and curl my fingers in the carpet to brace myself before kicking again. The light doesn't budge. A tear sneaks out, skating over my nose and stinging my eye.

I think of the day I first saw this carpet. It was the fourth time I'd helped Becca hide a body, and when she opened her trunk, I'd peeked through my fingers like normal, expecting the mangled remains of her latest victim. Instead I'd seen red and yellow swirls on a beige background with fringed edges.

"What's this?" I ask, reaching out to touch it before realization dawns and I yank back my hand.

"A carpet," Becca replies. "I bought it so you'd stop gagging all the time."

"Maybe if you stopped murdering, I'd stop gagging."

She rolls her eyes. "Doubt it. Now say thank you for the gift and grab his feet."

I kick again and again, missing as many times as I make contact. On the tenth try, when my sore foot is wailing and my thigh muscles scream, there's a faint scuffing sound and a whoosh of cold air. I peer over my shoulder. The light is gone, and in its place is a hole about the size of a wine bottle, through which I can see only darkness and the intermittent glow of the moon. I have no idea how far we've been driving or how far we have left to go. What I do know is that we're going fast, like we're on a highway, and I need an overachieving citizen to spot that missing light and report it before we reach our destination. It takes forever until I see the bright glow of approaching headlights, and my heart gives a hopeful lurch. Then the car shifts lanes to pass.

"How much farther?" I ask Becca. It feels like we've been carrying the body for miles.

"Stop complaining."

"That's the first time I asked!"

"Do you want to get caught, Carrie? Do you want to just drop her right here and let someone find her with your ratty hair stuck in her blood?"

I glare mutinously.

"I'm doing this to help you," she mutters. "Stop making everything so difficult."

It's an eternity before more headlights come, and again they glide by without incident. I let out a cry of frustration and feel around the perimeter of the opening with my toe. It's tight, but it's all I've got. Slowly, I wedge my foot into the gap. Wind rushes over my toes and turns them to ice, but I twist and push, feeling the ball of my foot pop outside and then my arch, shoving desperately until my heel is free. It feels like I've scraped off a layer of skin in the process, but I did it. My plan worked. Someone will drive up, spot my foot, and call the police.

Then we start to slow down.

And a few seconds later, we turn.

The paved highway morphs into something decidedly unpaved and bumpy, and we trundle treacherously over what feels like a million boulders. My ankle bone bangs against the metal opening as I try frantically to get my foot back in the trunk. It's stuck. No matter what I do, it won't budge, protruding from the taillight hole for any opportunistic animal or serial killer to find.

I struggle desperately, but it's no use. I'm trapped. *More* trapped. I'm an idiot.

I don't know how long we drive. Five minutes, maybe forty. The pain and cold and terror blur until time slows or ceases to exist altogether, I can't tell. When we finally stop, I don't know if I'm relieved or ashamed or petrified. I don't know anything.

It takes Footloose forever to shut off the car and get out, like he's got all the time in the world for whatever's about to happen. He slams his door, the sound echoing until it fades. And then it's eerily quiet, wherever we are, all hope of the highway and rescue lost in the distance. His footsteps crunch over dead leaves and twigs, mingling with the cheerful jingle of keys in his hand as he approaches the trunk. Then silence.

And more silence.

It's already dark, but I squeeze my eyes shut, like maybe if I can't see the horror that's about to come, it won't see me either. I know he's looking at my foot. Studying it. Perhaps reaching into his pocket to retrieve his favorite switchblade to begin hacking it off. Or maybe he has an ankle holster for a hunting knife, the kind with the ridges on the back and the swooping, low tip that penetrates deep and easy.

But instead of sawing off the foot I've served up on a platter, he laughs. He laughs loudly, which is perhaps more insulting and more frightening than the flick of a blade being opened because, when Becca laughed, it was never at something I'd find funny.

"What have you done?" he murmurs. I feel the gentle trace of his fingers on the sole of my foot. I'm too cold to be ticklish but not too cold to shudder in revulsion. "You're freezing," he continues, squeezing my toes in the warm palm of his hand. "Oh, that was stupid. You're not already dead, are you?"

There's a click as the trunk pops open, and I'm once again face-to-face with Brampton's last known serial killer. The car's interior light is still on, casting just enough shadow on his skin to make the moment even worse. The pale, bland face I foolishly trusted now looks scarred and lopsided, like the cracks are showing and his true colors are leaking out.

Footloose cocks his head and heaves a relieved little sigh. "Ah. You're okay. Thank goodness."

The Detective Schroeder glasses, trench coat, and badge are gone, but everything else is the same. The blond hair, the polite smile, the slight figure. The dead look in his eyes.

Behind him, the night sky is flecked with stars, treetops stabbing into the perimeter. It's hard to tell from this position, but it looks like we've stopped in some type of small clearing, not terribly unlike the night he first saw us in Kilduff Park. Or perhaps exactly as terrible as that night.

My teeth chatter. "Wh-where are we?"

He looks around like he's surprised I might not be delighted by our surroundings. "Oh, don't worry," he says. "We're not there yet. I heard you banging around like a trussed calf—or woman—and stopped to check it out. It's important you don't hurt yourself, Carrie."

The *I'm going to hurt you instead* part goes unspoken.

I try to sit up to look around, but my stuck foot makes the movement both painful and impossible. Still, in the second I was lifted, I could see what I expected: nothing. Not for the first time, I'm alone in a dark forest with a murderer.

Things get even worse when he reaches for my foot. I try to yank it back, but it's well and truly jammed in there, and all I succeed in doing is hurting myself more. My ankle bone wails as it smacks against the metal frame of the car, and Footloose tsks his disapproval.

"You know you're the first one to try this?" he asks conversationally. He reaches for my foot again, and I tense, expecting something awful, and am instead even more horrified when he takes my frozen toes and rubs them gently between his warm hands. "Kicking out the light wasn't a bad idea, but it wasn't great either, was it? I'd be mad if it were someone else, but I'm not. I've enjoyed getting to know you. You entertain me in a way those drug-addicted losers didn't. I mean, I suppose they did, for a while. But things were getting boring."

A shudder racks me. "Until you saw us in the park that night?"

He smiles widely, teeth flashing, taking the awfulness of being stuck in a trunk with a serial killer massaging my foot to a whole new level. "That's right. Your sister— what was her name? Bertha? Becky? I thought she might be my real competition, but she's nothing compared to you. She's…basic." He sneers the word like it's the worst thing he can think of. "You're interesting."

Very few people have ever called me interesting. Next to Becca, they hardly noticed me. And because I've spent a decade helping hide dead bodies, I haven't exactly tried to be noticed. Or interesting. I'm boring stationery-designer Carrie Lawrence, serial killer magnet.

"Anyway." Footloose claps his hands, the sound splitting the night. "We're getting off schedule."

I shouldn't ask, but the question comes out anyway. "What's the schedule?"

He smiles again, and again my heart stops. "You'll see. Sorry about this, by the way. It'll be worth it in the end."

He reaches into the trunk, and I feel a searing heat in my thigh, like I'm being branded, before sensation flees. I'm frozen, my muscles locked. And then the trunk closes and the moon disappears and he disappears, and darkness takes over.

—

It's still dark when I come to. I'm stiff and achy, my thoughts sluggish, and it takes awhile for my brain to catch up to my new reality. I'm sitting on what feels like a wooden chair. My arms are still bound, this time in front of me, resting on a hard surface. I flex my toes, confirming both feet are still attached but are now affixed to the chair legs.

I blink and then squint, though I can't see through the impenetrable darkness. Eventually, I realize it's because my head is covered. My breath gusts against the fabric, pulling it against my cheeks when I inhale. I'm warm, which somehow makes it worse. Without the cold, I can feel things, which means I'll be able to feel even more horrible things later. A terrified shiver travels through me.

"Ah." Footloose's voice penetrates the frightened haze. "You're awake. Right on time."

That can't be good. I don't say anything, don't move a muscle, not even as I hear footsteps approach and floorboards creaking. Fingers brush hair away from my neck as he unties whatever he's used to cover my head and pulls it away.

I see flames. They're so bright that they sear my eyes, and I flinch and look away. I hear them crackling in the fireplace on the other side of the room, a large dining table filling the space between us. A table, I see when spots stop dancing in my vision, that is set for two.

I occupy the guest-of-honor seat at the head of the table, and Footloose settles into the chair to my right. There's a plate with roasted potatoes, another with two cooked steaks sitting in their own juices, a tossed salad, and a bottle of wine. It's even more civilized and alarming than Becca's short rib dinner.

"What's going on?" I ask, because it's obvious Footloose wants me to ask. He's apparently gone to some trouble for this…date.

He smiles. "Are you hungry?"

I'm afraid to say no, but I'm more afraid to say yes. My stomach is tied in nauseated knots and, given everything that's going on, I can't imagine this food is safe to eat. "Not right now," I say finally. "I think the…medicine…"

He nods his understanding. "It fades quickly. You'll feel better soon."

I doubt it, but I nod, too. Apart from the fact that my hands and feet are bound, and I was brought here in the trunk of a car, and he's a deranged serial killer, this looks not unlike so many romantic nights in with Graham. It feels like a normal house, a large framed oil painting of a boat on one wall, a television mounted above the fire-place, a nice meal on the table. It's dark, and there are no windows. The small chandelier overhead casts shadows on more shadows, the walls a deep wood paneling, the table and chairs a similar shade.

"Is this your house?" I ask.

"Do you like it?"

"It's warm."

Footloose laughs, eyes crinkling at the corners in a deceptively sane way. The Detective Schroeder glasses are still gone, and he wears a dark-green sweater, the sleeves rolled up slightly to reveal strong forearms. "Good. I want you to be comfortable."

I'm not comfortable, and I'm instantly even less comfortable, though I try not to show it. I have a lifetime of practice hiding exactly how uncomfortable I am, knowing that revealing a bruise was just an invitation for Becca to press on it. When Footloose doesn't say anything, just stares at me with a tiny half smile, I feel myself tensing. I try to relax, but it's easier said than done.

"You said you had a schedule," I say, forcing the words past the lump in my throat.

Footloose blinks, like he'd forgotten. "There's no rush." He takes a sip of his wine, and I realize how easy it is for him to pass as normal. How easy it is for all of us. We get dressed, we go to work, we make small talk, we kill, we hide the bodies. If there were windows in this room, anyone peeking in would see a romantic dinner, a couple not pressured to make small talk, the pleasure of each other's company enough to fill the strained silence.

"You said I was interesting." I bite my lip, studying my bindings like I'm shy. Or terrified.

Footloose rests his chin on his hand. "You are," he says. "For so long, I've been going through the motions. I thought I had one purpose, and now I believe I was mistaken. I think we were destined to meet."

I try to look intrigued and not sick. "What was your original purpose?"

He exhales, and I think for a second that he's mad. That I was supposed to agree we were destined to meet and live happily ever after, or die happily ever after, or whatever he has planned. But then I realize that his eyes are fixed on the painting on the wall to my left, and I turn to study it, too. It's a sailboat on calm waters, a sunset in the background, the pinks and oranges spilling across the water. It's hard to see in the dim light, but there are figures on the boat, three little slashes of paint. They're not unlike the drawings we did in kindergarten, stick figure families standing in front of a house, the sun shining overhead, clumsy flowers dotting the foreground. He has a family. Then I look at his bare left hand. Had. Maybe he had a family.

"Drunk driver," he says, the words so quiet it takes me a moment to process them. He's still staring at the painting like he can see his family on the boat, remembering happier times. Like he can will them to join us, to see what he's done for them. I hate that I can follow his train of thought, but it's becoming clear.

"That's how you chose your…" I don't say *victims,* though that's what they were. Becca didn't consider her victims to be victims. She thought they were nuisances. Nonessentials. An obstacle she decided to go through instead of around. "You picked addicts and killed them before they could kill somebody else."

He drags in a pained breath and looks at me. "That's right. I knew you'd understand."

I have a lifetime of practice not showing my true feelings, and now I lie with ease. "I want to understand," I tell him. "I've *wanted* to understand. You…" I take a breath. "You interest me, too."

He doesn't blink when he stares at me. "You know, I didn't think I'd enjoy you this much. Compared to your sister, you were such a fucking loser. But she died so easily. And you haven't."

I wait for him to add the predictable *yet,* but he doesn't.

"How?" I say.

"How what?"

"How did you kill her?"

"Oh, that. It was easy. I went to her apartment, told her I had you and I'd make a trade. Her life for yours."

It's a nice story, but he's forgetting I actually *knew* my sister. "You're lying."

"I beg your pardon?"

"She'd never choose me over herself."

He laughs. "That's true. She didn't, so I drugged her and took her anyway."

"Did you bring her here?"

"No. I brought her to that old paper plant at the edge of town. They have a huge lot. When she woke up, I told her to run, and she did. Just not fast enough."

I try not to picture Becca running for her life and failing. Pinwheeling through the air, bones shattering and organs puncturing, before thudding to the ground, unmoving. But I don't need to imagine that part because he put a picture on my windshield so I could remember it forever.

"Why didn't you bring her here?"

"Because she didn't deserve it," he says. "And nobody comes here." His attention shifts back to the painting, and it's a minute before he speaks again. "For the longest time, I thought I was avenging them." The flames crackle in the fireplace, reflecting in his eyes. "The kid who killed them, he died, too. But that wasn't enough. His life meant nothing. One useless life for two with such promise? It wasn't fair. It wasn't right. And all those feelings I'd always had, the ones I thought I'd locked away forever, they came right back, like they'd simply been waiting. Like there was no reason to hide them anymore. No reason to pretend I didn't want to hurt somebody when I really, really did."

He twines his fingers together, twisting the thick silver ring on the fourth finger of his right hand. I have a flash of that hand flying toward me from my closet, connecting with my face. The ring breaking my tooth. Hours at the dentist. I run the tip of my tongue over my temporary filling. We can only hide our damage for so long.

"I was sure," he continues after a while. "I was positive. But after all these years, what had I really accomplished? No one even noticed those losers were missing. I began to wonder, was I doing the right thing? Until that night in the woods when I saw you. And again in your bedroom when you startled me."

When *I* startled *him*, the masked man hiding in my closet.

"That's when I thought, *that's* what I've been missing. Everyone had been telling me to get back out there, start over. But I didn't want a wife. I wanted a *partner.* All those years, those idiot drunks, addicts, prostitutes. I wondered why I felt compelled to do what I did, and finally I knew. My wife was leading me to you."

My eyes want desperately to bulge out of my head. Becca was fixated on me because I was her sister, because she'd entrapped me, because I'd been too young to escape. She hadn't chosen me. She hadn't imagined we were meant to be. She didn't think I was her fucking *destiny.* This is worse than I thought, and I was already thinking tonight was the worst thing to ever happen to me.

"Wow," is what I come up with. "That's powerful."

Footloose gives me a wry smile. "It's a lot to take in, I know. But you'll see."

"You said that already. What will I be seeing?" I want to gag at the thought of whatever guillotine-like contraption he likely has rigged up, lopping off people's feet as punishment for someone else's sins, but a partner would be intrigued. But not too enthusiastic, not right away. Becca wouldn't have made me her gravedigging accomplice if I'd liked it. The sense of power, control, and evil is what she enjoyed. But my audience of one is what she loved.

Footloose is no different, looking almost giddy as he stands and goes to the fireplace, retrieving a remote control from the hearth. Rejoining me at the table, he nods at my full glass of wine. "Have some," he orders. "You'll need it."

"I'm not really thirst—"

"Trust me," he says, like that's possible, or like I have a choice. There's a thread of steel in his voice now that wasn't there before. Then, as if to reassure me, he swaps our glasses, giving me the one from which he's already sipped. Sharing a glass is exactly 1 percent better than not, but I'm bound and powerless, so I use my zip-tied hands to grip the stem and bring it to my lips. He watches carefully as I take a minute sip of the red wine, the taste and smell sharp and strong. But it tastes like wine, not poison. In fact—

"It's your favorite," he informs me, though I'd already recognized it as the same kind Graham and I splurge on for special occasions. Perhaps Footloose hunted through my kitchen while stashing Shanté's severed foot in my fridge. Or while he framed me and filled my house with Soda Jack cans. Or hid in my closet for hours.

I take another sip, hoping my downward gaze helps to mask my expression, my horror and outrage at the extent of his invasion of privacy and my sheer inability to see the signs. Unintentional, perhaps, but Becca had helped him hide. Every misplaced item, every bad feeling, every wary gut instinct, I'd attributed to her. And now that she's gone and I'd dared hope that my life could be some kind of normal, another serial killer has decided to recruit me for his sick game.

I place the glass back on the table. "It's wonderful," I lie, knowing I'll never drink it again.

"I like it, too. It's pricey, but worth it."

I hide a shudder of revulsion at learning we have something else in common.

"The bodies you buried," Footloose begins, turning the remote in his hands, "how many did you kill?"

I can't imagine there's a point in lying. "Thirteen."

"Not in total. You, personally. How many did you kill?"

"None." The answer comes out too quickly, too defensive, and I instantly regret it. If he wants a partner, he might want someone whose stomach doesn't churn at the mere thought of an annual body-burying expedition. He might want Becca, not her incompetent sister.

"Not your co-worker? The one trying to steal your job?"

The reminder that he was listening to my conversations makes bile rise in my throat, but I say only, "No. Becca killed her. I've never hurt anyone."

"Hmm." He sounds disappointed and turns the remote in his hand contemplatively before giving a tiny shrug. "Well," he says finally, "this may be a bit…much. But it's important for you to know what I do. To see if we'd be a good fit."

If he cared for the truth, if he were at all capable of seeing exactly what's in front of him, he'd already know we're not a good fit. He'd know I want nothing to do with serial killers. That I was, in fact, looking for him, not to team up, but to kill him. At least, that's what Becca was going to do. I was going to help hide the body. But I don't have a choice. I never did.

"Let me know if you need a break," he says politely before pressing PLAY. "And help yourself to more wine."

I squeeze my eyes shut instinctively, expecting screams and gore to explode from the television screen. But instead I'm greeted with silence. I crack open an eye and feel Footloose watching me. Then I risk a look at the TV. It shows an empty room with a bare bulb hanging overhead, a white square outline on the floor, and a prone body lying inside it. After a minute, the body moves and slowly pushes to a sitting position. I swallow a gasp when I recognize Ron Anderson, the man whose smiling face, red hair, and freckles I'd seen in a frame on top of a casket at a funeral too few had attended.

Ron looks confused and then winces and rubs his hip. My own hip gives a sympathetic twinge, and I know he drugged them all. Drugged them, bound them, stuffed them in a trunk, and drove them...somewhere. Did their last nights alive begin with a steak dinner, a nice bottle of red, and a movie?

On-screen, Ron starts coughing. The volume is too loud, and the sound makes me jump. Footloose murmurs an apology and lowers the volume but never looks away from the TV, riveted by his work. There's a cut, and a new camera angle captures Ron on his hands and knees, coughing and fumbling his way around the room, the scene growing misty with something white. Smoke, maybe. Poison, perhaps, sprayed into the room. It makes him weak, and he collapses onto his stomach, trying to cover his face with his sweater, legs twitching.

"He didn't get very far," Footloose explains as the screen flickers and we're in the same scene but with a new player, someone the police have yet to identify, and may never. It's a woman with shoulder-length dark hair and tan skin, her eyes wide and afraid. She pounds on the walls and screams at the camera, dropping to her knees as the white mist overtakes her. Her body is racked with cries and poison, but then her right hand catches on something in the floor, and she fights to stay conscious, pulling on whatever she's found. All of a sudden a trapdoor opens, and she falls through, dropping out of sight.

The next room is darker than the first, but there are

multiple cameras here, too. Some of them reveal the others, tiny red dots glowing like eyes. This room has some kind of pool, if the splashing is any indication. The display switches to something hazy and green, like night-vision goggles. It allows me to see the woman from the first scene trying to escape the pool, but she can't. She keeps trying, gripping the sides, flinging herself at the edges but slipping back. There's something preventing her escape. She disappears under the water, and I count the seconds. One, five, ten. She emerges, gasping for breath, and tries again to get out. Fails again. Back under the water. It happens over and over until I count to ten, and she doesn't reappear. Not when I get to twenty, thirty, a hundred.

I risk a look at Footloose. He's riveted. His homemade torture porn, and his newest, and possibly first, audience member. I take a larger gulp of wine, willing my expression to appear respectfully interested when he checks on me, pausing the video.

"It's really elaborate," I say, because it's true. He'll know I'm lying if I'm too effusive, and he won't want to partner with me if I tell him it makes me sick to my stomach, more sick than anything Becca did. Becca's crimes were stashed in trunks and wrapped in murder carpets. His have been recorded, edited, saved. Shown. Telling the truth will land me in his house of horrors, assuming I'm not there already. "Your home is amazing," I add tentatively, hoping to stall so I don't have to watch anymore.

"Oh, that's not this place." He chuckles. "This is home. That's my...cabin."

He makes *cabin* sound like a bad word, but I just smile encouragingly. "Did you design it?"

A proud nod. "Designed it, built it."

"You're very talented." I gesture at the furniture. "Is this your work, too?"

"Oh, no. I'm not a carpenter by trade. It's just a hobby."

"What do you do?" It's a risk to ask, to make him suspicious, but he just shrugs.

"I'm retired."

"So young."

A small smile. "But I was a butcher. You'll see."

My stomach tries to leap out through my mouth as he presses PLAY again, and my mind fast-forwards through the pool and its drowned victims, imagining whatever room must wait for those unlucky enough to escape the water, those who fight for their lives and never win the battle. What's their prize for surviving too long? A butcher's table? A homemade guillotine, fed through feetfirst? Because no one wins, I've always known that. Becca never fought fair; her targets didn't even know she had them in her sights. Footloose chose people who were already struggling and then drugged them and drugged them again, asking them to play a game he'd rigged from the start.

Two more people drown in the pool, a man and a woman. It's too dark to recognize them, to know if I'd attended their funerals. The fourth victim disappears under the water, and I begin my countdown, jolting in my seat when there's a loud rushing sound and the pool begins to drain.

The camera cuts to a new room, a safer-looking room, with a couch and a towel and a confused, staggering, dripping-wet Shanté peering around, eyes wild and terrified. Carefully she reaches for the towel, pinching it between two fingers and shaking it out. On the screen, Footloose's voice sounds soft and quiet, making me and Shanté jump.

"Go ahead," he says. "Dry off. Make yourself comfortable."

She whips around but doesn't find the source of the voice. It's rigged. Not just the game. The whole house. Cameras, microphones. I think about my house and Becca's apartment. He knew she'd found something, and that's why he killed her. He knew about Detective Schroeder because he heard me discuss him. Maybe he even watched me. Those times in my home, he wasn't just leaving severed feet and Soda Jack cans. He was placing cameras and microphones. The thought makes me almost as sick as what's happening on the screen, watching a horror movie where you know the heroine doesn't survive.

Footloose monitors my reaction with an intensity that belies his casual posture, the glass of wine held loosely in his hand. "You knew her," he remarks.

"We'd met."

"You liked her."

I try to shrug. "It was only a couple of times."

He turns back to the television. "I liked her, too. She was smart. Not everyone made it this far."

"But they all died."

"I overestimated them. I thought they would all make it to the end." He lifts a shoulder. "But they didn't."

On-screen, Shanté paces, drying herself with the towel. She eyes the neatly folded change of clothes but doesn't touch them. She's waiting. It's all she can do. Wait and stare at the cameras that capture her final moments.

All of a sudden there's a loud whirring sound, and two doors are revealed on opposite walls. They each expose a staircase, one up and one down. Shanté stares between them, knowing as I do that neither one leads anywhere she wants to go. A high-pitched whine starts, not too bad at first but quickly growing louder, and just as quickly becoming unbearable. Shanté covers her ears and falls to her knees, her eyes clenched shut with pain. Suddenly, she lets out a blood-curdling scream. "Is this what you did to my friend?" she shrieks. "Is this what you did to her?"

In response, the whining grows impossibly louder. My heart pounds, and my own head starts to hurt, and Footloose must feel it, too, because he lowers the volume more so we can't hear; we can only see. Shanté crawls toward the nearest stairwell, the one leading up. *No*, I want to tell her. *Not that way.* But she disappears into the darkness, and after a minute, an eternal minute of nothing, the screen fades to black.

I blink. "That's it? That's the end?"

"For now. What did you think?"

What I think is definitely not what I'm about to say. What I think about instead is what Becca would do. What she would say. And most important, what she would want to hear.

"It's so different," I tell him. "I feel…" I'm not pretending I'm at a loss for words. I don't know how to finish the sentence. "…special," is what I settle on.

Something flashes in Footloose's eyes. It might be delight or it might be suspicion. He's insane, so it's hard to pin down.

"The whole world is obsessed with you," I continue hurriedly. "They want to know who you are, and how you do what you do, and why you do it…And you chose me."

The corner of his mouth moves like he's trying to hide a smile. "Did you love your sister?"

The question is as simple as it is startling. My mind forms several questions before my mouth settles on an answer. "Yes, of course."

"But she made you a criminal. An accomplice. Her bitch."

I try not to flinch. "I didn't say I liked her."

"That's an interesting distinction."

"We had an interesting relationship."

I hide my distaste at the implication that he knew about our relationship because he'd watched it, filmed it, saved it. "How about your wife?" I ask instead. "Did she know about your…interest?"

He smiles. "Just my interest in building things, dabbling in engineering. She was a good person. You remind me of her."

My insides curdle. "I do?"

"Your hair," he clarifies. "When I saw you that night in the forest, I thought you were her. Just for a moment."

I force a flattered smile. "Oh."

"But better, in a way. Because you *knew*. You knew your sister. You knew her dark side, and you helped her. I've never had anyone who really knew me. Not like that."

"Her dark side wasn't all she was," I say, because it's what he wants to hear, not because it's true. "She was good, too."

It's hard to tell in the dim lighting, but I think he blushes.

"What happens now?" I hope I sound curious and not nauseous, not desperate to have these bindings removed so I can restore circulation to my hands and feet and make a run for it.

He cocks his head slightly. "What would you like to happen, Carrie?"

"I'd like to know your name."

"Maybe later."

"And I'd like to know where my sister is."

"Maybe later."

I give myself a mental kick. For a split second, I

forgot he was a lunatic, a narcissist. Becca, just in a different form. He doesn't care what I want. He doesn't know how to care. "What would you like to happen?" I ask instead.

He smiles because I knew the right answer after all. "I'd like you to pass a test."

There was never a world in which I would like his answer. It was never going to be a good answer. Something nice, sane, easy. But…a test. What kind of test? Crawling out of a poison room? Not drowning in an impossible pool? Picking the right staircase, knowing, deep down, that death waits at both ends?

"I love tests," I lie. "I got straight A's in school."

His teeth flash when he smiles. "Of course you did. Student council president?"

"Treasurer."

The smile widens. "My house is too challenging."

"You want me to help you make it easier?"

He sips his wine, still smiling as he shakes his head. "I want better participants. People who really test me."

I freeze. "What?"

"I want you to bring me someone you think will survive."

"You want me to choose the next player?"

"Sure, let's call it that. Who would you choose, Carrie? Who's the best *player* you can think of?"

I stare at him, wishing desperately that I could read his mind. It'd be twisted and nightmare inducing, a tortured fun house even more unspeakable than the one he built, but at least I'd know what he wanted. Because Becca always knew. Becca never asked me what I wanted. She asked me to tell her what she wanted to hear.

"Becca?" I whisper.

Footloose goes very, very still, like a marionette whose strings are pulled taut. Then he laughs, turning up his palms like he's the one who's completely helpless. "That's the best you can do?" he asks. "A dead woman?"

My heart pounds so hard it hurts. For the tiniest second, I'd allowed myself to believe Becca wasn't really dead. That it was all a trick, a demented ploy to get us to this stage of the game. But it's not. The answer is somehow even worse. Who else would he want me to nominate? I don't know that many people. My parents? My co-workers? One's already been murdered. Who else? Rudy from Accounting? Gene from Concepts? Troy with the hideous shirts? Or maybe Mr. Myer across the street, always trying to nose his way into my business?

"Detective Greaves," I say, even as the truth settles on my shoulders with a weight that threatens to crush me.

Slowly, Footloose shakes his head. He doesn't even say the words, but I know he's thinking them. Two strikes. I only have one more try.

But I can't. I can't say it. I can't say Graham's name because he's the nicest guy I've ever known, the best man, the sweetest, kindest guy who didn't even believe in Foot-loose but has always, despite my most horrible secrets, believed in me. He saw the best part of me, the part I want desperately to be my whole life now that Becca's gone. Now that the worst is supposed to be over.

I open my mouth, willing myself to cooperate, to play my part. *Graham. Two syllables*, and the ultimate betrayal. Maybe he'd make it through the house. Maybe I could help him somehow. Two against one. We could take down Footloose together. But I'm strapped to a chair, and Footloose doesn't fight fair, and I know he wouldn't start now. He'd drug Graham, and maybe worse. He'd make him run that losing gauntlet, and the only thing that would be different this time is that I'd be forced to watch.

Footloose clicks his tongue, his disappointment unmistakable in the sharp sound. That was the real test. And I failed.

"Well," he says, pushing back his chair. The wooden legs screech over the floor, making my ears ring. "That was a waste of fucking time, wasn't it?"

"You're a cheater," I say, knowing it's my only play. That if he's too mad at me, he'll lose focus. He'll get clumsy. And he'll forget Graham and only make one of us pay for my sins. "No one makes it out of that house alive because you cheat."

Footloose rolls his eyes and goes to the fireplace, grabbing a small, flat box from the mantel. "Don't be righteous, Carrie. It's a game. Someone has to lose."

He opens the box and retrieves a syringe and a small

vial. He stabs the needle in violently, pulling back the plunger, filling it with his drug.

"And you only choose losers," I say, pedaling with my feet as best I can, backing away as he stalks toward me. "You said it yourself. They were losers. You tried to make it into something special, claiming you were avenging your wife. But you were being a coward. You made a stupid house of horrors, and you picked weak people to play, congratulating yourself when they lost. But they were already lost. You only told us what we already knew."

He's fighting to keep his composure, but the muscles in his neck are tense, and a vein on his forehead bulges. "I guess you'll confirm the theory," he says. He grabs me by the hair, yanks my head back, and slides the tip of the needle into my skin.

———

The good news is I'm alone, and Graham is nowhere to be found. The bad news is everything else. I'm lying on my side on a floor, wrapped once again in Becca's murder carpet and its accompanying stench. My face and feet are freezing, exposed to the cold air of what I imagine is Footloose's cabin. I peek through my lashes, doing my best not to move.

The room is dark, the only light coming from a door on the opposite wall with a tiny window above it, no bigger than a hardcover book. Light from the full moon trickles across the wide expanse of shiny dark floor like a path to freedom. I don't need his home movies to tell me this is the last room in his house of horrors, the one scene he didn't show me.

"Carrie," Footloose croons, his voice echoing off the walls, "I know you're awake. I can see your eyes moving. It's time to start the game."

I give up pretending and struggle to a sitting position, the murder carpet falling away, the icy winter air pricking my skin. The room spins and sways, and I lean against the wall behind me, feeling the rough-hewn wood poke through my shirt. Nausea hits in a wave, and I gag. I thought the rancid smells were from the murder carpet, but that was wishful thinking. They're here, in the room. Sick and blood and fear. Death.

"Let's go," Footloose orders. "You know the rules. Escape or die trying."

What I know is that everybody died and there is no escaping, because that's not the outcome he wants. Even from here, I can see that the door is too good to be true. The moonlight filters through the window, but there's no light at the base of the door, nothing to suggest a frame. It's just an illusion, a mirage. The naive idea of escape.

I turn instead to look behind me. There's a click and a whir, and I whip back around. In the upper-right corner of the room, a red dot blinks and moves. A camera. A quick scan reveals four in total, capturing my final moments.

Just over my shoulder is a doorway, a real one. A few feet past it is a short set of well-lit stairs that I assume lead down to the room with the couch and the towel, where I last saw Shanté. That direction seems like a much better option than whatever lies ahead, but before I can move, the choice is made for me. The unseen light casts a yellow circle on the wall at the top of the steps, and now a dark, unmistakable shadow moves into view. Footloose. He was just a voice in the movies, but now he's part of the show. I don't know if he was always this hands-on or I'm the exception, but I suspect it's the latter. Becca hit people with a car because it was easy. Like her, Footloose doesn't want to do the hard work. He just wants to watch people try and fail so his name-calling is justified.

"Move, Carrie."

Obviously, moving is the worst thing I can do. The rooms in the video had no clear goal. No door in the poison room, nothing in the pool. The towel room felt safe, innocuous. He comforted his victims, made them feel a little better, and then forced them to flee, terrified and in pain, stumbling into this room and the false hope lurking outside that fake door. Somewhere in the twenty feet between me and the opposite wall is where they lost their feet. I know it. I can smell it. He used to be a butcher, but I wasn't lying before. More than anything, he's a coward. He invented a cowardly excuse to kill people when the real reason was that he, just like Becca, simply wanted to do it.

I hear a faint sound, like Footloose is taking a breath, ready to speak again. He holds his tongue when I push to my feet, still a little wobbly from the drugs. My neck hurts from the needle, and there's a bump on my head that wasn't there before. Maybe I fell out of the chair when he drugged me, maybe I made the trip here in the trunk, or maybe he dumped me on this floor like so much human garbage. Maybe all three.

I brace my hand on the wall and kick tentatively into the room, waiting for something to happen. I think of movies with explorers in booby-trapped caverns with spikes dropping from the ceiling, darts shooting from the walls, and a line of fire tearing across the floor. But nothing happens.

Bending, I roll the carpet and then scoop it up and heave it into the room like a log, tossing it five, maybe six feet. It skids across the floor and falls flat on its side, unfurling partway. The remaining cameras click and hum as they come to life, zeroing in on the intruder, but nothing else happens.

A stair squeaks behind me as Footloose starts his ascent. The shadow on the wall looms larger, and I imagine him with a syringe in one hand and a cleaver in the other, ready to take things into his own hands if I don't follow his deadly script.

I ease into the room. One cautious step and then another, just a few inches apart. Immediately the smells start to intensify. The tang of blood is strong, twining with perspiration and other bodily fluids. But the floor beneath my bare feet feels smooth and clean, and I can see enough to ascertain that there are no noticeable objects or puddles on the floor. The smell is coming from somewhere hidden, unseen.

I approach the carpet like it's a raft in the ocean and have almost made it when my foot catches on the edge of one of the floorboards. I find my balance before I can fall, breathing hard. Carefully, I crouch to collect the carpet, teetering like I'm walking on a tightrope instead of a floor. My fingers have just curled over the edge of the rug when Footloose speaks behind me.

"You're so slow, Carrie."

Startled, I topple forward, my elbow planting hard in the unrolled carpet. The floor underneath gives way, and I sink in several inches, the carpet catching my arm like a net. I cry out in surprise, the sound masking the thud of a board smacking the wall of the pit below, a trap sprung.

His laugh is cruel. "You're such an idiot. Everyone wanted to make a run for it, but you—you love the punishment, don't you? It's why you helped your sister all those years. You whine to make it sound like you didn't enjoy it, but you had all the opportunities in the world to leave and you chose to stay. And here you are, taking your time all over again. Not leaving."

When I glance back, he's leaning against the wall next to the doorway. His hands are empty, but I can feel the evil in his eyes. The eyes from the dark trees at Kilduff, the eyes from my closet, the eyes that watched my sister die. The eyes hoping to watch me die, too.

"No, I'm not," I protest, letting my voice quaver. I pretend to be feeling blindly around the floor, but I'm easing back the corner of the carpet to examine the hole that's opened up beneath it. I gag as the stench of the hole is released. It's the smell of blood leached into earth, of tears, of death. It's the smell of Jacinda Moon and Ron Anderson and Marcy Lennox and Shanté Williams and too many others.

It's too dark to see much, but the moonlight glints off something at the bottom of the hole, something small and raised, like a button or a sensor. A few inches above that, nestled into the side of the trap, is what looks like a blade. The kind that might chop off the foot of someone running toward the door, to freedom, their foot falling into the hole, stomping on the button, and activating the blade.

I got lucky a minute earlier when just my toe touched the corner. But not the corner of this trap, a different one. The floor must be full of them. It's why Footloose hasn't followed. He doesn't need to. But he should have. Because from where he's positioned, he can't see what I've seen. He doesn't know I know.

"Where will you bury me?" I ask, trying to think, to buy time. I can't have come this far just to lose. "With Becca?"

Footloose chuckles. "Who said you need to be buried? You've been kind enough to bring along your very own grave. I'll just roll you up in that filthy carpet and dump you in a field where someone will find you in a few days. Or weeks. What will the police think when they test the carpet? All that DNA, all those missing people. They'll be preoccupied for years."

"They—"

"Enough stalling," he says, pulling a knife from his pocket. It's not a cleaver, though, and I remember Becca's story about trying to chop off somebody's arm, the guy we buried on the golf course. How difficult it was. Footloose isn't going to use a knife to cut off my foot. He's going to use his traps; the knife is just a prop.

Leaving the carpet over the opening, I shoot a wary look over my shoulder and crawl toward the door, feeling with my fingertips for another weak spot in the floor. I find one almost immediately, my heart pounding as I make a mental note of its location. My palms slide along the wood, and I try to go slowly, to be cautious, but the smell of filth and decay is so strong it's taking all my strength not to retch and give away my discovery.

"Just a little more," Footloose murmurs behind me. His tone is encouraging, but there's a note of excitement as he waits for the finish line.

A glance back confirms he's entered the room a little more, just two or three feet, wanting a close-up view of what's about to happen. The red eyes of the cameras are zeroed in on me, recording this for posterity and whatever else he does with his creepy home movies.

I peer up at the fake door, the window at the top a deceiving beacon of hope.

"Why did you kill Shanté?" I blurt out.

"Who?"

I press my fingers into the floor in front of me. There's no movement; it's solid. "You put her foot in my freezer."

"Oh, her. *Shanté*." He drawls her name in a slow, mocking way. "Because she saw me at her friend's funeral."

"She wasn't even allowed inside."

"Not inside. Outside. After. When you three were talking. And filming."

And suddenly I know what Becca found. I'd sent her *three* videos, not just the two I'd used to run my own failed comparison. I'd taken a third video outside the church while talking to Shanté and Laurel. I'd told the others to play along and they had, posing and taking selfies. Shanté had paid the price for a discovery I didn't even know I'd made.

Footloose takes another step, leaving just five or six feet between us. The fake door is just as far. Two deadly options.

"Don't come any closer," I beg, holding up a hand like that might work. "Please. I'm—I'm going."

His mouth quirks. "Are you?" He makes a movement like he might lunge for me, and I react in kind, pressing hard on the spot on the floor I know is firm and collapsing forward, like it's one of the traps, the rolled end of the murder carpet blocking his view.

I scream as though I've hit a trap, my hand severed, my cry loud and tortured. It's the sound of someone who, of all the people who have died in this hellish room, most deserves to be here. I scream for a decade of complicity, for Becca, for Shanté, for everyone who no longer can.

Over my shoulder, I see Footloose watching, his whole body tense, expression giddy. I flop flat on the floor, scratching with my good hand, trying to lift myself up and failing. I don't know how long it takes to die this way, so I writhe and twist interminably, eyes rolling, before slowly letting the life leach out of me, all the exhaustion and terror draining away. I keep my eyes open, staring blankly, and see Footloose studying me, committing this moment to memory, although it's already committed to film. He seems to be counting, making sure I'm dead, and after everything I've been through today, staying still is the hardest part. Not flinching when he finally moves, his eyes on the floor as he notes the safe places to step, approaching my lifeless body.

"Aw," he says, one finger tracing lightly over the sole of my foot. "A hand. Not quite as exciting as a foot, but perhaps more appropriate, given how you helped your sister, hmm?"

He sniffs the air, searching for the smell of fresh blood, but the odor from the open hole is too rotten, too powerful. "Now what am I—"

I shove up as fast as I can, startling him. He'd crouched to inspect me and now topples back, scuttling like a crab.

I lunge for him and he jerks away, his cry of rage quickly silenced as his arm plunges into one of his traps. There's a click and a soft whoosh before his eyes widen and he screams, a roar of pain and outrage and disbelief.

I hurl myself over Footloose, pinning him down, forcing his arm to remain in the hole so he can't bring it up, can't try to stanch the flow of blood. The mineral tang is so strong it makes my eyes water. He claws at me with his good hand, his knees flailing, hitting me hard in the thigh and knocking me sideways. I use the murder carpet as a buoy, keeping me safe from the deadly floor, holding on for dear life as he tries to kill me with his final breaths. He grabs my elbow and rolls his body, attempting to force my arm into the same hole, but he's losing energy fast, his breath coming shallow, grip easing.

I keep him pinned, my eyes on his face as I watch the life seep out, one slow second at a time. His chest stops rising and falling, his legs stop twitching, and still I don't move, not trusting, not believing. I've seen too many dead bodies, but I've never seen anyone die.

I don't know how much time passes. Too much, definitely. I'm stiff and sore when I finally dare to move, shifting cautiously, waiting for Footloose to come back from the dead. But he doesn't. His mouth is slack, eyes closed, and when I use a finger to lift an eyelid, he stares vacantly at the ceiling.

I push at the floor, trying to convince my shaky legs to stand, my hand slipping in a pool of warm blood.

I thud back down onto Footloose, his body grunting grotesquely, like I've knocked the last of the breath from his lungs. Over the sound of my own panicked whimpers, I hear something metallic clink in his pocket and fish it out: car keys.

His left hand is still attached, palm up, fingers bare. Reluctantly, I shift to peer into the hole and there, at the bottom, glittering in the trickle of moonlight through the window over the nonexistent door, is the hand with the thick silver ring, the one that broke my tooth. My father wears a ring from his college football days, and one of my high school teachers wore a ring with his family crest on it. When I asked for Footloose's name earlier, he said maybe later. Later's no longer an option, and if I want any chance of learning who he is—who he was—this is it.

Nausea wells up fast and hard as I reach into the hole and snatch up the severed hand. I clutch the thumb, still soft and warm, and resist the urge to hurl it across the room, instead dropping it onto the floor and staring at it like, well, a dead man's hand. It takes four tries before I can convince myself to touch it again, holding it down by pressing two fingers into its palm and twisting the ring. It slides off easily, bumping over the knuckle and off the tip of his finger like it was meant to be mine. Like I've earned it. I wipe it clean and stuff it in my pocket.

For what is hopefully the last time ever, I unroll the rug. Parts of it are drenched with Footloose's blood, a literal red carpet. Becca would have loved that joke. I crawl across the carpet to the stairwell, finding three more trapdoors and springing each one, revealing their horror. I'm shaking with exhaustion when I reach the hallway, the hum of the cameras my only company. I stare at their glowing red eyes, the only remaining witnesses to this show, to my crimes and confessions. As much as I need to tell someone about this, to let the town know it's finally safe from the serial killer it knew and the one it didn't, I can't. Both have trapped me, even from beyond the grave. Becca by planting evidence on the bodies; Footloose with his records from my home, his home, and here. If the police discover this building, they'll be able to find the recordings, wherever they are.

I descend the stairs to the room below. There's a new door open on the far wall, one I didn't see in the movie. It leads into yet another room, this one small and cool, a desk light shining on a computer with two monitors, a microphone, and too many wires and unidentifiable devices. I could spend hours smashing the pieces, but no matter what I do, there's someone out there who can put them back together, revealing the misshapen puzzle that tells my story, however right or wrong. Mostly wrong.

A handle glints on the wall, a dead bolt painted black just beneath it. I twist the lock and the door swings open to reveal a dark forest. I walk the perimeter of the building, my bare feet crunching over dead leaves and pine needles. For all the horrors hidden inside, the cabin looks deceptively harmless, crude and imperfect, a roughly shaped box designed to blend into its surroundings.

Finally, I find the car. It's old and unremarkable, the kind no one would notice or remember seeing, even with a busted taillight. My suitcase sits discarded next to the passenger-side door, probably intended to be thrown away later to support the theory that I'd left for the airport and never made it. I retrieve the keys from my pocket, trying three before finding one that fits the ignition. The car starts and stale, cold air pulses out of the vents. Relief makes me want to cry, but as much as I want this ordeal to be over, it's not. Not yet.

There's a cigarette lighter on the dash, and I push it in, waiting for it to glow red hot. I'm exhausted and filthy, but I get out of the car to scoop up huge armfuls of leaves and pinecones and bring them into the house, covering the floors and stairwells. Footloose lies where I left him, gazing blankly at the ceiling. I go back out for more kindling, gathering small sticks and setting them up in random piles in the rooms like miniature bonfire towers.

Finally, I hunt through my suitcase, pulling out a change of clothes and the bottle of hair spray I'd packed for my trip. I strip and dress quickly in warm, blood-free clothes, tossing the case into the backseat of the car. Returning to the house, I pump hair spray on the clothes and the murder carpet and each stack of sticks and use the rest to create a trail through the rooms. I make sure to douse the computer area so nothing can be salvaged, should anyone later find this place and think to investigate. On the desk is a Soda Jack can, its tab already gone. It's ancho chile flavor.

I jog back to the car. My breath hangs in the icy air, but I can barely feel the cold. The cigarette lighter glows bright orange, and I pinch it from the dash between two fingers, hurrying back into the house to touch the lighter to the sticks and the leaves, watching tiny flames spring up, catching, jumping, spreading quickly. I start fires as I retreat, thick smoke filling the air and making me cough.

In the computer room, I light a stack of leaves on the desk, watching a tiny spark flare and then die. No. No. I snatch up a stick and hustle back into the main room, touching it to the growing fire. It lights up, and I run back to the office, setting it on the glowing wet patch of hair spray. It catches fire immediately.

I cough again and turn for the door, stopping when I hear a dull thud. Then another, and another. Each more frantic. For a second, I think it's Footloose, pulling his mangled body through the burning house, seeking his revenge.

But then I look down. It's coming from beneath my feet, the floorboards rattling.

Then somebody screams.

CHAPTER 10

H elp!" It's a female voice, hoarse and desperate. "Please, help! Don't leave!" She breaks off in a fit of coughing, the pounding beneath my feet stopping for a second as she hacks.

I stare back into the house, the fire spreading slowly but surely. I scan the computer room, looking for whatever evidence it holds against me. I can't afford to have anyone find this place, to find Footloose, whoever he is, to know what he knew. It needs to burn. I can't stop now. But Becca is the murderer in the family, not me.

The fire on the desk snaps, making me jump. The bottom of one of the monitors has started to warp and melt, a spark leaping onto the cheap chair and smoldering. Footloose is the one I want to erase, not the woman beneath the floor. And technically, I haven't murdered anybody. He hurt himself, and I just stopped him from getting help forever.

The pounding resumes, weaker this time. "Help!" she cries again, her voice breaking. "Please don't...Please don't..."

I drop to my knees and feel around the floor for any type of hinge or handle. "I'm here!" I call. "Where's the door?"

There's a pause, like she's astonished to have gotten an answer. "Over here!" she shouts, her voice more muffled. "Under here!"

The floorboards under the burning computer desk bounce, and I spot another lock, black and silver, catching the firelight. I scramble over and turn it in my hand, but it needs a key. My eyes water from the smoke, and my throat starts to burn. There's nothing in this room to use as a weapon, not that I'd be able to smash through a lock with an ax, even if I could find one.

I cough painfully and shove to my feet, racing back outside, gasping in the cold air. The rusted muffler spits clouds of exhaust as I run to the car, yanking open the door and snatching the keys from the ignition. The engine sputters in complaint, but there are five keys on this ring, and one has to work.

I cover my mouth and nose with my shirt as I return to the house, dropping to my knees and fumbling with the lock. Next to my head, the fabric on the chair sizzles, still struggling to catch fire. The desk and equipment have had no such problem. The flames lick up the walls, burning away all evidence of Footloose's crimes. And hopefully mine.

I jam the first key into the lock, but it doesn't go more than half an inch. Same for the second. The third slips in but doesn't turn. My cheeks and forehead feel like they're burning.

The woman bangs on the floor, whimpering and pleading and choking, her words muffled by the crackling of the fire. There's a loud whoosh in the next room followed by a muted bang as something explodes in the flames.

The fourth key works. Tears stream from my eyes, and my fingers shake uncontrollably as I fumble to release the lock, forcing the hasp free and hoisting up the door to reveal a pale, gaunt face surrounded by stringy red hair. Cold, musty air emanates from the opening, like an old root cellar. In the firelight, I can see the packed-earth floor, shadows extending into the darkness beyond.

"Please," she mumbles, her fingers scraping the edge of the floor, unable to find a grip. I try to grab her forearms and pull her up, but I'm not strong enough, and neither is she.

"Wait." I shove her back, the smoke making it nearly impossible to speak, to breathe. The chair is smoldering but hasn't caught yet, and when she backs away from the opening, I shove it in, stomping with my foot to jam the chair through the tight space. I hear wood splinter as the floor gives way, and after an agonizing minute, it's through.

Beneath me, I see firelight flicker in red hair as the girl crawls back and rights the chair, climbing up and wobbling dangerously as she reaches her hands to me, like a child being collected from a crib. I wrap my arms under hers and lift, and together we topple into the burning room, faces turned toward the open door.

"We have to go," I say, feeling her tremble next to me. "There's no time."

She's sobbing, and even through our clothing I can feel the sharp stab of her ribs, her hip bones. Fiona McBride disappeared a week before we buried Angelica in the park, and was missing more than a month. She's been here this whole time, waiting for her turn to run Footloose's gauntlet. And while she waited, he played another game.

I crawl toward the door, the cool air a boon on my burning skin, my cheeks feeling sunburned and itchy. When I glance back, Fiona has pulled herself up next to the burning desk and stands completely still as she gazes into the flaming abyss beyond.

"Let's go," I say, staggering to my feet.

She turns to look at me for a haunted minute, like whatever happened to her in that cellar is not worth living to remember, and then gives herself a hard shake, voluntary or otherwise. She shoots one last look at the hole in the floor before walking past me out the door.

The smoke is thick and sticky now, and I can see dark patches of soot on my clean clothes. My instinct for self-preservation is screaming at me to run after Fiona, get in the car, and drive away from here as fast as we possibly can. But the way she lingered and the way she looked at the hole in the floor are making my other instincts shriek in warning. I've had this feeling before, too many times to count. *Don't do it*, they're saying. *Don't look*. But my legs move of their own volition, away from safety and into the fire. I drop to my knees, the air slightly less choking at this level, and peer into the cellar, my eyes watering in the acrid smoke. The chair lies on its side, and the glow of the orange flames licks over the damp earth, like I'm peering into hell. My eyes burn, making it impossible to see, even as I stick my head down farther, craning for a closer look at something I don't want to find.

And then I see it.

A faint yellow glow, tucked far enough back I would have missed it if not for the light from the flames growing around me. The synthetic yellow of Becca's puffy jacket, stained with dirt and worse, glimmering like a beacon that's fast losing hope. It's too dark to tell if there's more than just a jacket down there, and I really don't want to know, but I snag the edge of a branch from one of my piles of kindling and plunge it into the hole.

It's only a coat. The shadows on either side are dark, and there's no blond hair, no legs, no body. She's not here. I don't know if I'm devastated or relieved.

He killed her and hid her body, and like the families

of Becca's victims, I may never learn the truth about what really happened. Maybe that's what makes me cry. Or perhaps it's just the smoke stinging my eyes. But the karmic irony that I know the answers to thirteen families' heartbreaking mysteries and will likely never know the answer to mine makes my chest ache and my tear ducts work overtime. I sob pitifully as I crawl away, my palms scraping over the floor, every movement more arduous than the one before.

Finally, I'm outside. I collapse on the leaf-littered ground and gulp in mouthfuls of clean air, swiping the back of my hand across my sweaty, tearstained face. It comes away black with soot. My whole body is begging me to lie down and close my eyes, but I know I can't. The sky is dark enough that the smoke is obscured by the night, but it's not impossible that someone, somewhere, will notice something amiss. We have to go.

I stumble to the car and get in. Fiona is slumped in the passenger seat, unconscious. Jamming the keys into the ignition, I search until I find a switch for the lights, high beams bumping against a thick wall of trees. I shift around, scanning every direction until I spot a slight opening in the forest about ten feet behind the car. I navigate the perimeter of the house, smoke billowing out the roof, and steer us onto a narrow lane, the tires bumping over unseen rocks and divots. The old car creaks and bangs as we trundle away into the darkness, my fingers gripping the wheel to steady myself for every jolt. Beside me, Fiona is slouched in her seat like a rag doll, the seat belt the only thing keeping her upright.

After ten minutes or so, we come to a road. It's two lanes, roughly paved, with no signage to indicate where we are or which direction we might want to go. Fiona is still out cold, so I make a left and slowly press down on the gas, wanting to get as far away from this place as possible but also wanting to make sure that if Fiona wakes up she won't be able to lead anyone back.

It's another thirty minutes before I pass a faded green sign, one corner missing. It says the turnoff for Highway 95 is six miles ahead. I drive a little faster. Highway 95 cuts through the state from north to south, but I have no way of knowing where we are in relation to Brampton. The car is so old it has a tiny clock to tell time, both hands stuck at twelve as if in prayer, giving me no sense of how far I've traveled or have left to go.

There's no warning about the approaching highway, just the abrupt end of the thin wall of trees on our right to reveal six lanes of silent road. I still have no idea which direction I'm facing so I cut across and carry on in the way I'd been driving, the moon our only witness. Eventually, I see an overpass in the distance, dark shapes bolted to its side. I steal another look at Fiona, but she's snoring softly, her hands folded protectively over her middle. The highway signs come into focus, and I see that the next exit is Newport Village, where I attended Jacinda's funeral.

Brampton is thirty miles past that. If I keep driving, I'll be home in an hour.

I glance at the gas gauge, now at a quarter full, and slow the car to make a gentle U-turn, careful not to wake my passenger. I'm running on little more than adrenaline and panic right now, relief at having survived the most horrific ordeal of my life held at bay by the fear that I still have to figure out what I'm going to do to prevent anyone else from finding out about it.

I drive for another hour, watching the gas gauge tick lower and lower. By the time it's hovering near empty, the pale glow of the sun has started to emerge over the horizon. Every time I see headlights in my rearview mirror, my heart jumps, praying this isn't the Good Samaritan who decides to point out my missing taillight. My eyes are burning and fatigue is setting in, and I can't hang on for much longer. All I want is to curl into a ball and sleep like Fiona, but I can't. Not yet.

Another sign announces a rest stop in ten miles, and I find it abandoned when we arrive, the small wood structure advertising bathrooms and drinking water. I pull in and park. Fiona stirs but doesn't wake as I remove the keys, pull the car key from the ring and replace it in the ignition, and then put the rest in my pocket, just in case.

I get out and pace, plotting our next move. Then my eyes lock on the trunk of the car. While we navigated our way out of the woods, the car had bumped and jostled, and I'd attributed the noises to the car's age and undercarriage.

Now I open the trunk, the metal parting with a soft squeal. I hold my breath as I peer in, expecting the worst.

What I find is a twenty-four-count case of Soda Jack with one can missing.

It's a variety pack, six flavors arranged in rows of four. I peer closely to see the tab on the red cans, ancho chile flavor. HA! it says. I scan the row. HA! HA! HA!

My eyes sting, and a hot lump lodges itself in my throat. Becca would laugh if she were alive to see this. She'd think it was hilarious that the man who meant to kill me thought it was funny, and she'd think it was hysterical that I'd survived. This whole thing has always been one big joke, and my life is the punch line.

"Hey."

I scream and slam the trunk closed, revealing Fiona on the other side, where she'd gotten out of the car without my noticing. She screams, too, and trips over her feet, sprawling on the pavement in terror. The cries shatter the stillness of the morning, and somewhere an owl hoots, a low, haunting sound.

"I'm sorry," I say, covering my face with my hands and slumping against the car, my legs suddenly too weak to stand. "I'm sorry, I—"

"No," Fiona says, struggling to get up. "I'm sorry, I didn't mean to scare you."

"Everything's scary right now."

She hesitates and then cautiously rests next to me on the trunk. "Not anymore."

I drop my hands and gaze ahead at the trees that surround the rest stop and line the highway, the ones that hid Footloose from the world so efficiently that he killed a dozen people in his house of horrors and no one even guessed.

"I don't know where we are," I say finally.

Fiona glances around. Her eyes are struggling to focus, and there's a gash on her cheek I hadn't noticed earlier. It must have split open awhile ago and festered without treatment, the skin dark and rotten around the edges. It pulls her face up on one side, trapping her mouth in a permanent sneer.

"Me either," she says. "I remember you opening the door, then…nothing. This."

I stare at her, trying to gauge her sincerity. Somewhere in the distance, a train whistle sounds. Fiona doesn't even blink, like she can't hear it.

"There wasn't much gas," I lie. "Just enough to get out of the woods. I found the highway and drove until we reached this place. We're almost out."

Then she does blink, a tear slipping from her cheek. "We're still close, then? To…him?"

"Yes." I gesture to the woods on the opposite side of the highway. "Over there somewhere."

She's wearing a pink hoodie, just like in the missing posters her mother hung around town, but now it's so stained with dirt and soot and whatever else that there's only the occasional splotch of pink visible. "So he can still come?" she asks, voice breaking. "Take us back?"

"No." I stick to the truth. Sort of. "He wanted to burn us alive, but while he was setting the fires, he fell into one of his traps. He cut off his hand and bled to death. That's how I managed to escape."

Tears roll down her cheeks and drip off her chin, but she doesn't move to wipe them away. "No one escapes," she whispers.

"We did."

"That's what he said. No one escapes."

"Well," I try, nudging her gently, "we did."

"The other girl didn't."

I freeze, thinking of Becca. "Did she stay with you?" I ask. "The other girl? In the…basement?"

Fiona shakes her head, her long red hair so greasy and matted it doesn't even move. "I don't know who it was. I never met her. I think he…forgot about me. He was getting the house ready for my turn, and then…he just wasn't. He said not yet. He had better things to do."

"What about the yellow coat that was down there?" I ask, trying not to let my desperation show. "Who did that belong to?"

"I don't know. I kept shouting that I was cold, and one night he threw it in and told me to shut up."

"Did he tell you where it came from? What he was doing?"

Another twist of the head. "No. I could just hear him

working. He was happy. Excited. Always in that room. Sometimes I heard him whistling."

A semi-truck rumbles past on the highway, but neither of us moves to flag it down.

"I heard her," she says softly.

"Heard who?"

"The last girl."

I grip the edge of the trunk. "She talked to you?"

"No." Fiona's face crumples, and she uses the cuff of her dirty sleeve to swipe at her eyes. "But she screamed. She said, *Is this what you did to my friend?* He hurt her. A lot."

My stomach twists. Shanté. The last player to die in his sick game. I did that. Becca did that. If we hadn't buried Angelica at that place on that night, none of this would have happened. And if we hadn't decided to start our own investigation, we'd have never met Shanté, and she'd have never met Footloose.

"Could you hear him talking to her?" I ask, because I have to. I have to know what Fiona could hear down there. "Anything else?"

She shakes her head. "I covered my ears. I didn't want to hear. And I don't think I could have heard anyway. There was stuff on the ceiling so I could only tell when someone was walking. Or screaming. And then when there was fire. I could smell the smoke. That's why I started shouting. I didn't think anyone could hear me. He never did."

"Did he tell you his name?"

"No. Did he tell you?"

"No. But the newspapers call him Footloose."

She sniffles. "Why?"

I decide to delay her discovery of the details of what made Shanté scream, of the fate that awaited her. She would have nightmares of her own to deal with.

"I don't know where we are," I say again, pushing away from the car. "And I don't have my phone."

"Me either." She thunks the side of her hand on the trunk. "And this thing is, like, a million years old. Before GPS."

"We'll have to flag down a car. Someone will come. Someone will rescue us."

Fiona lets out a broken sob and then flings herself into my arms, pressing her uninjured cheek into my chest. "You rescued us," she sobs. "*You* did it."

When I hug her back, all I feel are bones.

———

Fiona and I confirm to the police that the man who abducted us was Footloose. Fiona describes her time in the cellar, the screams she'd heard from an unidentified woman and then later from me. I tell them about the room with its fake hope and its trapdoors designed to sever feet. I tell them the same thing I told Fiona about Footloose's attempt to set the place on fire and then falling into his own trap and dying, allowing me to escape and rescue Fiona in the process.

Neither of us can guess where the house was located. Fiona because she was unconscious, me because I was blinded by darkness and terror. Footloose had wiped down the car, and the only fingerprint in it that didn't belong to me or Fiona was unidentifiable.

We tell the stories over and over again to different detectives in different places. I spend a night in the hospital while Fiona stays much longer. She tells the police I'm a hero.

It's a week before anyone dares leave me alone. Graham has been stuck to my side almost nonstop, breaking away only when my parents came for a three-day visit, which was long enough for us all. Graham feels guilty for everything—not offering to fly with me to Phoenix, not sensing that the fake Detective Schroeder was insane, not realizing I was in a house of horrors instead of my parents' home—and hasn't stopped apologizing, though I've practically begged him to. He feels like this is all his fault. I tell him it's not, though I can never tell him why.

Today is the first day Graham returned to work since my abduction, and because I don't know how long this quiet time will last, I immediately hurry to my bedroom and retrieve Footloose's ring from where I stashed it under my mattress. I'd hidden it from the doctors, the police, and Graham, and now I open up my laptop, studying the design I'd already committed to memory. It's thickly woven silver with an intricate etching of a G inside some type of triangular emblem. Above it are the words MASTER MASON. I do an internet search for the term, immediately finding a slew of images of rings with similar designs and links to websites dedicated to Freemasonry.

I add the word *Brampton* to the search and find a link to the local chapter. The website is sparse, mostly text, briefly explaining who and what Freemasons are, and includes a contact form. There are a handful of links at the top, and I click on them in turn: About, Supplies, Volunteer. And there, pictured on the Volunteer page, promising rides to those who need help attending appointments for cancer treatment, is Footloose. He smiles at the camera, his light hair longer than I knew it, slightly tousled, his eyes crinkled at the corners. He wears khakis and a white button-up shirt, the distinctive ring visible on his right hand. DANIEL NILSSEN, VOLUNTEER COORDINATOR, is typed beneath the picture.

For a second, my heart stops. The man in the woods, in my closet, in my nightmares, finally has a name. Daniel Nilssen.

I do a few searches for Daniel Nilssen in Brampton and the surrounding towns, but nothing comes up. This is all of him. His name and his smiling, helpful face. The mask he showed to the world. Gone forever. A volunteer coordinator, a jewelry store salesperson, a novelty stationery designer. The people you would never expect, never notice, never remember.

The Freemasons will wonder what happened to their brother, the police will waste their time searching for a serial killer, and only I will know the truth. I close the website, delete my search history, and flush the ring down the toilet.

———

Two weeks after our escape, Fiona is released from the hospital with huge fanfare. I watch the news from my couch, Graham at my side. It's dark and cold outside, the early December wind rattling through the trees. Through the curtain, I can see the faint glow of Mr. Myer's Christmas decorations, cheerful and abundant. The furnace rumbles from the basement, and heat seeps through the house, and despite the ordeal we've just been through, I feel…safe. Like it's finally, completely over, and I've seen the proof for myself. No more Footloose. No more Becca. Just me.

On the television, I watch Fiona and her mother, their red hair pulled back in matching buns, blue eyes squinting against the afternoon sunshine. I knew there had been a press conference earlier today, but I'd chosen not to go. The police have been happy to take credit for Fiona's rescue, and I'm happy to let them, as long as it keeps my name out of the papers.

"Fiona!" a reporter calls from the throng off-camera. "How does it feel to be going home?" The sun gleams against the white stucco of the hospital like a spotlight.

Fiona's smile is shaky. "I can't wait."

"We're so happy to have our daughter back." Her mother wipes a tear from her pale cheek. "We're not going to let her out of our sight."

Something subtle shifts in Fiona's stance, her eyes flickering to the ground in front of her, like she's trying to compose herself, stay still, stay strong. Or maybe she's trying not to roll her eyes. I only went to visit her once in the hospital, but she was weak and tired so we didn't talk much. I held her hand, and she squeezed my fingers, and after a while I left.

The news has been vicious; equal parts heralding her safe return and harping on her sordid past. Sound bites play on repeat, her parents begging for her to come home, forgiving her for her sins and all the things she's done wrong. Her drug use is highlighted along with her penchant for running away, a year spent in juvenile detention for petty theft and unsubstantiated rumors of an affair with a teacher. Even when she's the victim, she's the villain.

I really don't want my side of the story made public.

"What are you looking forward to most, Fiona?" Another disembodied voice rises above the crowd. There are clicks and flashes as photos are taken, the dark head of a microphone slipping into the shot before being quickly pulled back.

"Peace," she says softly. "And a fresh start." Tears spill, and her lower lip quivers as she stares down at her hands.

"Okay," her mother says, tugging her elbow. "That's all for today. Thank you. Thank you so much."

"Fiona!" someone calls as she's led away to a waiting car. "Do you have anything you'd like to say? To the person who rescued you?"

Fiona's father is in the driver's seat of the gray sedan, and her mother holds open the back door, gesturing her daughter in first. Fiona pauses, her hands tucked into her pockets as the wind pushes strands of loose hair out of its knot. She looks into the camera, her blue gaze steady. "Carrie," she says, "I need to talk to you."

Beside me, Graham stiffens with surprise. He knows the whole story, of course, or at least the one I've been telling the police. But neither one of us knows why Fiona would want to talk to me or why she would make her request so publicly. After a lifetime of being at Becca's beck and call, all I want is to be left alone.

I can almost hear Graham cycling through a dozen responses, trying to settle on the least offensive one. On television, Fiona and her mother duck into the car and close the door as a dozen reporters shout the same desperate question: Who's Carrie?

"Why would she want to talk to you?" Graham finally asks the question I'm asking myself. We were separated almost immediately upon arriving at the hospital, and beyond my brief visit, there was nothing much to say. I've read about survivors of trauma using one another as a support system, finding comfort in people who'd been through the same ordeal, but Fiona and I had very different experiences. There's nothing I can do for her. No answers I can—or will—give.

My phone rings on the coffee table, the sharp sound shattering the comfortable evening. I pick it up and see a local number on the display, not one I'm familiar with. I show it to Graham, who shrugs. I answer.

"Ms. Lawrence?" I recognize Greaves's low voice. He'd interviewed me twice after our rescue, and neither time had given me the sense that he was completely satisfied with my version of events. Still, he couldn't dispute Fiona's story that a man had abducted her, put her in the cellar, and tortured another woman before my arrival.

"Yes," I say. "Hi."

"I'm sorry to call you this late." He doesn't sound sorry. "I'm relaying a message from Fiona McBride."

My eyes flicker to the television, which Graham has muted. The news has changed to a story about an adoption drive at a local animal shelter, the homeless dogs and cats wearing Santa hats as they're posed for photos.

"She'd like to meet with you," Greaves continues when I don't say anything. Fiona doesn't have my contact information. She never asked, and I never offered.

"Did she say why?"

"She's not adjusting well. It might help to see you."

I hesitate, but I can't think of a reason to say no. Because I'm too traumatized? Fiona had it worse. I was abducted for twelve hours while she'd been held for a month. I think about the reporters shouting after the departing car at the hospital. *Who's Carrie?*

"Where?" I finally ask. "Where would we meet?"

Graham looks at me in surprise. He knows I just want to put this whole thing behind me. He thinks I'm not dealing with my grief. He's never considered that I feel guilty.

"Here," Greaves says. "At the station. She could be here tonight. She's been very insistent." He pauses. "Did you see the news today?"

"I just watched."

"I think…" Another pause. "I offered to call you myself. To relay the message more…directly. I know you're worried about your sister and would prefer to keep a low profile." What he's really saying is that Fiona will continue to ask about me publicly if I don't meet with her privately. I tell myself this isn't an echo of Becca's manipulations, it's a scared girl asking to meet with someone who might understand, but I can't stop the way my skin prickles with irritation.

"Okay," I say. "I can come."

"Tonight?"

"I'll be there in half an hour."

"All right. I'll arrange a room for you two to talk. You can tell the desk sergeant you're here to follow up on your sister's case."

I hang up. Graham is staring at me again, trying to figure out what to say. He's heard enough to know what's going on.

"I have to go to the police station," I say anyway.

"I'll drive you."

"You don't have to."

His eyes are sad. "I want to."

We don't talk much on the ride over. The night is crisp and cold, the forecast promising snow later this week. Christmas decorations light up houses and businesses as we pass, falsely bright and cheery. The whole time I'm rehearsing my story, what I told the police and what I told Graham, making sure the details line up.

We hurry into the police station, the squat building well lit and strangely welcoming. There's a different officer behind the glass partition today, and I tell him I'm here to meet Greaves. He nods and picks up the phone, and seconds later the sliding doors open to reveal Greaves on the other side. This time he's wearing a navy suit and a red tie, looking like a politician.

"Dinner plans," he explains.

"Do you have any news about my sister?" We follow him through the crowded squad room. No one's listening, and I already know the answer anyway.

"We're still investigating." He leads me past his desk in the corner to a heavy metal door I hadn't noticed the last time and swipes his ID. There's a click, and then he gestures me and Graham into a long hallway that smells like sweat and coffee. The walls and floor are the same depressing beige, and doors with tiny windows are interspersed at even intervals. We reach the door at the end and stop. Through the glass, I see Fiona sitting alone inside, her red hair loose, obscuring her face. Her head is bowed, hands clasped on the small table in front of her, like she's praying.

"We'll give you some privacy," Greaves says. Graham is ready to protest, but I shake my head. I don't know what Fiona's going to ask, and I don't imagine they won't be watching, but it'll be easier to lie without him sitting right beside me.

Fiona looks up when I enter, the fluorescent lights overhead making her pale skin appear jaundiced. The scar on her face is no longer bandaged, standing out in a stark red gash on her cheek. There's a large mirror on the far wall, and I picture Graham and Greaves on the other side, ears pressed against it.

I force my attention to Fiona and offer a small smile. "Hi."

She wears a bulky winter coat and fingerless gloves, as though they might help to hide her fragility. Her eyes are watery when they meet mine, and after a second she stands, holding the back of the chair for support. "Thank you for coming."

"Of course," I say, though I hadn't wanted to. We hug awkwardly, and she smells like baby shampoo.

I take a seat, the metal feet of the chair scraping along the linoleum floor, and Fiona does the same. Two Styrofoam cups of water sit on the table, one marked with pink lip gloss. For lack of anything better to do, I pick up the clean one and take a sip.

"How are you doing?" I ask when Fiona doesn't speak.

She runs a thumb along the rim of her cup. "Not good," she says finally. "I feel like…like, they don't get me."

"Who? Your parents?"

She nods but says, "Everybody. Them. My friends. Neighbors. The police."

"I'm sure it's a hard time for everyone."

"They watch me constantly. I can't even take a piss without my mother hovering outside the door."

I think of the way her mother said they were happy to have their daughter back, how they wouldn't let her out of their sight. The way Fiona flinched at the words.

"They're worried about you."

She scoffs like that's doubtful. "They want me to do a bunch of interviews. Someone even asked me to write a book. And I mean, we need the money. I need it. But I don't want to write a book. That's not going to help…" She gestures to her scarred face, the scars we can't see. "*This.*"

"You shouldn't do anything you don't want to do."

"What about you? He took you, too. How's your family treating you?"

My mouth opens and then closes. "It's been a rough time," I say, thinking about who's on the other side of the glass. "My sister is…missing, and my parents don't live here. My boyfriend has been great." I don't have to fake the tears I wipe away. "But it's still hard."

Fiona looks interested. "Your sister? Was it…him?"

I shake my head. "I don't think so." *Definitely.*

She clears her throat and sips her water. "I'm sorry."

"I guess we're all adjusting."

She laughs roughly. "God, don't say that. That's what my mom says. 'It's an adjustment period.' Yeah, like you can *adjust* after something like that. Come back to your regular life, and after a few weeks it'll be fine again. It will never be fine. It can't be. There's no way—" Her voice breaks, and a tear slips free. She swipes it away with the edge of her glove. "I wish I hadn't gotten out," she whispers. She says it so softly that I can barely hear it. Even if the room has microphones, they wouldn't be able to pick up her voice. I picture Greaves on the other side of the mirror, trying desperately to make out the words.

"Don't say that." The response is automatic, just like the impulse to reach across and squeeze her hand. An encouragement, and a warning.

She shakes her head, more tears falling. "I know. I know I shouldn't. I just feel like, like, there's no one I can—" A hiccup. "No one I can talk to. The person I was before is gone. Everyone just sees all those stories they're printing about me from the past and the ones they're printing now. No one sees *me*."

For the past weeks, Graham has been taking care of me. Buying groceries, making dinner, doing the laundry, taking out the trash. He's held me when I cried, threw away the used tissues, and didn't complain when I woke up screaming in the middle of the night and nearly gave him a black eye.

"You're still you," I tell her. "A little bit different, but the same. Just stronger."

"Just deformed," she says, waving at her scar.

I think of my chipped tooth. "Repaired," I say. "Fortified."

She stares at me like I'm insane and then laughs. And laughs. After a second, I laugh, too. Her scar is visible, and everyone knows how she got it. My scars are hidden but no less real. But they're healing now.

"You're funny," she says when she finally calms. "That was funny."

The words are simple and not really true, but they still touch me. They're even better than Graham's kindnesses these past weeks, the obligatory compliments and reassurances. They're sincere. They're new.

"Well," I say, "I should get going. It was good to see you. To know you're okay. Even if you don't think you are."

"I'm glad you came."

We stand, and this time when we hug, it's not awkward. We step apart when Greaves opens the door. Behind him, I see Graham and a flash of red hair. Fiona's mother.

"You've been eating," Fiona says as I move to go.

I pause. "What?"

She pats her stomach, the way Becca used to do when she saw me with a donut or a slice of pizza. "I haven't been able to eat since…that day. I can't keep anything down. But you can. That's great."

Her mom scurries in and ushers her out, darting me a look that's half pity, half apology. Greaves studies his shoes, doing his best not to make eye contact. A hot wave of fury washes over me as I see myself in the mirrored wall, bloated in my winter coat.

"She didn't mean it like that," Graham says, putting an arm around my shoulders and pressing a kiss to my temple. "It was a compliment. She wants to be like you. A survivor."

"She survived, too."

"Because of *you*."

He means it to be reassuring, but all I feel is a sour pang of regret. The words and the casual way Fiona flung them at me are too familiar. Too deliberate. Like one source of my pain died with Becca and another took its place.

An hour ago, I'd told myself her public plea wasn't manipulative, it was just what it sounded like, a plea. But after a lifetime of experience, I know better. It was someone testing the waters, trying to see how much I'll tolerate, how much they can dig in and torment me.

And the answer is nothing and not at all. That chapter of my life is closed, and I'll do anything to make sure it stays that way.

CHAPTER 11

Despite the fact that Brampton's finest have been unable to even identify him, finding Footloose's house is not that difficult for me. I spend an hour searching online for stories of drunk drivers and eventually locate one mentioning the deaths of Emma and Rae-Anne Nilssen seven years prior. They'd been waiting at a bus stop when a twenty-two-year-old college student, returning home from a party, lost control of his car and jumped the curb, killing them instantly. He'd died two days later at the hospital.

A search for Rae-Anne, Footloose's daughter, turns up a few archived social media posts from friends mourning her loss, including pictures from school dances where a group of young girls posed in front of a normal-looking house in a normal-looking neighborhood. Appearances can be deceiving.

Walking to school alone sucks. I miss you, RayRay, says one post with a picture of a lonely pair of too-small shoes on a sidewalk.

Who'll be the yin to my yang? asks another, wearing a black crescent costume and holding a matching dot in her hand. *Halloween will never be the same!*

Hard to cheer, but I know that's what you'd want, says another, accompanied by a picture of two skinny tweens in green-and-gold cheerleader outfits, BROOKLINE BOBCATS stamped across their chests.

I find a more recent post on the Facebook page of the Halloween friend. On the anniversary of the deaths, she'd stopped by the house to visit Footloose, bringing a basket of homemade snacks, unaware he'd found a less healthy way to fend for himself in the seven years since losing his family. She shared a photo of the two of them standing in the front yard of the same pale-yellow house that was featured in the earlier pictures. In this one, the number 45 is visible over their shoulders.

I do a quick online search for the Bobcats, confirming they're the mascot for Brookline Middle School in the neighboring town of Westchester. If Rae-Anne walked to school, that means their house is somewhere in the vicinity, and so forty-five minutes later I'm driving in slowly widening circles around the school, scanning the houses like a stalker. It takes another half hour, but I find 45 Poplar Street, comparing the yellow house with white shutters with the images on my phone, confirming it's the same one. A string of dark Christmas lights dangles along the edge of the roof, and a wreath hangs askew on the front door. A silver SUV is parked in the driveway.

I check the time. It's almost 6:00 p.m., night settling in fast, cloaking the street in darkness. I drive a few blocks and park before jogging back, the silver 45 winking at me in the light from the streetlamp. The house is black and still when I knock on the door, prepared to bolt if someone should answer. There's nothing. I ring the bell, hear it chime inside, and count to ten. Still nothing. Things are going according to plan, but I'm still terrified by what I'm about to do.

It's freezing, and my only company is my breath hanging in the air like a ghost, telling me not to go through with this. But I have to. Eventually, someone will notice that Daniel Nilssen hasn't shown up for his volunteer shift or that his car—not his murder car, apparently—hasn't moved from the driveway or that his Christmas lights are still up in February. That someone will knock on the door or call the police, and they'll go inside and find...something. I don't know what, but if Footloose was recording me at home and his victims in the cabin, there could be evidence here, and I didn't survive his creepy date night just to be caught on camera admitting I helped my sister bury thirteen bodies.

I glance around, but the street is empty. Lights are on in the house to the right, but the house on the left is dark, so I go around that way, the frozen grass crunching under my feet. There's no fence, and the backyard is compact and tidy with a little deck and a door flanked by two windows, very similar to mine. I pull the keys I'd saved from my pocket, trying three before one slides into the lock and turns. The sound of the tumblers falling into place echoes too loud in the quiet night. I wait for a dog to bark or someone to demand to know what I'm doing, but the neighborhood is silent, and after a second I ease the door open and slip inside, closing it behind me.

This isn't the first time I've entered the home of a serial killer, but it's the first time I've been so afraid my knees are quaking. *He's dead*, I remind myself, over and over again. *You killed him.* But it doesn't matter. Becca's been gone for weeks, and I can still feel her. Evil lingers.

I use the light on my phone to peer around the tidy kitchen, the counters clean. There's a pot and a pan on the stovetop, and when I open the fridge, it's full of normal things, like milk and orange juice and eggs and a rotting head of lettuce. No severed feet. I check the freezer, just in case, but its only occupants are a tub of mint chocolate chip ice cream and a bottle of vodka.

Next to the kitchen is a small home office with a desktop computer and a large whiteboard that functions as a calendar, noting what I assume were Footloose's volunteer shifts. He has a standing appointment at eight o'clock every Monday morning to take someone to the Westchester Hospital for dialysis. He's missed two shifts so far.

I proceed down a short hallway to the living room at the front of the house. I turn off my phone, using the light from the streetlamps to see a couch, two chairs, and a television. A set of stairs occupies the wall in front of the door, and I peer around for the dining room he'd set up for my failed test, but there's nothing more on this level.

I eyeball the stairs and then blow out a shaky breath. Even as common sense urges me to sprint back outside and give up this desperate plan, I know I have to go up there. I have to make sure the past stays in the past.

The worst thing about the house is that it's so creepily similar to mine. Older but well maintained, with all the dusty traces of his family. Pictures line the wall as I climb the stairs, starting with Rae-Anne as a baby, watching her grow into a young girl, gap-toothed and smiling widely for school photos. There are the expected staged family pictures, featuring the beaming Nilssens wearing matching sweaters or tacky Christmas pajamas. They're the things you would expect to see in a normal home. We had them in our house, too, when I was growing up. They're the things you use to mask the truth.

The upstairs has two small bedrooms and a bathroom. The tiny lilac bedroom smells like lemon furniture polish, and my light reflects on the buffed nightstand and head-board. Stuffed animals lie neatly along the pillows on the bed, waiting for Rae-Anne to return. There's a matching collection of toys and dead flowers tucked into one corner of the room like a makeshift shrine. I creep closer, finding glittery cards and sequined homemade picture frames sitting in a pool of dried rose petals, showcasing a smiling Rae-Anne. He saved it all.

Unlike his daughter's meticulously preserved room, the master bedroom has obviously been lived in. The bed is unmade. The evidence that he'd lived here, slept here, and plotted here makes me want to retch. It proves he was real, not a figment of my imagination. The single closet is still divided down the middle, men's clothes on one side, women's on the other. The floor shows the same arrangement with shoes, his wife's heels and strappy sandals organized by color, each pair standing obediently upright, like she might return any minute to pick a pair to wear out dancing.

I blink back tears, thinking of Becca's apartment, flash-frozen in the last moments of her life. The dishes in the sink, the open tube of toothpaste, the dirty clothes scattered on the floor. I still haven't decided what to do with her things. She's not officially dead, just missing, but holding on to them, clinging to the hope and fear she might return, seems wrong. More wrong now that I've seen this place. This is what happens when people continue to live in the worst moment of their lives, letting those broken feelings slice through their humanity, creating wounds that fester and rot them from the inside.

I return to the living room, the steps creaking under

my feet. If Footloose had indeed brought me to his home for dinner—if he cooked the steak and potatoes and paid for the electricity—then the dining room has to be here. But where?

The front door waits at the base of the stairs, and kitty corner to that is another door. The winter coat hanging from a hook on the back made me assume it was a closet, but now I knock the jacket to the floor and turn the knob. Locked. Pulling the keys from my pocket, I try the smallest one. The door opens with a loud squeal, revealing a dark staircase.

A terrible smell wafts out, like it's been waiting for me. It's sweet and rotten and makes my eyes water. My brain begs me to run even as my hand reaches for the string attached to the ceiling, tugging on it, a bare bulb flickering to life and illuminating the narrow space. My feet start the descent, moving of their own volition. Narrow wooden planks serve as steps. Footloose must have dragged my unconscious body up and down them on the night of our failed dinner date, explaining some of my heretofore inexplicable bruising.

The basement is divided into two parts. One is the stereotypically creepy furnace room found in most old houses with unfinished concrete walls and floors, exposed ductwork, and cobwebs in the corners. The other half has yet another door, propped open by a wooden chair, likely because Footloose's hands were full of my newly drugged body as he carted me out of the house and off to his murder cabin. The light from the stairwell stops just inside the room as though it, like me, can't bear to enter. The smell of rot and decay is strong.

I aim my phone inside the room, my eyes squeezing shut in self-defense. I force them open and then slump with relief. This is indeed the source of the odor, but it's just the decomposing remains of our untouched steak dinner, not a pile of dead bodies.

It's been nearly three weeks since we were here, and the fire is out, the dining room full of the damp cold that comes with basements and old houses. I remember the chandelier and feel along the wall just inside the door, my fingers grazing a light switch and flipping it on. The room is illuminated, and I scan it quickly before stepping inside. A click and a whir make me freeze, looking over my shoulder, expecting Footloose or Becca or perhaps Detective Greaves to catch me in the act. But it's none of them, I realize when I can breathe again. It's a small black camera tucked into the far corner, its red eye welcoming me back.

I force myself to focus and step cautiously into the room, eyes scanning the floor for any obvious torture devices. There are none.

Unless Footloose stored all his videos and editing equipment at the cabin, this has to be his control center. The room is deceptively sparse and functional, but that camera filmed me confessing to my crimes during dinner, so there must be something saving the recordings, storing them for later manipulations. Something I need to destroy. Burning this place down has crossed my mind, but I don't want to make arson a hobby. Setting fire to an isolated murder shack is one thing, but starting a fire in a family-friendly neighborhood is quite another.

Ignoring the flies buzzing on the rotten meat, I check the fireplace, shoving at the mantel, pressing on the bricks for a hiding space. Nothing. I look behind the television, but there's nothing there. I pull the boat painting off the wall, expecting a safe of some sort, but it's just a wall. I look under every chair and then peer beneath the table, feeling along its thick wooden legs for a hiding spot, a button, anything, but apart from the camera, there's nothing obvious.

I think of Footloose's cabin and his penchant for trapdoors and scan the floor more carefully, looking for anomalies in the wood. I'm on my hands and knees, pressing, feeling, hunting, and then finally, I spot it. Under one of the table legs are two pieces of wood with matching cuts that don't flow with the otherwise-staggered pattern of the floorboards. I shine the light from my phone for a better look, and it's definitely a hidden panel. Standing, I lean all my weight into the heavy table, moving it approximately an inch. I try again, gaining another inch. The table weighs a million pounds, and my already-stressed heart is working overtime.

Something shrieks, and I scream, jerking upright and banging my arm. It shrieks again and again, and I realize it's my phone ringing, the sound too shrill in the quiet house. I bury my face in my hands and try not to cry, terror and adrenaline making my hands shake. I can hear Becca now, cackling madly. *Who breaks into a house and doesn't put their phone on silent?*

Snatching the phone from my pocket, I see Graham's name on the display. He's supposed to be at a work dinner. I hope he's not at my place, wondering where I am on a weeknight.

I try to sound composed when I answer, but I'm still trembling. "Graham?"

"Carrie? Hey." There's the murmur of voices in the background, dishes clinking. He's still at the restaurant.

"What's up?" I ask.

"I just wanted to check on you. Are you okay? It sounds like you're struggling to breathe. Do you need me to come over?"

"No," I say, wiping sweat off my forehead. I'm definitely struggling. "No, I'm fine. Don't come. I just, uh…I'm…" Oh God. Don't say it. "I'm…moving furniture."

A pause. "Which room? I thought your place looked fine the way you had it."

"Yeah, it does. I just wanted to try out a new look." Fuck. Now I'll have to rearrange the living room when I get home, and I'm exhausted.

"Okay, well, I look forward to seeing it. Have a good night."

"Thanks. You too."

I hang up, grit my teeth, and shove the table with everything I have. The effort buys me another two inches, but that's all I need. The hidden panel is exposed. I drop to my knees and feel around the edges. Prying with my fingernails, I can't get enough leverage. I dig in with one of the keys, lifting the thin wooden panel just enough to lever it out. And there, in a nook the size of a briefcase and twice as deep, are three laptop computers, humming as they work. There's also a box of labeled USB sticks and several colorful cords. I scoop everything out, replace the panel and the table, haul a chair to the corner to yank out the camera, and take everything with me upstairs. I find plastic bags in the kitchen to bundle up my stolen goods and then slip out the back door, down the dark streets, and make my final escape.

CHAPTER 12

The next day, I drive to the outlet mall on the outskirts of town and park at the edge of the huge lot, at least a hundred yards between me and the next car. Here I do a cursory search of Footloose's laptops and USBs, knowing that, no matter what I find, it will be horrible.

And it is. The labels are in some type of code or shorthand, so I can't simply find my name or Becca's, forcing me to fast-forward through each one to review the contents. They contain raw footage of the victims made to navigate Footloose's house of horrors, all losing their lives in the end.

Finally, on the seventh flash drive, I hear Becca. *"Do you know what your problem is, Carrie?"*

I suck in a sharp breath. *"It's the two serial killers in my life,"* my recorded voice replies.

"*You're too negative,*" Becca says. "*You never look on the bright side.*"

I fumble with the laptop, pausing the playback. Hearing Becca's voice is almost as painful as imagining her running the deadly gauntlet.

I look around the parking lot, the sun out, the sky bright and blue, belying the cold weather. In the distance, holiday shoppers rush back and forth to their cars, bags bursting with gifts and decorations. And here I am, watching murder home movies on a serial killer's stolen laptop and hearing my dead sister's voice.

I close the laptop, get out of the car, and line up the computers and USBs with my four tires. Then I get back in the car, put it in drive, and roll forward, hearing them crunch. I reverse over them. Then drive forward again. Then back again. I do it until I see a woman in a bright-red winter coat bustling toward the nearest car. I stop and feign interest in my phone until she drives away. When she's gone, I get out and gather up the shattered equipment in two bags, confident the fragments can never be rebuilt. I take them to the dumpsters behind the mall and sprinkle them inside like confetti.

Footloose chose to dwell on the most awful moment of his life, let it grow bitter and rot and spread until it became the excuse to commit his unspeakable crimes. But I'm not going to repeat his mistakes. He's dead, Becca's dead, and I have no excuse. I'm leaving death behind me once and for all.

———

My house looks normal when I pull into the driveway, a snowman decal on the door, fake holly berries twisted around the stair rail, my lame effort to blend in. It's already dark, and through the closed curtains I see the flickering glow of the television in the front window. Without fear of Becca's unannounced visits, Graham has been spending more and more time at my house, and I like it. It finally feels like a home.

I wave to Mr. Myer across the street and jog up the steps. The welcome mat is skewed. I straighten it with my foot and then stick my key into the lock and turn. It doesn't move. For a second, I think the lock has been changed, but then I realize the problem: It's already open. Everyone in Brampton locks their door now, even those of us who know the monster is dead.

I step inside and stumble to a surprised stop. Fiona sits on the couch, a glass of milk balanced on her lap, the television remote on the cushion next to her. She lifts a hand in greeting, like this is normal, like I haven't spent a lifetime finding manipulative women in my home. I look around warily.

"Where's Graham?" Having learned my lesson, I'd put my phone on silent while watching Footloose's movies, and now I feel for it in my purse, cursing when I find a hairbrush and hand lotion and two tubes of lip gloss but no phone.

"He left to get takeout," Fiona replies. "From that Indian place you like."

I find my phone and yank it out, swiping my thumb across the display. One missed call and four unread texts, all from Graham.

Hey, are you hungry?

Fiona is here???

I'll go grab some food. How about curry?

I'm getting curry.

"So," Fiona says, muting the television. On the screen, a sitcom family gestures dramatically as they argue over Christmas decorations. She smiles, but I don't smile back. Becca's dead; I don't need to pretend I buy the act anymore.

"How did you get my address?"

The smile disappears, and she shrugs. "Detective Greaves called you the other night. When we got to the station, I asked if I could use his phone. He said sure, and I checked the list of outgoing calls and copied the numbers. Then I reverse-searched them. And here I am."

"You need to go."

She heaves an exaggerated sigh. "I'm sorry for what I said." She sounds like Becca when she'd insulted me in front of our parents and they'd mustered the energy to scold her. "I didn't mean it in a bad way."

I stare at her, unyielding. She's seventeen; I have a decade more experience on my side.

Another sigh, this one less dramatic, and she stands and twists her hands in the front of her hoodie. "I need to talk to you about the book."

"You said you didn't want to write a book."

"I know," she mutters, scrubbing her hands over her face. "And I don't want to, but I can't be here, in this town. I hate it here. I always have. And now, with everything that's happened, it's even more of a fishbowl. It's unbearable. I have to leave."

"So go."

She chews her lip. "I can't go anywhere right now. I'm broke. That's why I'm going to write the book. They said they'll give me an advance." Her stare is calculating. Gauging my reaction, my interest, my fear. She knows I don't want my name connected to this story, but she doesn't know the real reason why.

She waits for me to say something, but I stay silent.

"I really don't want to do it," she says finally. "I don't. I want to respect your privacy."

"Then why are you here?"

"Because I need to see it."

"See what?"

"The house. Where he...kept us."

I try not to show it, but I go numb at the mention of the house. Because of where we were picked up and my vague description of how we'd gotten there, the police have had no luck locating Footloose's house of horrors. It was dark enough when I set the fire for the smoke to be muted by the sky and damp enough for the fire to extinguish itself.

"It burned down," I say. "Remember? Footloose tried to burn us alive, but he got hurt and couldn't escape. That's how we got out."

Fiona is shaking her head. "It doesn't matter. I just need to see it. To know that it's really gone. To have closure." The words sound rehearsed, and she must see the doubt on my face because she laughs, embarrassed. "That's what my therapist says, anyway."

"Your therapist told you to return to the house where you were held captive for a month?"

"No. She told me to find closure. And I think that's the way to do it."

I'm not buying it. "And then you'll write the book?"

"Well. I need the money." Her eyes flitter to my open closet, the hanging coats. My purse on the hall table behind me. The flat-screen television.

"I'm not giving you money."

She shifts awkwardly. "I didn't ask you to."

"And I don't know where the house is."

When she looks at me, her eyes are clear, like a curtain has fallen away, revealing the behind-the-scenes machinations. To anyone who hasn't grown up with a psychopath for a sister, it might look like pleading, but I recognize it for what it is. Plotting.

"I know what you did," she says.

"Saved your life?"

"What you and your sister did."

Shock washes over me, but I make myself say, "My sister is missing."

"I know. Because Footloose killed her. Just like she killed that girl you worked with, and you helped her hide the body in the park. Just like she tried to chop off some guy's arm but couldn't, and you buried him at the golf course."

"You know nothing," I say, but she does. Somehow she knows what was on the equipment I just destroyed.

Fiona eyes me contemplatively. "I don't need much. Just enough for the first year. Then I'll be eighteen, and my mother can't do anything about it." There's a pause, like she's calculating. "Fifty thousand dollars."

I stare at her. "What?"

"That's how much money I need." She reaches into the pocket in her hoodie and pulls out a small black rectangle. It's a flash drive. Of course there was one more. There's always one more. Maybe he'd made a copy to bury with my body, so when and if I was found, the police would be sent on another chase, hunting for even more lost souls.

"I took this from his house," she says. "Before we left. It was on the desk but hadn't caught fire yet. I didn't know what it was, but I thought maybe there was something on it, something about Footloose. Evidence. But it wasn't about him. It was about you. And your sister."

"You're lying," I say. "Again."

She tosses me the flash drive, and I catch it against

my chest. She's written a phone number on the side in sparkly silver marker.

"I'm not," she says. "That's a copy. Listen to it. Watch it. Call me."

She strolls past me to get to the door, her arm sliding over mine, making me shudder with fear. Rage. Revulsion.

"I didn't want to do this, Carrie." She puts on her shoes and tugs a wool hat onto her head, fluffing out her hair. "You saved my life, after all. And I'm grateful. But it sounds like you've done a lot of bad things, and going to jail would probably be good for you." She laughs. "At least, that's what Mom's always saying to me."

My heart pounds so hard I can barely hear.

"But," she continues, "more than justice for your crimes, I need this money, and I want it now."

"I don't have fifty thousand dollars."

She reaches for the doorknob. "Sell your house."

Then she strolls out into the street where holiday decorations glow cheerfully, like it's just a normal day, like she hadn't just tried to manipulate me, just like Becca, like Footloose.

I close and lock the door, pressing my back against it. I squeeze the flash drive so tightly I hear it crack, and press my hands to my eyes, digging them in, letting it hurt. I'll check the flash drive, but I believe her about the contents. I think she knows enough about Becca to get everything she wants, whether it's fifty thousand dollars or a book deal exposing Brampton's two successful serial killers and their one loser accomplice.

But she doesn't know me.

———

The plan is to call Fiona from a pay phone. They're not easy to find anymore, and almost immediately my plan threatens to fail. Eventually, however, I locate one next to an old video store, long empty, its blue facade peeling. I dial the number on the side of the flash drive and wait a second for the tinny ring to start. To be sure, I'd plugged the drive into my laptop immediately after she left the other night, confirming she had enough damning recordings to put an end to my newly reclaimed freedom.

Fiona answers on the second ring, her voice suspicious. "Hello?"

"It's me."

There's a pause. "Oh. Do you have it?"

I hesitate, part cold, part nerves, part performance. "Yes. I can meet you."

"When?"

"Whenever you're ready to go."

Another pause. "Tomorrow night. I'll come to your place at ten."

"Okay." My voice shakes. "And, I, um—"

"What?"

A semi rumbles past on the highway, drowning out my answer.

"What?"

"I think I found it." My voice is barely a whisper.

"Found what?"

"The…"

"The house?" Fiona asks. Now she's whispering, too.

I swallow. "Yes. After what you said about closure, I went—I went looking for it. I must have blocked out the details while we were running away, but I could just…feel it."

"And you found it? It's definitely the place?"

"Yeah. It's gone." My voice breaks on the last word. "It was totally burned down. Seeing it again was like reliving the whole nightmare. But it's gone, Fiona. There are only ashes. So you can have your closure."

There's a pause that I wait for Fiona to fill.

"I want to see it." Her voice is smug.

"There's nothing left!" Another truck roars past, forcing me to raise my voice.

"I don't care. I want to see it. Tomorrow night."

"B-but it'll be dark. And cold. It's in the woods. And—"

"So bring a fucking flashlight, Carrie. Jesus. Where's it at?"

"It's not a good idea," I say weakly. Across the street, the sun burns over the forest, the treetops piercing the blue sky.

I can practically hear Fiona roll her eyes. "You said he's dead, right?"

"Yes, but—"

"Then there's nothing to be afraid of. Where's the house?"

I hesitate. "Barr Lode Trail."

There's silence, and I'm pretty sure she's searching the name on her phone. The trail has been abandoned for more than a decade, closed when she was just a kid. It's the perfect place for a serial killer to bring their victims.

"I'll meet you there," Fiona says finally, sounding satisfied. "Ten o'clock. Don't be late."

"I—"

She hangs up, the dial tone ringing in my ear. In the dusty shop window, a blue-and-yellow sale sign hangs at an angle, a promise made too late. The store name was removed when it closed, but the white imprint of the letters remains, like a reminder. Like what happens when we refuse to change course while we still have the chance.

—

I get to Barr Lode Trail just before ten. It's pitch black, the moon a scythe in the sky. The wind whips fiercely, pelting my face with sharp flakes of snow, enough to hurt but not enough to cover the ground. The parking lot is overgrown, frozen blades of grass and scraps of wood and garbage crunching beneath my tires. My headlights slice through the night, catching a tiny pair of eyes before they scurry into the underbrush. The wooden board that used to mark the trail entrance is long gone. A rusted chain with a dented NO TRESPASSING sign has taken its place.

My car is warm, but I shiver as I sit, lights off, checking to make sure the doors are locked. I know Fiona said ten, but if she's anything like Becca, either she'll be late, laughing as she pictures me waiting in the woods, or she's already here, hiding and watching.

At a quarter past ten, a set of headlights sweeps over the trees. Barr Lode Trail leads off a tiny logging road that runs parallel to the highway. At this hour, there's no reason for anyone else to come this way, and when the car turns into the parking lot, I squint through the glare to see Fiona in the driver's seat. She's alone.

She parks and climbs out, the slam of the car door deafening in the still night. I take a deep breath, grab my flashlight, and get out, taking care to close my door more quietly. Like me, Fiona is dressed warmly in a thick jacket and jeans, hiking boots, wool hat, and gloves. Unlike me, she's excited.

"Where is it?" she says by way of greeting.

I gesture toward the trespassing sign. "Back there. Twenty, maybe thirty minutes up the hill. It's really steep—"

"The money," she interrupts.

"Oh. You want—"

She arches a brow as I pop the trunk and round to the back of the car, pulling out a black duffel bag. There's a tire iron there, too, but I leave it for later.

Fiona snatches the bag out of my hand and unzips it, shining her flashlight on the mass of unbundled bills and combing through it with her fingers. It's obvious she doesn't know what she's counting. I couldn't possibly get fifty thousand dollars without someone noticing. "This better be all of it," she says.

My lips are already frozen with cold. "Of course."

She tosses the bag into the backseat of her car and slams the door again, smirking when I jump. Something small hits me in the chest and clatters to the ground. I look down to see the flash drive. The original. My freedom. I crouch and pick it up, stuffing it into my pocket. I should be relieved, but I'm not.

"You're welcome," Fiona says, then flicks her wrist, her flashlight slicing through the dark. "Now lead the way."

"You—you still want to see it?" Something icy washes over me, something final, like a door slamming, the lock tumbling into place.

"Of course. Let's go." She sounds like an executioner ordering me to my death.

I turn on my own flashlight, the beam bouncing off the sign as we circle the wooden posts flanking the path and start up the trail. It's nearly impossible to see the path now, covered in inches of dead leaves and pine needles, stray rocks and sticks. I trip over a hidden tree root almost immediately, falling to my knees and tearing a hole in my jeans.

Fiona snickers, and I force myself back up, gritting my teeth.

"You could stay, you know," I call out over my shoulder, the wind whipping the words away.

"I know."

"It's just one more year. Finish high school, write your book, then take off."

Our feet crunch over the dead leaves as we ascend. The trail is steep, and my thighs ache. The cold becomes heavier, wetter, as the trees block the wind and wrap us more tightly in the dark.

"You wouldn't understand," she says finally.

"I could try—"

She cuts me off. "Tell me about your sister."

I slip on a frozen patch of mud and nearly fall again. My arms flail, the flashlight beam careening through the trees, finding nothing. No witnesses this time. No Footloose lurking, listening.

I force my voice to stay steady. "What about her?"

"Why'd she kill those people?"

I've asked myself the same question a million times. I'd even asked Becca, but the answer, while probably true, offered no insight.

"Because she felt like it," I say eventually.

"That's cool."

"I thought she'd killed you," I tell her. "When the missing posters first went up. I thought that's what happened."

Fiona scoffs. The glow of her flashlight, steady at my feet, jerks to the side as she loses her balance before righting herself. I don't laugh.

"I wish," she says after a few steps.

"Trust me. You don't."

"I do. All I did was sit in a hole in the ground for a month, pissing in a corner and eating stale bread. Everyone's waiting for some amazing story, and that's the whole thing."

"Is that why you want to see the house?"

"I want you to tell me about it," she says. "Everything."

The same images that haunt my nightmares come to mind now. The dinner, the television. The house with blades in the floor. Footloose, blood spraying as I held him down, watched him die.

I swallow, my lips numb. "I already told the police."

"They won't tell me anything. But I need to know. For my book. The story you can't tell. I'll say it's mine. Then you'll get closure, too."

To date, my whole life has been a story I can't tell. Even with Becca gone, and now Footloose, I still can't tell it. Can't live it.

"He showed me a movie," I say, my tongue struggling to shape the words. "About the house. And the people he'd trapped there."

Fiona catches up to me, walking closer, almost side by side, so she can hear.

"Are you recording this?"

She shakes her head, and there's nothing in her eyes but curiosity. "I'll remember it," she says. "And embellish."

"Sure."

She presses a hand over her heart. "I swear."

"That means a lot."

Her teeth flash when she smiles. "Best I can do."

Reluctantly, I tell her about the poison room, how some had made it out and some hadn't. I describe the pool, watching the players disappear under the water, resurfacing once, twice, then no more. Talking about it brings me back to the time in Footloose's dining room, watching the movie, feeling the increasingly desperate need to put an end to this nightmare once and for all.

"Here," I say. I stop abruptly, and Fiona stumbles beside me. I'd hiked up here yesterday to support my story of rediscovering the remains of the house and left a red hair elastic wrapped around a branch that jutted out into the path. My heart is pounding from the exertion, and now that I've stopped talking, I can hear Fiona breathing hard, too. It's a steep incline for the first mile, and we've climbed quite high.

She looks around the dark path. "What?"

"This is where I first came out of the forest. I remembered that branch. The way it sticks out, like a hand."

She frowns and shines her light over it. It just looks like a branch. "Okay."

"Anyway." I turn to the left, the dense wall of trees. "We came out through there, then just stumbled down the hill. His car was in the lot."

I don't want to do this anymore. I don't want to be here. I don't want to tell this story. I don't want to tell her how

it ends. She's so much like Becca with her awful, domi-
neering side and her curious, attentive side. My whole life
has been spent trying to balance those two things, but one
side always won. The scales were never even.

Fiona bumps my elbow with her flashlight, harder
than necessary.

"Lead the way," she says, nodding toward the trees.
Like she's the one deciding.

I take a deep breath. The cold freezes the inside of my
nose, but I plunge forward into the forest, retracing the
steps from yesterday, from ten years ago.

"Keep going," Fiona orders.

A spiderweb sticks to my cheek. "I am."

"With the story."

I swipe at my face, struggling to focus on the tale
when my mind is on each footstep, the unreliable terrain
beneath.

I'd tried to count my steps yesterday, how far from
the trail to the edge of the cliff from which Becca had
dumped Shanna all those years ago, but I can't remember.
It wasn't far. It wasn't far enough.

It's so dark now. The tiny sliver of moon can't cut
through the trees, and we have to shift our bodies sideways to press forward, unseen fingers snagging on our
jackets and our jeans. My toes are frozen in my boots,
aching every time they kick into a rock or a root.

"C'mon," Fiona says, misinterpreting my silence.
"Tell me."

"After the pool, there was a new room with two sets of stairs," I say, my voice swallowed up by the trees. They're too thick to allow for wind or snow, so it's deathly quiet. The only other sound is Fiona. I understand now why Becca was never afraid when we ventured into the dark to hide the bodies. She never had nightmares; her mind never whirled with terrifying what-if scenarios. She was the watcher in the woods, the figure in the closet, the monster under the bed. She was always the worst thing.

"They had to pick one," I add. "Up or down."

I spot the moon, the tiniest spot of light in the darkest sky, and reach out to find the trees with my hand. The night meets the cliff the way the ocean turns into the horizon, impossible and inevitable and all at once. I move slowly, my steps shorter. Just inches. Waiting for my toes to find the edge.

"What did they choose?" Fiona asks, breaking my concentration.

"What?"

"Up or down. Which set of stairs?"

I think of the book she'd like to write, the story she'd like to tell. Her own version. Scarier, braver. Much better than a girl who disappeared into a hole in the ground, her body never recovered.

"Down," I say, my eyes adjusting enough to see where the black of the cliff edge twines with the dark of the night. The trees stop like soldiers, awaiting their instructions to jump as the ground erodes around them.

I turn to the right, away from the cliff, just a single row of trees separating us from the nothing that waits. The wind is sharper here, colder, but if Fiona notices, she doesn't point it out. She still wants her story.

I take a few tentative steps forward, like the house is here. Like there's anything here.

"And?" she prompts, her voice a whisper. She bumps into me and mumbles something automatically. An apology.

I close my eyes.

"He brought me to the last room," I say. "There was a small window on the far side, and I could see the sky. I could see the moon. I thought it was the way out."

"But it wasn't?"

I shake my head. "I didn't know that yet. But Foot-loose was coming, forcing me into the room. I didn't want to go."

"What was in there?"

I stop. "Do you know why they called him Footloose?"

"Because all the bodies were missing a foot."

I think of Shanté. "There were holes in the floor. They were covered, and if you stepped on one, you fell in and it sliced off your foot. That's how people died."

"But you didn't."

I turn and face Fiona. There's a small gap in the trees beside us, and I can see the moon. Its false hope. Fiona turns her head and sees it, too. Registers the emptiness. But she's not scared yet.

"No," I say. "I didn't."

"Why not?"

"Because my sister was dead." I don't realize I'm crying until I taste salt on my tongue and feel the tears slipping over my numb lips.

Fiona looks confused. "So?"

"So I'd just gotten my life back. It wasn't fair that this was happening."

"Tell me about it." She scoffs, flipping the flashlight back and forth behind me, trying to find the house where it all began, where it was supposed to have ended.

"I am telling you," I say.

The wind picks up, slicing through my coat, but I'm too numb to feel it. I've been numb for a long time.

"Then what?" She shivers, sounding irritated. "He forced you into that room. How'd you get out?"

"I pretended."

"What?"

The wind is howling now, like a warning.

"I pretended," I repeat. "I pretended I was weak so he would follow me in. So he'd think it was his idea."

Finally, finally, realization dawns on her face. The moon doesn't provide much light, but it's enough to see this. She grabs onto a tree and looks around frantically, but there's nothing there. Nobody to help. Nobody but me.

"Then I killed him," I say. "I killed him to get my life back."

"You—you had no choice." She's backing up.

"No, I didn't."

"And then you—you saved me—"

I think of her pounding on the floorboards, her desperate cries for help. The smoke and the flames and the decision I'd made. The wrong one.

"I just want my life back," I tell her.

"You have it," she says, stumbling. Her hand comes free of the tree and flails for another one.

"Almost." I take a step forward, forcing her to take one back. She grabs another tree, but it's the wrong one. It's the last one. Now there's only empty space behind her. I think of Becca tossing Shanna over the edge, how quickly she'd disappeared. How easily.

"I'll stop," she says, tear tracks glinting on her cheeks. "You can have the money. I won't—I won't tell anyone."

Becca. Footloose. Fiona.

They all fed off this power, off someone else's powerlessness. Mine, in particular. I didn't like it then, and I don't like it now. I don't want to hold this much power over someone's life. I buried those bodies, went to those funerals, watched Footloose die, saw Becca's lifeless face. I don't want to be the last one standing, the sole survivor. But it's better than the alternative.

I shove Fiona off the cliff.

She screams, which I wasn't expecting. It's sharp and loud, swallowed up by the wind. It's too dark for me to see much now, but yesterday when I came here, I'd knelt on this ledge and peered over in the bright sunshine, mentally calculating the sheer drop, the bottom too far away to register, too distant to ever be found.

I hike back down the mountain, use the tire iron to smash the window of her car, and take back my duffel bag and its thousand dollars in loose bills. Fiona thought she could buy a new life with fifty thousand dollars, but I know better than anyone that the price of freedom is much higher.

———

I've spent most of my life thinking like a sociopath. It's the only way to stay one step ahead, out of the path of a speeding car, dodging a deadly trapdoor. Now, as the holiday season gets into full swing—houses glowing with decorations, carolers in the downtown streets, men and women in Santa Claus hats soliciting donations in front of the drugstore—I'm thinking about my sister's dead body and where Footloose may have hidden it.

I'd already driven out to the paper plant at the edge of town, the lot peppered with frozen clumps of dirty slush, making it impossible to determine if a woman had been murdered recently, but the body wasn't there. I'd crept around the perimeter with a flashlight, shining it into the waving stalks of dead grass and weeds, but there were no signs of Becca. No lingering sense of malice or mayhem. Nothing.

I've done my best to forget about it. To let it go, to move on. I know what obsessing over vengeance did to Footloose, and he was grieving two innocent people. I'm not. Still, every time I cross the bridge into downtown Brampton, I think of the night I snuck out here and hurled Shanté's severed foot over the edge, adding one more name to the list of missing people no one's looking for nearly hard enough.

They've identified five more victims from the bodies buried at Kilduff Park, three women and two men, all having fallen prey to addiction or poverty or sheer misfortune long before crossing paths with Daniel Nilssen and his misguided sense of justice. I'm sitting across from Detective Greaves at his desk at the Brampton Police Department, politely studying the names and photos of the newly identified in case I recognize them, given my curious and unfortunate relationship to Footloose and his crimes.

The photos are from better times in their lives, people basking at the beach or smiling at a family dinner, their expressions filled with hope and happiness, the way they're best remembered. I recognize one as the woman from the murder video who'd escaped the poison room and drowned in the pool, but I don't tell Greaves. It won't help anything. It won't help her. And it won't help me to admit I'd watched home movies at Footloose's actual home, giving Greaves another thread to tug on. Because it's obvious he has doubts about my story, that I have too many connections to Brampton's most notorious serial killer—the one he knows about—and he'd love nothing more than to continue inviting me here and asking me questions until I give myself away. But I grew up sharing a bathroom with a master manipulator, and he's got nothing on my sister.

"You're sure?" he says when I return the stack of photos and confirm I don't know the victims.

"Positive."

He stares at me, his expression neutral. "We're still looking for your sister," he says, his idea of give-and-take. He gives me nothing, I give him something.

"Thank you."

He waits, like I might say more, and then nods. "We'll let you know if we find anything."

"I appreciate it. And of course, let me know if I can be of any more assistance."

His mouth twitches, but he doesn't smile. "Absolutely."

I show myself out. The bulletin board near the entrance has a poster of Fiona with a new picture and a fresh red MISSING stamp above her name. I ignore it.

Outside, the December air is damp and cold. I drive from the police station to Kilduff Park, abandoned at this time of year. It's late afternoon, the sun tucked behind gray clouds, growing dark like the last time I visited, when I carted a body in a carpet to a clearing in the woods, when one killer first met another, when a new game started, a game with only one winner.

Now I'm the last player standing, trekking through the forest until I find myself once again in the middle of the circle of trees, the branches and boughs overhead bending under the weight of the snow. The ground here is brown and icy, torn up and frozen from weeks of investigation, bodies collected, analyzed, identified, discarded.

The police finished their search two weeks ago, re-opening the park to curious locals and morbid visitors, internet sleuths and clairvoyants who promised to get to the bottom of things but never did and never will. Perhaps they've given up, or maybe the cold has kept them away, but I stand alone in the center of the clearing and turn slowly, scanning the trees.

If I were Footloose, this is where I would have dumped Becca's body, returning her to the place it all started, closing the circle. But there's no sign that she's here, and no indication that she ever was. As the winter sun sinks out of sight, I stay where I am until the forest is black and the trees are quiet. I peer into them, unafraid, undaunted. I see no eyes staring back, no monsters, no ghosts. There's only darkness.

ACKNOWLEDGMENTS

Writing has always been a very solitary pursuit for me, so having the support of a wonderful group of people has been amazing.

I'm eternally grateful to Jill Marr for offering to represent me and for her determination to find the best home for this story. Thank you as well to Andrea Cavallaro for her diligent work on the contracts, a task I am both unqualified for and too easily distracted to tackle alone.

Enormous thanks to Alex Logan. It's been an awesome experience to work with such a skilled and diligent editor, and undoubtedly she has made both the book and its writer much better.

Thank you to my friend Jenn for agreeing to read an early version of this book and its rewrites, helping me puzzle through feedback, and being a generally encouraging and fantastic person when I truly needed the support.

And of course thank you to my parents for getting on board with this path I've chosen. I look forward to the day we get to stand in a bookstore and read these words together. Well, some of them. Not the whole thing. Maybe just this page.

ABOUT THE AUTHOR

Elaine Murphy is a Canadian author who has lived on both coasts and several places in between. Among other things, she has volunteered in Zambia, taught English in China, and jumped off a bridge and out of an airplane. She has a diploma in writing for film and television but has never worked in either field. She recently took an interest in the dark side and began plotting suspense and thrillers. She enjoys putting ordinary people in extraordinarily difficult situations and seeing what they do about it. She lives in Vancouver, Canada.